Occupational Death

By M.F. Thurston

To Shifu Paul, who keeps trying to teach me!

MFT

Copyright © 2018 by M.F. Thurston

All rights reserved. No part of this publication may be reproduced, distributed, or transmitted in any form or by any means, including photocopying, recording, or other electronic or mechanical methods, without the prior written permission of the publisher, except in the case of brief quotations embodied in critical reviews and certain other noncommercial uses permitted by copyright law.

TO MY BEST FRIEND, MY PARTNER IN LIFE

CONTENTS

Prologue	1
Chapter 1 Richard	7
Chapter 2 Days Past	13
Chapter 3 Interview	19
Chapter 4 Watch	37
Chapter 5 Grayland	47
Chapter 6 Felicia	61
Chapter 7 Garden	69
Chapter 8 Regus	83
Chapter 9 Emergence	87
Chapter 10 Lineage	105
Chapter 11 Points of Light	111
Chapter 12 Many Rivers	113
Chapter 13 Hope	121
Chapter 14 Smiths	129
Chapter 15 Bloodlines	135
Chapter 16 Learning Curve	139
Chapter 17 Cave	149
Chapter 18 Paperland	157
Chapter 19 Thomas	171
Chapter 20 Hard Day's Work	177
Chapter 21 Vision Quest	185
Chapter 22 Moving On	193
Chapter 23 Choice	199
Chapter 24 Home	213
Chapter 25 Letters	223
Chapter 26 Sorted Emotions	227
Chapter 27 Then There Were Four	233

Epilogue

PROLOGUE

There was nothing. Void. Empty blackness. From a single point, light exploded and was sent in all directions as far as could be imagined. The wave of light moved in and through the empty spaces that were. The wave of light pushed out the dark empty spaces, bringing energy and substance to the absence. The light was great but it couldn't put out all the darkness. The Light stretched far and wide as did the small bits of matter and gases which danced and collided with each other and the light as it escaped into the beyond. There was a moment of peace as light, gases and particles settled throughout the expanse. Nothing stirred or moved, all was settling into its rhythm. Then the Darkness, in between the places of light, stirred and started to form in those spaces that were absent of light. Patches of darkness collected the other pieces of darkness, they split leaving some darkness behind as it grew on its own. The Darkness moved and solidified, arranging into a single darkness. Darkness started to reach out to touch lighted areas all around and recoiled from the light. The Darkness preferred the cool lightless spaces, where it could spread and gain strength and continue its dominance through darkness. It probed the light, where it didn't shine so bright. It was able to start to take over those places of weak and dim light, snuffing the light and prohibiting the spread of the Lights influence.

The Light sensed the cool dark, it knew that it had lost some of its presence. It pushed back upon the encroach of the invading darkness. The Light spaces collected and coagulated, creating a fortress of light to stand against the darkness. The light grew and readied its consciousness for the darkness. Darkness had tried to put out the Light once, and the Light knew it would try again.

Tentacles of pitch shot out of the Darkness and attempted to envelop the Light taking it with brute force and a will that wanted only the lightless spaces. The Light recoiled from the attack of the massive long black appendages. As the tentacles reached for the Light, tendrils tried to circle and kill the Light, extinguishing it forever. The Light organized, forming arms of gigantic proportions to fend off the attack from the Darkness. The battle raged on while each opponent tried to get the better of the other. After a while the fighting had stopped. An agreement was brokered between the Light and the Darkness. It didn't last long.

The Darkness plotted and schemed and tried to catch the Light off guard. The Light, aware of the incoming attack, tried to reason with the Darkness. The Light tried to convince the Darkness that fighting wouldn't get them anywhere. Peace had worked, but they both had to want peace. The Darkness rebuffed the negotiations and continued his assault. As the battle raged for longer than before, The Light and the Darkness had formed bodies, two arms and legs and a head. These two leviathans waged war upon each other. They hurled considerable mass and space bodies that had formed around them as weapons. As much as the Darkness wanted the Light gone it could not gain the upper hand. Remnants of their battles littered the spaces in between light and dark, these pieces, the energy left in time and space were ignored and discarded as the battle raged on. The Light and the Darkness made no headway in their battle so they discussed another peace. The immense bodies stood across from each other and extended their hands, open and empty. Each grabbed the others hand, they moved their hands up and down once in a synchronized effort, squeezing once more then letting go and they agreed to stop the fighting.

A great time passed and the fighting had not resumed. The Darkness was plotting, biding his time. Darkness took parts of himself and formed an army of homunculi and armed them with weapons and sharp teeth. Some of them had scales and slithered from dark places, others walked on two legs, half the form of Darkness and the other half covered in fur, and more still were created with wings to move fast on the Light and attack him not from below but from all around. These dark things, these little fiends were the first of their kind. The agents of the Darkness would strike fear and help Darkness overtake the light. They marched on towards the Light murmuring low growls and threats, whooping and hollering, cursing the Light and all that it prevented the Darkness from accomplishing. They ran across space and time to battle the Light. The Light battled the homunculi but there were so many. These monsters bit and clawed, swung and leapt upon The Light. Winged creatures distracted the massive Light being all the while, parts of the Light were ripped off by dark claws, teeth and weapons. These bits of light fell and formed homunculi made of light and they assisted the Light, while other piece of the light drifted on in the expanse. Soldiers and creatures of light took up the fight with the Light to drive back the monsters and creatures that served the Darkness. While the Light was distracted the Darkness struck. It laid itself on the large body of Light and tried to smother the light with its own darkness. Light tried to remove the inky black layer of its assailant. It struggled and fought, it spun and flailed trying anything to rid itself of the Darkness that was consuming the Light. Darkness had the upper hand, it was winning; it was close to snuffing the Light. The last patch of light was slowly shrinking. The light began to focus, pouring all of its power into the last light it had. A single beam of potent light pulsed and grew bright and powerful. The Light pointed the beam at the Darkness and it rent Darkness. Pieces of darkness fell away as did the monsters that were in the path of the beam. Darkness moaned and howled at the pain the Light has caused it. Darkness was now reeling from the Light. Light ripped the shredded pieces of darkness from its body and hurled the pieces with all its strength. The Darkness flew and kept going farther and farther. Darkness sailed through the void, passing the wave of light that had started all these problems for the Darkness.

Light waited, knowing that Darkness would return and try again. This time Light prepared for the conflict by creating avatars of itself. These avatars were given names and were created in many different images so that Light could keep track of them. Light gave them tools and a purpose, to watch over certain parts of the light. He warned them of the Darkness and told them that they might have to work with their enemy in the future. The Light knew nothing would truly be made without cooperation between the two aspects. With that knowledge, the Light thought and dreamed further and further into the future. It stopped and started collecting gases and space bodies that formed and surrounded the lighted spaces. It scooped up the particles and added them to the gases and breathed its breath on them. Collecting some of the remnants of darkness that had been left from the previous conflicts, it too was added to these forms and creations. These were special so they were kept close to the Light. They were tended at regular intervals, making sure they were just right, that they had all that was needed to fulfill the purpose in which they were created. The Light gathered more of the substance of the Universe, but never every last bit. Some was left behind. It took parts of itself, adding them to its next creation. With a mighty arm, these next creations were thrown out into the farthest reaches. The Light nodded, knowing that they would find a place and take root. The first creations of the Light remained close. They were tended by the Light and its avatars for these creations had to be just right. It all was to come full circle. There was a spark of something else, a new aspect, not light and not dark. The Light acknowledged it and accepted it. Now that it started to grow, it was a part of the greater scheme. It was added to the canvas of the future, as was the Darkness. The new aspect drifted on through space and time. Light knew that it wasn't his but something else entirely.

Darkness finally came to rest. There was nothing around just the emptiness of the void. Darkness took in the absence of light, enjoyed oblivion for just a moment. Darkness then went to work as well, creating avatars. Once the avatars where given life, they went to work collecting the nothing that resided around their master, they gave the collected absence to Darkness. He knew that he had only so much time, the Light was coming, ever expanding across the cool comfort of the emptiness. Darkness warned them that they too would have to work with the Light at times, just to further the Darkness. Darkness released his creation, not throwing them. He wanted them to find a proper place where they could do the best or the most malice so they slithered and flapped, clawed and crawled to their places. The Darkness sensed the creation of another. It sensed that it was coming to dark places as well. The Darkness knew this new aspect wasn't his either, so he let it drift, finding its own way.

And that was the end of the first day between Light and Darkness.

CHAPTER 1

Richard

The alarm went off. Samuel reached over to his bedside table and turned it off. Maggie rolled over and smacked her lips, which prompted a blind hand to search her bedside table for her water bottle. Samuel returned to his back and looked over at Maggie. His eyes coming awake were still adjusting to the darkness as well as sleep that remained. There he could make out the silhouette of Maggie as she put her water back and let out a small sigh. She then reached out for Samuel and put herself right next to him with her head on his chest. Maggie was still sort of breathing that deep sleep breath. Samuel put his nose to her hair. She washed every other day, but he could still make out the faint traces of her shampoo. Maggie didn't lay on Samuel every morning, but the mornings she did made it easier for Samuel to get up and face the day. The weekends it was more likely to happen as they didn't each have to run out the door.

"What time is it," Maggie asked with sleep in her voice after a yawn. Samuel just chuckled, "you know I don't change my alarm each day just to mess with you." As he chuckled he craned his neck slightly to kiss her on the forehead. They stayed like that for a couple more minutes before getting up and going about their normal morning routine. After the preliminaries, Samuel made his way downstairs to get a cup of coffee, then back upstairs to Marcus' room. Samuel knocked on Marcus' door walking in after no answer, even though he knew there would be no answer because his son slept like the dead. Samuel turned on the lights and approached Marcus. *He sleeps like he's in a coma; a freight train could crash through the house and wouldn't even make him stir* thought Samuel. After a gentle rub on his leg Marcus rolled over.

"You know the drill son. I'm going to stand here until you get two feet on the floor and don't flop back over to go back to sleep," said Samuel over top of his coffee. With that, Marcus pulled the covers over his head. "Well, good at least you hear me this morning. Gotta manage your time better by, oh I don't know, going to bed before 11 having to wake at 5:45" Samuel finished. He pulled the covers and blanket off and deposited them on the floor. He then proceeded to spin his son's legs over the edge of the bed and pull him up to sitting by his arm. "I'm going to check on the twins. I'll be right back." Samuel went down the hall passing Maggie and stole another kiss as she left the hallway bathroom, Maggie liked the shorter toilet. Recently Samuel installed a taller toilet in their bathroom. He wasn't a tall man, about average, but the smaller toilet would cause his legs to fall asleep while he would go to the reading room. It could have been considered a handicapped toilet and seat because it was taller, but Samuel didn't care. He just hated when his legs fell asleep while doing his business.

He opened the twins' door and used the dimmer control to turn up the lights enough that the twins would come out of a deep sleep to something that Samuel could work with. He returned to Marcus to find him, two feet on the floor, lying flat on his back. With a sigh, he went back to the twin's room to retrieve his tool for waking his son. A couple of squirts from one of the water pistols had Marcus shielding his face saying "I'm up, I'm up" then he sat up and began his labored march. Samuel let the walking dead slide by to make its way toward the bathroom. Samuel made his way back to his bedroom to pick out something to wear for today's interviews.

Maggie's phone rang, her feet thumped down the hall on the way to her and Samuel's room. Samuel dodged his wife as she jogged to the phone. Expecting Maggie to simply say hello, Samuel turned to see Maggie hesitant to answer the phone.

"It's Grace," Maggie said showing the phone to Samuel. She stared at the phone letting it ring once more. Samuel stopped what he was doing knowing that this wasn't normal. Grace was Maggie's sister in-law, married to her brother Richard. She had strained contact with her brother over the years. Maggie went off to live her life while most of the family understood, Richard wasn't one of those people. His wife, Grace, was even less understanding, being down right critical of Maggie and Samuel. That however, was a story for another time. Maggie finally answered the phone. "Hello."

She sat down quickly on the edge of the bed, barely sitting half on the edge of the bed, then sliding slowly to fall off the bed before catching herself on the way to the floor and finally resting with her back against the side of the bed. Samuel quickly went to her seeing her posture. *What happened?* He crouched down to her level. Her eyes were wide and alert, they did not have the normal sleep look that she would have been walking around with in the morning. Her hand went to her mouth. After a minute of listening to her sister-in-law she managed a weak "goodbye".

"Richard is dead. He died in his sleep. They think it was a heart attack. Grace will call me later with more." Maggie's voice was monotone and she spoke quickly and softly as if volume might lend credibility and weight to what she just said. Maggie spoke as if she didn't want to acknowledge the truth of her brother's death; *the shock of the news was still registering with Maggie. She doesn't want to believe what Grace just told her, neither do I for that matter. We've had enough loss in the past six years we don't need more.* With that he got down on the floor and put an arm around Maggie and rested his head against hers. They sat there until they heard the twins from their room. With that

Samuel got her up and walked her down stairs to get her some coffee.

Once Maggie was down stairs, Samuel guided the twins to his bedroom and put the TV on for the kids. Taking charge, Samuel made sure that Marcus was up and ready for the bus. The twins would ask questions about Maggie which Samuel would hint at with words like, sad and upset as well as phrases like "the heart stops or doesn't breathe anymore" when referring to Richard all the family knew about Richard, just not the details of his and Maggie's relationship. Marcus could see the emotions plain on his mother face. The news about Richard was bothering his mother. Maggie squeezed the life out of Marcus and planted a kiss on his cheek. Marcus knew that his mother was upset when the hug lasted longer than normal so he kept hugging his mom. Samuel came around Maggie's back and just nodded on his way to the sink. Marcus returned the squeeze and only after Maggie hesitantly released her son, did Marcus kiss his mom on the cheek and let go with, "love you mom".

Samuel walked Marcus out after Maggie took a seat, and explained to his son what had happened. Marcus had only met Richard a couple, maybe three times. His expression of concern was more for his mom. Even Marcus knew about the strained relationship between his mother and his uncle. Samuel told his son that he loved him as the bus arrived and walked back inside to get the twins ready for school.

The twins were at school, Samuel had dropped them off and needed to get back to his wife to help in whatever way he could. *The relationship between Maggie and Richard had never been the best. They barely spoke but that doesn't make this any easier for her. I know when my dad had died six years ago, he and I had time before he died to make things better. Dad and I had our ups and downs, mostly downs later in his life, but we did get back to a better place eventually. Maggie really didn't have any good times with her brother. We had always talked about her trying to reach out to him, but with her career...that could have been on purpose, or maybe an excuse not to reach out to Richard. Maggie will never be able to mend the relationship now. Now that Richard was gone, it's done, just as they had left it.*

Samuel reached out to his brother and sister, Carl and Susan, and told them what was happening. Each of them knew that Maggie and Richard were estranged, and offered condolences and help if needed. Samuel knew that he would probably stay with the kids and that Maggie and Marcus would make the trip. Samuel made sure to tell his siblings that he loved them. He pulled into the drive and walked into the garage and entered the house through the door that was attached to the kitchen only to see that Maggie really hadn't moved, sitting with her back to the door he just came through. He closed the door and she sniffed and wiped away her tears. It was difficult to see Maggie like this. She didn't normally show a lot of emotion but when she did you knew it to be deep and genuine. He walked by and saw that she hadn't really touched her coffee.

"Would you prefer some tea?" Samuel asked taking a seat on the edge of the "C" shaped booth, opposite her, so that he could take in all his wife's emotions, her gestures. She shrugged and kind of cringed at the offer. Her eyes not moving from some distant point, perhaps only seeing Richard. Perhaps reviewing one of the good times or several of the bad times she had shared with her brother.

"Why did I let things go so long? Now I feel horrible that I didn't try to repair things with Richard. He's gone...just gone," Maggie said not even looking up. The house was utterly silent when they weren't speaking except for the ticking of the grandfather clock in the dining room. Samuel just listened and waited for Maggie to lead the conversation. Maggie didn't really heap guilt on herself but these were feelings she was going to carry. She would chain herself to the idea that it was her fault alone. Samuel knew that it wasn't just Maggie's responsibility.

Richard was to blame as well for the lack of communication, although it wasn't the time to mention that Samuel knew he was right. As he thought about his siblings and what it would mean to lose one of them, he knew that both Carl and Susan, tried. *Actually we all tried and made an effort to stay in touch, to make sure the lines of communication stayed fresh. It wasn't easy with family. Past issues would surface when someone wanted to take a jab at the other and that could be hard to let go of at times. We always seem to work through it, that is what family does. You don't just leave it on the floor and walk out the door. Maggie and Richard had both done just that, they left it unresolved; they learned it from their father.*

"Grace hasn't called back yet. When she does I'll make arrangements for Marcus and myself to go to the service, if she'll have me," Maggie finished with indignation and another sniff. Each time Samuel and Maggie spoke it felt like a roar over the silence of the house.

"What can I do for you?" Samuel asked sliding closer and reaching out and grabbing her hand. Maggie shook her head as she blinked away another tear. "I love you" Samuel said letting go of her hand and any chance of her talking while the wounds were fresh. He got up and left the table to get things ready for Maggie and Marcus.

CHAPTER 2

Days Past

Mesopotamia 5925 BC

The valley was wide and flat. With mountains to one side, desert to the other, the land of two rivers growing, thriving and supporting those that tended it. Patches of green lined the river and became sparser the further they grew away from the river. The air was warm and dry as birds soared overhead looking for water, food and a place to nest. It was the start of the growing season and the crops were growing healthy and strong, promising a good year and a bountiful harvest. Many small clay huts, set close to the crops, buzzed as the day's activities were in full sway. Pens kept goats and sheep close by the clay huts. Men tended the fields making sure that the crops were getting enough water. Others were wading into the shallow waters and casting their nets to bring in fish. Greetings were exchanged and pleasantries made as life and community took firm roots in this land of abundance. Women went about collecting water as well as watching that their children would not wander too far. Dusty dirt trails connected the houses as well as fields in a web of life, growth and expansion. A few carts were moving supplies and clay pots from here to there, the busy concert of life was starting on a new day.

    A small trail of dust rose off one of the dirt paths as a young boy ran as fast as he could back to his family, hoping he was on time. His skin, deep brown was unlike the lighter dried dirt he ran on, a simple cloth covered him. His breathing was fast and deep as his hut came into view, a speck among other specks in the distance. His grandfather had fallen ill and he wished to see the kind old man before it was too late. Ignoring the calls from neighbors and friends he doubled his effort and picked up his pace. His feet were hot and thick with calluses, but he continued to run. His grandfather had taken ill days ago, suddenly without warning. One day the man was happy and working strong, and the next it seemed, the heat was too much for him. When this first happened his family started to prepare a place beneath the house as was the custom since coming to the valley. His grandfather would be the first to be put to rest in this new place. His grandmother, sick before they started traveling to this fertile land, fell on the trail here as she had been ill for a long time. The Boy could still see her face. Her warm dark eyes and her mouth in a perpetual smile, especially when surrounded by her grandchildren, came to mind as he ran.

    The Boy remembered his grandmother's face, but not much about her because he was young when she died. His grandfather had become a large fixture in his life as he told stories that would make him laugh and make him cry. His older brother was too mature to entertain these stories and his younger brother was too childish and only wanted to play. The Boy, as he ran, remembered one such story that Grandfather told and this brought the quick flash of a smile. Grandfather's story went like this; to make collecting wood more interesting, one boy would climb to the top of the tree. When that boy reached the top another boy at the base would cut the tree down. The one at the top of the tree assisted in bringing the tree down, riding the tree to the ground. They did this to make a game of an otherwise boring chore. It was dangerous, but it did assist in quickly felling the tree.

Grandfather told about how the people would just roam from place to place never really having anything permanent, dealing with hardships like others trying to take what they had hard fought and won. Grandfather spoke of the uncertainty of day to day life; would there be enough food or water? It was a question that this new land answered for them. With the help of his Grandfather and father, the Boy was being taught how to hunt and fish. Still too young, he now worked the fields waiting to come of age and take his turn hunting and fishing with his older brother and father.

His home in sight, the Boy sprinted the last distance seeing a few people talking and congregating outside. The sheep and goats made nervous noises at the crowd that had gathered. The looks of their faces long, their tones were hushed with respect for Grandfather and the family. Trying to catch his breath, he gently pushed the coarse cloth door out of the way. Most of the occupants of the house turned. Another group of sad faces and whispered tones greeted him from inside the house. His mother and father hovered close to Grandfather. Only after a few seconds, did they look to see it was their middle son who had finally come home. Others came and went throughout the day, not sure if this was grandfather's last day. Grandfather had seen much in his days and warranted the attention of others who live close as his words were respected and heeded. They gathered to honor him as much as hope to catch his last few precious drops of wisdom before passing.

The sun low in the sky and family united, the friends and neighbors left, giving this family their quiet respect and heading home for their own evening meals. The boy took his mother's place as she rose to finish preparing what might be the last meal as a family. With his face in obvious discomfort, Grandfather's breaths came slow. All of them, the father and all three brothers expecting it to be his last. With each breath in or out, there came a pause. The family would hold their breath, then Grandfather would start again, this went on for some time.

Then suddenly his breath became normal. No longer was his face tormented, but relaxed and at peace. His eyes opened, startling the four of them. He pointed to his wrist and a metal band appeared. All of them were frightened for metal was very rare and used only for tools. The band disappeared again and then he started speaking, barely a whisper, which betrayed his breathing and his body posture.

"I was blessed with a gift. I have not shared my complete tales with you all. That will change tonight for the last tale I tell is also to prepare you all for what is to come. I am a vessel of something greater, something that will stretch to the ends of time. The band that you saw appear and disappear calls me to perform my duties not here but places away from here. The things I have seen could blind you, things I have done you would never believe. My time is almost done. Once I am gone the band will appear to one of you and then that one will have to take my place, serving as the new vessel. I was told I was the first. It is to be passed down from generation to generation. Who will receive this honor I cannot tell; Take strength and hold to the course of your duty."

Grandfather went on, only taking breaks when the mother would come to check him or serve food. Then he would resume his weak and haggard form. The father didn't touch his food, didn't move. He sat with utter reverence, hanging on Grandfathers every word. The Boy too sat with reverence, not touching the food, waiting for each word. These words were like sweet water, the sweetest the boy had ever tasted. The oldest brother picked at his food and half heard the tales. The youngest would pay attention when he wasn't playing in the dirt or with his food. Once dinner was through Grandfather continued preparing all of them as much as possible for what was to come. When he finished they all sat calmly, each looking from one to the other. The father believed every word, you could tell by his solemn face. The brothers, old and young, just kept shaking their heads, thinking none of this possible, tricks of the heat and the mad ravings of grandfather dying. A raspy choke brought the father and the brothers' attention back to the grandfather. The middle boy sat still, looking around the room first at grandfather, then to his father and then to each of his brothers. The Boy held up his wrist, the metal band reflecting the low light from the fire. The metal band was all one piece. The father tried to pull it off, but the band moved only slightly up or down the boy's arm. Grandfather spoke again, the father and three brothers were intent, hanging on his every word.

"I knew it would be you. You have a belief, a faith in you that you share with your father. Your love was evident my grandson, in how you listened to my every word. Your love of me helped guide you to this moment. Your father will be sad that I am gone, that is likely why he wasn't chosen. Be strong, I know this is something that will test everything that you are and will be," grandfather finished stroking the boy's face. Grandfather went limp as his last breath left him. Father's shoulders slumped and he placed his hand on Grandfather's forehead. Father began to mutter to his father. The brothers could only make out a few of the words of the final goodbye between father and son. After he finished father looked at the Boy. The brothers rushed to Grandfather's side, followed by the mother, who came across the room crying, joining the family. Gently they touched grandfather saying their last goodbyes, first the mother and then the three brothers. The boy's eyes were fixed, still staring at the metal bracelet as the family wept, touching the smooth, cool metal. Hearing his grandfather's words over and over again is his head, wanting to remember this moment. The boys were in tears, but not the middle boy. The goats and sheep started to stir and bleat drawing the family's attention away from grandfather. The animals didn't stop, but in fact got louder as if something was very wrong. The families concern for the animals took them to the door to look. As soon as the family appeared in the door, the animals stopped their cries, nothing was out of place. There was just enough light reflected in the sky for all to see that all the animals were well. The family turned back to go inside knowing the animals were safe. The single room was empty expect for a few clay pots, mats for sleeping and Grandfather's lifeless body. The middle boy was nowhere to be seen.

CHAPTER 3

Interview

Samuel was still in his house clothes which consisted of comfortable, loose fitting, yet holey pants and an old Steely Dan concert t-shirt. He was sitting at the booth where his family took most of their meals. The kitchen a few hours earlier was abuzz with activity. Marcus was the first to head off to school. A hectic Maggie was next, taking the twins and dropping them off at school. Samuel gazed into the muddy reflection of his coffee. *I haven't ever seen Maggie upset for this long. Granted, Richard's funeral was three weeks ago and I know that has something to do with it. Maggie hasn't been affected by a death quite like this, Richard's death was unusually sudden. When someone is gone that fast you have the rug pulled right out from under you, and you are lost for a while, unsure. With her Mom she had time to prepare; with my parents we were prepared, with Richard not so much…I'm guessing Maggie will dive into work and come out the woman I love, which she's done before with less significant life hiccups, like her husband not keeping a steady job. I have to have faith in her. This also brings up the pain I experienced in losing my parents. I know it's not the same as a sibling, but I really miss my parents. Sure they got to see Marcus, but he was so young and they were really good with Marcus. It would be great to have them here and now, playing with the twins… helping me with a job. HA! Dad would have said I raised you, you can figure it out. Still, Richard's death has opened some old wounds.*

Samuel glanced at the stove. He wouldn't be able to finish his coffee. Leaving the morning's half-cup of coffee, Samuel got up from the table. "Time for the interviews," he sighed aloud. The routine of the interviews had become dressing, traveling, interviewing and then disappointment. Samuel had gotten used to it even as he dressed for this next interview. He glanced at his resume, making sure he was still familiar with it, before shutting it in his briefcase and collecting his keys. Samuel's eyes gazed at the comforting sight of his coffee as it breathed out the last breath of steam.

"Another time," whispered Samuel as he walked out to the car. On the drive to the interview Samuel went over his employment history in his head. The longest job he'd ever worked was the paper route he had in junior high and senior high school, mustering a total of six years on the job. *You can't think like that going into the interview. Those are things you can't change. You can change your present employment situation.* With the thoughts of the past drifting away, Samuel thought about the company he was interviewing with. He had looked at their webpage the night before so that he would be familiar with the company's operations. It wasn't terribly important but Samuel could use any advantage he could scrape together since this most recent job drought. Recently he had been working as a substitute teacher which paid the bills, but the kids could be tough. He felt that they looked at him as a joke, or was that how Samuel looked at himself? Before the substitute teaching position, he had worked with an old friend of his as an assistant office manager. Today's interview was for another assistant office manager position.

Maybe I should reach out to Mary Patricia. She was a good person to work with and has helped me find a couple of positions in the past. I just hate reaching out like that to her though, it makes me feel like some charity case. She had good luck with jobs and keeping them. It couldn't hurt. But I'm not going have to reach out to her be-

Occupational Death

cause I've got this! Today will be different. He had landed a couple of positions with Mary Patricia Dooley suggestions, although she seemed to have luck at finding and keeping positions. The same was rare for Samuel.

Samuel left the interview with mixed feelings. He had presented himself in a professional manner, he answered the questions to the interviewer's satisfaction, hopefully, and it turned out checking out the website for the company had paid off. They had asked him a couple questions about where the company was going as well as his opinion on where they could grow and enrich the employee experience. Even with all that in his favor shreds of doubt seemed to cling to him like an Irish pennant. He glanced at his watch and saw that he had time to stop for a bite; *a little reward seems apropos.* There was a deli shoppette that was close that made a mean Italian cold cut; the meats, cheeses and veggies were good, but the dressing just made the sandwich. No parking was available on the street so Samuel pulled into a parking garage close by.

Things seemed to be going his way as he walked in the door of the sandwich shop with no one in line even though it was midday, he walked right up to the counter. He ordered his sandwich and a fountain drink. He didn't normally drink soda, but when they had cherry coke, from the fountain, he made an exception. He stepped out of the shop, took a sip of his drink and let out a sigh of contentment. He took the stairs back to his car.

As soon as the door closed on the 3rd floor of the garage Samuel heard the echoes of a struggle. The first thing he saw was a man standing, then he saw a man kneeling with his fist poised to come down onto a third man on the ground in the center of the down ramp. In those seconds Samuel could tell that the man on the ground was being beaten. The man standing was looking up the garage ramp when his head started a slow turn towards Samuel. Samuel ducked behind the car trying to be as small and as quiet as possible. Threats continued to echo in the garage; they weren't shouts but the tones were enough to shake Samuel to the core.

"All this can stop" came from one of the two assaulting the lone man on the ground. "Give us your wallet and your phone and we will leave you be."

Samuel hunkered down to avoid being seen, got close to the car to his right and raised his head just enough so he could peer through the window. The images were distorted through a couple panes of auto glass but Samuel could see the two standing over the one. The two were stomping and heckling the one, taunting him, while using fear to keep him on the ground. Samuel noticed that the ice in his drink was shaking, so he pulled his hand close to his body so that it would be steadied and the rattling ice would cease its chattering. The two had their backs turned to where Samuel was hidden. Skin on skin slaps echoed down the ramp sharp and clear like the two had made a career of slapping, slapping their girlfriends or little sisters perhaps. The echoes drifted down to where Samuel was hiding. He hunkered down again afraid to be seen, as he tried to be one with the paint on the side of the car. He was petrified. He couldn't move if he wanted to. Fear held him in place, fear leached from his body causing him to shake uncontrollably. His ears strained to hear if the men were coming closer. He simply wished he could turn his ears off, to stop hearing the taunts and the slaps that the one on the ground was suffering.

A vehicle not far off beeped as if being unlocked remotely. The two stopped their assault and ran off, their hurried steps echoing closer. *They are coming this way!* The footfalls where closing in on Samuel. He cringed and he tried to make himself invisible even though it was not possible as he cowered. He could hear the two as they ran right past him, as if he were simply not there. The door banged open as the one in the lead slammed into it and both continued on their way. Samuel's heart was banging like cymbals in his ears. His breathing was fast and shallow. The door to the stairs clicked closed, and only then did Samuel open his eyes. He heard the scrapes of the one trying to pick itself up off the ground in the middle of the ramp on level three of the parking garage. The sound of sniffling and possibly tears filled every aspect of the third floor of the garage. It choked the air, it bounded off the cement walls and it seemed to dim the lights just for a moment as Samuel nervously got to a crouch and peered through the glass again just enough to see the one attempt to rise in the middle of the ramp. A woman was walking down and saw the man. She rushed over to the man "Oh my God, are you ok?" That was all that could be heard clearly, after that he could see their lips move, he could hear hushed conversation, but not all of the words were lost. Words like police and nowhere along with the occasional sniffle and scuffle of feet bounced off the walls and found a way to Samuel. The rest of the conversation was lost to the pounding in his ears and the concrete of the parking garage. The smooth gray walls seemed to swallow not just the words but the color as well. Samuel became aware of what the third floor of the parking garage presented. The bright lights that came through the gaps on this level washed everything in gray. He rose from his position and watched the lady help the one to his car. Only then did Samuel realize that he was sweating, not a good work out sweat, it was the sweat of sitting in a sauna turned all the way up while wearing a parka and ski gear. His shirt was soaked through and his sport jacket was wet from his pits to his waist. He ran quickly and quietly to his car, unlocked it, jumped in and locked the doors. His heart was hammering from the short run and being witness to the mugging. He looked down at himself and realized that he was still holding the sandwich and cherry coke his rewards for doing a good job in the interview. He cracked the door and flung the contents of his arms on the floor, the cherry coke spilled and ran away from the moment just like Samuel. He closed the door and jammed the keys in the ignition, or tried to as his hands wouldn't stop shaking. After several attempts with the keys, he took one steadying breath and inserted the key, turning it, bringing the car to life. The car was thrown in gear to back out and thrown in gear again as Samuel sped down two levels to the street.

The afternoon was beautiful, that's what someone would say if trying to cheer the beleaguered middle-aged man. The shortage of jobs this time around has been running longer than usual, but that was the furthest thing from Samuels mind now. He has vowed to be a great father and good husband; everything else would fall into place. He didn't particularly feel like a great human being let alone a great father or a good husband. Samuel drove in circles knowing that he would eventually have to go home. Home meant having to face what he had witnessed after his interview.

Why didn't I help that person? I'm a coward that's why. I'm a runner not a fighter. If it were my family I would have fought, or am I just telling myself that to make it all better. No. I would have fought poorly, but at least I would have made a stand, not acting like a child frightened of the monster in his closet. The truth did little to comfort Samuel. At a stop light Samuel ripped off his damp sport jacket putting it in the passenger seat. Then loosening his tie, he violently ripped it from around his neck. The act of ripping the tie was so exaggerated that a button was ripped off as well, it hit the windshield and was gone. The windows were down and that helped to start to dry out his pits and slow his breathing. The light changed as Samuel started to question everything he was, everything he had been. The interview went well, but how could he focus on that when he was paralyzed by fear. All he could hear were the struggles of the victim in the parking garage.

Forget the job Sam you're not even worthy of that job. You left that person. You left him to fear and torment. Why? Just because you were afraid of getting slapped around? No you were afraid of leaving Maggie alone with three kids to raise. You were afraid of not seeing Marcus graduate. You were...not the person you hoped you would be. Samuel blew out a huge sigh. *That person on the third floor of the parking garage could have worked in the office where you applied, and if you'd have stepped up, you could have counted on a job.*

Samuel was so bewildered and distracted he almost ran a stop light. He slammed on the breaks and his tires just went past the crosswalk line into the intersection. People went about their day not paying any attention to Samuel who just had a good interview and a dreadful personal experience. With his hands over his eyes, breathing hard, not quite knowing how he was going to get home when a car pulled up next to his at the intersection and his ears picked up on music. The driver of the car next to him had the volume up as the lyrics drifted across the way into Samuel's ears and let him breathe easier for just a moment.

The less that you have water,

The more that you can falter,

The less that you have air,

The more you feel despair,

So breathe...breathe deep...center yourself

Drink... drink deep ...and put your trouble on the shelf.

A musical interlude filled the speakers for a few seconds then the singing continued.

Then listen to your heart...

Samuel took his hands away from his eyes when a horn honked behind him, he snapped out of his trance, saw the light was green and accelerated through the intersection. He reached for the radio power button and listened to the music. It was an artist he was unfamiliar with whose voice wafted out of the speakers and he found that listening to the music slowed his respirations. He hummed the music, not knowing the words. The song ended and another followed. Samuel, with each passing song, could feel himself relax, could not hear his heart in his ears anymore and felt he could make it home without wrecking the car. The music floated by as he drove and then the interview found its way back into his head. He felt he had done a pretty good job in the interview as his mind turned to the good points of the day just like the wind rolling around the inside of the car and the music that kept him company. He was starting to dry off from the downpour of sweat, and that started him rethinking as to why he was wet in the first place. He started to think about the episode in the garage, but instead he turned up the radio, letting the episode of the two versus the one fly out of his head. Letting the memories and fears fly right out the window and get swept by in the traffic like a plastic shopping bag drifting on the highway. Samuel took his exit and kept listening to the good tunes the DJ's were playing. He knew that he had to make a stop at the grocery store, he just wasn't sure if he was up to being around anyone at this point in the day. He collected himself and started to evaluate himself as he sat in his car in the parking lot of his local supermarket.

Jobs have never been easy for Samuel to hold onto or to find, and the marital stress because of the lack of a job wasn't helping matters. It was a run-away engine with no oil, just waiting until the rpms hit their cap, then boom! The oil, lubrication, was the job. That lack of oil was starting to wear on the engine of his marriage. Maggie wouldn't put that stress on him or make those analogies to him, it was just a fact of life. Now being a father is all Samuel was truly good at, he thought; *now don't get me wrong I don't think I am arrogant, but I am a good father, it's just …I've always thought confidence comes in drops while arrogance in showers. Besides its all I have to cling to now.* Samuel took all of this in stride as his strides took him into the grocery store and deeper into considering his job as a father, which was one of the steady positives he had going for him. *Marcus has been withdrawing* he thought as he started placing his items on the belt for checkout. This was to be expected with Marcus being in his teens. Samuel and Maggie had noticed the change and weren't sure how to proceed. Now Marcus wasn't Samuels's son but he had been there when he was born and always treated Marcus as his own, going as far as to adopt Marcus. The bond Marcus and Samuel shared had always been based on trust and love, until now. Something was rearing its ugly head and Samuel didn't know what to make of it. Pulling into the driveway and parking the Subaru, Samuel let the music of Moody Blues Tuesday afternoon take him to another place, briefly.

Samuel had been a child when they were big, but the love of music was something his dad instilled in him and Samuel kept it alive. That passion even extended into Samuels learning the saxophone. Music was therapy. As the song ended Samuel moved into the house knowing the kids would be home soon and dinner needed to be started. Putting out the flowers for his wife Maggie was the first business. Flowers for no reason, well a slight reason, were some of the best flowers you could get a woman. Working on something that Samuel could completely control would help take his mind off of the ups and down of the day. Even his concerns about Marcus rolled away as the beef and broth came to a rolling boil. Later he added carrots, potatoes and onions to the mix and Samuel was well on the way to a good beef stew. The vegetables were half way done when the clamor of the two youngest took Samuel away from preparing the meal. *Hmmm, I didn't even hear the bus.* Samuel moved with haste to greet and hug Denise and Robert. Samuel was not a big man, about average, but the kids were still young enough to be scooped up in one big hug.

"Hi Daddy," they echoed, one trying to be louder than the other.

"Did you both have a good day at school?" Samuel asked knowing full well the routine.

"We-ee-ee-ee, HA HA HA," the children carried on with trying to answer as Samuel put a gentle repeating squeeze on his children causing them to stutter with each squeeze then break out in laughter. *I used to do that with Marcus, where has the time gone?*

I better enjoy it with the Denise and Robert as long as I can. Setting the children down they began telling of the day's highlights. Samuel went back to the stove and the kids dug into their backpacks pulling out the day's work. There was a cut and paste and a couple of number sheets that the kids showed Samuel. Each of the kids picked their best work and hung it on the refrigerator.

"Have either of you seen Marcus?" Samuel questioned as he stirred the contents of the pot checking the carrots and potatoes; they always took the longest to cook. Samuel looked up from the simmering pot to see the answers on the kid's faces as much as hear their responses. Samuel asked, knowing the children might not have an answer because of the difference in schedules. Marcus came home between 2:00 and 2:30 while the kids about 3:30, depending on the buses. Both stopped for a moment, looked at each other, and then their unsure eyes came back to Samuel, then quietly said "no," as they went back to the table and their backpacks. The twins never lied except when it came to Marcus, Samuel knew that would change eventually. They both looked up to their big brother and didn't want to betray that. Samuel knew they weren't completely truthful but wouldn't push the kids and put them in the middle. *Sometimes you have to let the kids go on a lie. This one concerning Marcus I'll especially let go. There were many times when Carl, Susan and I were in that same situation.* They were good kids and loved their brother. Half-brother really, but with the Willis family, like Samuel was taught by his father, it was all or nothing when it came to family. Working on dinner Samuel heard the automatic garage door opener start. Two minutes later Maggie came into the house with dry cleaning in one hand and her cell phone in the other.

She is going to know, she always does. No matter how I try to hide what I'm feeling she knows. She has watched me for years. I don't even know all of my tells, but man she has my number. I could blink slightly slower and she would know that something was up. I guess that is a good thing, having someone you know you can rely on, even if you can't rely on yourself.

Samuel let out a sigh and accidently dropped the spoon he was stirring with. Samuel picked up the spoon went to the sink to rinse it and went right back to the simmering pot. The kids scrambled spreading their affections and dancing around Maggie looking for a little mommy love. Clap! The phone was down and the dry cleaning hung on the door jam, Maggie now crouched on their level listening, gasping, and animating to engage the children with expressive eyes and large smiles. Maggie's brownish red hair which hung just past her shoulders, was simply beautiful. He loved that she constantly pushed her hair behind her ear and right on cue, her hand came up and pushed the hair back. Samuel chuckled. He could still smell her shampoo even after a day of work and hustle. Dressed in a gray suit and matching skirt, Samuel sighed looking at her legs and seeing her smile. That smile seemed to have a magic of its own. She was a wonderful woman and mother as well as an amazing wife. *I'm repaying all this by not holding up my end of the stick. She would never call me out on a lack of employment, but I know she is distracted; distracted about bills and money. I know that it will all work out with a job I just need to stop being so hard on myself, that's what Maggie would say. Still, I can see the worry on Maggie's face as she plays with the kids. Marcus could be picking up on it as well. He is smart enough and old enough to know that life can be difficult.*

"Mmmm, smells good. What's for dinner?" Maggie asked throwing a quick arm around Samuel's neck looking into his eyes then planting a peck on his lips. *She knew something is wrong and still she didn't ask me. She also seems to be in a better mood than this morning. I'm too damn lucky.* In typical Maggie fashion she collected her cell phone and called through the doorway to the stairs, "I'm gonna go get in comfy clothes, hang up the dry cleaning and I'll be down before dinner."

Samuel knew this meant that she would work till the family was half way finished with dinner and come down for a few bites only to feign being stuffed then return to their bedroom to continue business. *Real estate has saved us, so I guess I really cannot complain. God knows I haven't been putting that much bread on the table so to speak. Teaching is paying, but it's not really sustainable. I'm also glad she didn't pry too hard into my day, I'm not ready to relive what happened in the garage. Just like when Richard died she wasn't ready to really talk and only recently has she hinted at starting that conversation.*

Everything went to plan, except, no Marcus. Cleaning up after dinner, Samuel put the leftovers away; while putting portions away for Maggie's lunch and covering a plate for Marcus, he was wondering again where his son had been. *Where is Marcus? He's never this late.* Satisfied with the cleanup in the kitchen Samuel moved to the office of Margaret (Maggie) Lynn Willis, aka their bedroom. Samuel stood in the doorway in silence watching her move and waiting for a break in the shuffle. The room was warmly lit while papers covered the desk and the double bed. That had been their first bed, and the one Maggie spent most nights working on. Pushing the hair from her face with a sigh she noticed Samuel who smirked at the hard-working love of his life.

"Hi dear. how goes it," Samuel questioned crossing the room to plant a kiss on his wife.

"Good, two possible sales and I have two new referrals. So...no luck on the interviews huh?" "We'll see," said Samuel with a shrug.

"Well that's ok too, we are making ends meet and a little more. So why the troubled brow my love," Maggie asked gently putting her arms around Samuel's neck as he joined her sitting on the bed. *She is truly wonderful. I put more pressure on myself than Maggie ever does. She knows something went wrong. I just don't have the heart right now to go into it. 'The interview was good sweetie, I just let a mugging happen and did nothing to stop it.' No I'll just let her believe that the interview was no good. I'll explain later.*

Pulling himself from his thoughts with a quick subject

change "Marcus isn't home yet?" Samuel probed shaking his head and pausing for a moment not sure whether to continue or not. "Have you noticed how he has withdrawn lately?"

"He is being a typical teen; his grades are up so we agreed not to push. I mean his chores have started to slack a little, but I don't think that is any reason to really come down on him," Maggie said looking at Samuel at first then moving her attention to another pile of papers.

"You don't suppose he is doing drugs do you?"

"No, Marcus isn't like that. He's more like his old man, walking his own path."

"Do you mean me or Daniel," Samuel retorted knowing that was a sensitive subject, for himself most of all. Daniel was Marcus' biological father. A couple years back, Marcus showed interest in finding his dad. Samuel did what any good Dad would do and encouraged Marcus. It took some time but Daniel was eventually found but wanted nothing to do with Marcus, much to Marcus' dismay. He took it really hard, but bounced back quickly. Samuel's father had given him some advice when he was still a boy. Like any good father Samuel made sure he passed it to Marcus. Samuel could hear that three pack a day, deep and raspy voice of his father saying; *Don't chain yourself to the past or look too far to the future that you might trip over something very good, in the present;* well something like that. Marcus was a tough kid and Samuel respected him for that.

"You Samuel; you're his old man. You've been there to wipe tears, brush skinned knees and drive him to his first dance," Maggie said again wrapping her husband in her arms and pulling him close. Looking deep, drilling with intensity into Samuel's eyes to make her point, she knew Samuel had hang ups about the dynamics of being Marcus' father. Samuel reading the look, "I know, I just can't help but wonder if we should try and sway him to making another effort, I just don't want any lingering doubt."

The papers that Maggie was holding floated gently to the ground at their feet and with a soft and loving look in her eyes, "I love you Samuel Willis, you are a good man and have been great with Marcus and the kids. I can tell the lack of job is affecting you, but don't let that translate to your relationships with Marcus, Denise and Robert. They are smart and will pick up on it," she finished by planting a soft and slightly wet kiss ever so gently on his lips. *Sigh, I am truly blessed, lucky or maybe, just maybe both.*

"Thanks hon, you're the best." Samuel couldn't hold it in anymore he told Maggie what had happened in the garage after the interview. She listened with no expression. Once he finished his account, he visibly slumped as if recounting the misfortune allowed Samuel to shrug off a hundred-pound backpack. She rubbed his arm letting the silence take hold, making sure that Samuel had nothing more to add.

"I love you. I married a man whose strength is inside, not out. What would have happened if they had knives or worse guns? I think you did all that you could. Only you can say if you should have or would have done more. I'm glad you didn't. You came home to me and the kids, made us a delicious meal and that is good enough for me."

"But the fear, Maggie, it was petrifying. What if that were you or the kids?"

"You would have stopped them and protected your family. I know that, I believe that with every fiber of my being," Maggie finished, standing up and pulling Samuel into her arms. The embrace lasted long, longer that Samuel expected but Maggie just kept squeezing. Each of them let up at the same time. "You're the best, Margaret Lynn Willis."

"Sometimes," Maggie replied, seeing that Samuel was slightly better after the talk. He stood a little straighter and didn't have a defeated look in his eyes. Maggie went back to work figuring the issue resolved, for now at least. Samuel however didn't have her faith. But speaking of faith Samuel remembered, "I do have to start those cookies I said I'd bake for the Sunday school class. Don't work too hard." Samuel winked and returned to the kitchen. The cookies helped him take his mind off rehashing what happened in the garage for just a bit. Something that traumatic doesn't just leave, it lingers like a fart in a car. As Samuel wrapped up the cookies and finished cleaning, his mind wasn't clear enough for sleep.

Looking to the garage door, Samuel knew relaxation and peace of mind rested behind the door to the garage. *One garage caused issues, the other holds a means to quiet the emotions of the day.* One side contained Maggie's Explorer; the other half was filled with bicycles, balls and other toys, including Samuel's. His Saxophone was resting on a stand. He retrieved it, wet the reed and fingered the keys. It had a couple of tiny dents, nothing to affect the sound really, and it was tarnished and in need of a good cleaning. Samuel sat on one end of the children's play bench and began to play. The sounds that escaped were clean and smooth unlike the instruments body. It was so easy for Samuel to get lost in the sweet sounds. The highs and lows of the notes, playing the saxophone was otherworldly as far as Samuel was concerned. He was just learning but that was the point to try something new and keep working at it. Working through the sweet sounds and the horrible squeaks, was all a part of the process. Samuel stopped just to marvel at that feeling, the tingle that passed all over his body, closing his eyes to wrap himself in the moment. The knots of his mind began to loosen. A few deep breaths helped along the purging process and the problems seem to unravel, making the world just a little easier to deal with. It was at this moment Samuel was clued into the entire goings-on around the house, every creak, his wife's footsteps upstairs as well as the compressor on the fridge kicking on, and then the front door opened. Waking from his trance Samuel put back his saxophone and listened before moving into the house. Walking to the door slowly Samuel could swear he could hear a conversation; a muted conversation with a hint of duress. Walking up the couple of stairs, cracking the door that lead to the kitchen and then opening the door all the way Samuel found only Marcus. Marcus spun quickly and looked at his old man; Samuel noted his son's eyes were wide like saucers and his hands were curiously behind his back.

"Hey Marcus, who were you talking to?" Samuel asked peering into the dimly lit kitchen to see who else was there.

"Nobody!"

"Come on, I could swear I could hear a conversation. Were you talking to yourself? If not, I won't be upset if you have a friend over either." Samuel closed the door, looked around the kitchen, then closed the distances between Marcus and himself. Samuel witnessed something he would remember for years; Marcus retreated with fear in his eyes from his old man. The look in Marcus's eye froze Samuel. *What have I done or not done for that matter to have Marcus this afraid of me? I can't believe it's happening right in front of me.* Trying to deflect, Samuel tried again, "Marcus are you ok? It is late Bud, I have some supper wrapped for you if you're hungry." Trying not to focus on Marcus' retreat or that he was hiding his hands, Samuel just wanted Marcus to talk. Still Marcus retreated slowly, carefully, seeming very unsure of the moment, but nonetheless he continued his retreat.

"No I'm just tired" Marcus, said with hands still hidden. Trying to make light of the situation Samuel put his hands behind his back.

"Is this the way kids hang these days?" Samuel asked and Marcus rolled his eyes. "No Dad", and was backing his way out of the kitchen showing a slight sign of coming out of his posture, but then went right back to it, guarded and fearful.

"Something is going on son. I can tell. Why don't we just sit down and talk about...whatever," Samuel, matching his son's pace with his hands extended and then back at his sides was almost asking for a hug as his son rounded the corner and was gone up the stairs. Samuel followed thinking *Marcus is fast.* A slightly winded Samuel reached the top of the stairs huffing and puffing.

The upstairs was dark; the exception was the light that came from under Marcus's door. The light seemed brighter than normal as Samuel squinted at the bright light walking to the door and knocking. "Marcus? Can we talk?" The knob turned easily and the room was as it should be, posters plastered this way and that. Music of various types and artists stacked on the dresser. The light in the room seemed less than it did in the hallway. On Marcus' bedside table there was a small reading lamp that provided the room's light, but didn't seem as bright as when Samuel topped the stairs. Marcus rarely used the overhead light which Samuel switched on and off quickly, trying to make sense of the bright light. Samuel was ready to talk to Marcus.

The only thing that was missing to complete the picture of the room was Marcus. The closet door was open, *not in there.* The curtain whispered to hint that Marcus might have fled into the night. Samuel went to the window looked out and saw nothing. The screen had been patched where Marcus used to cut small holes to break into the house. These holes in the screen he would use in order to get the screen out and climb through the window. Marcus was notorious for losing his keys and this window, slightly cracked would allow him in the house without telling Samuel or Maggie he had lost his keys again. But that hadn't happened in years.

"The kid is a regular magician," Samuel said closing the window not locking it. Samuel always wanted to leave an option for his son, he didn't want him to feel trapped, like there was no way out. *Tomorrow bud, we will talk about this tomorrow.* Samuel walked to his bedroom to talk to Maggie about Marcus.

"Did you get Marcus' text? He said that he was heading to

Nelson's to finish up a project and might spend the night if they don't get done what needs done." Maggie said showing Samuel her cell as he scratched his chin. This wasn't out of the ordinary as Marcus and Nelson usually teamed up for projects. This left Samuel's mind slightly at ease but he couldn't help but think, *I could have sworn Marcus was in his room.*

CHAPTER 4

Watch

The next morning Samuel checked Marcus' room before looking in on the twins. The room was undisturbed, bed still made, window slightly cracked and everything where it was the night before. Closing the door with a sigh, Samuel went to his usual spot in the morning, sitting on the toilet and talking with his wife as she prepared for work. Pulling the lid down on the seat Samuel started with a raised voice, "Marcus didn't come home last night." The conversation continued after the hair dryer stopped, Samuel sat in typical thinking man pose.

"He's a teenager Sam, they go through periods when they don't talk and want to be on their own. I would try and talk to him but you and I both know that will result in a screaming match, followed by Marcus and I not speaking for weeks." Maggie was right about Marcus and herself especially in the last couple years. Before that it wasn't as bad. History and personality similarities dictated that if Maggie approached Marcus it would end up ugly. Maggie checked herself in the mirror and reached for something out of her make-up bag. She did a little more touching up here and there. She looked back to Samuel with her hand on the light switch, Samuel stood and left the bathroom. "I'm gonna be late if I don't motor." Maggie said as Samuel followed her down stairs. Maggie opened the fridge to retrieve her lunch and smiled as she closed the door. She presented the container to Samuel which had a sticky note on it saying, 'love you wife' and then placed it in her lunch bag along with an apple from the fruit bowl. In this way they were like high school kids, leaving notes for each other, whispering sweet nothings in each other's ears and long kisses when no one was looking. "I love you too Samuel and I know we, mostly you, will figure out what is bothering Marcus because we both know you are better at it than I am. One foot in front of the other right?" Maggie asked blowing Samuel a kiss and was gone. *Maggie is sure that things will work out...I'm not so sure. She didn't see the expressions on Marcus' face, she didn't see his posture, odd and chary. It wasn't a side that I've ever seen of Marcus.*

Denise and Robert were up and playing. Another normal morning of dressing, brushing, eating and running for the bus. With a chance of showers later that day, Samuel handed Denise and Robert an umbrella each. Sword fighting with the umbrellas, Denise and Robert were typical brother and sister acting out one of Samuel's bedtime stories. Robert played El Mustachio, an over the top hero with flair and panache as well as an immaculately groomed mustache. He dressed in exaggerated outfits with flowing capes and scarves, and vanquished his enemies by poking them in the bottom with his rapier. Denise was playing the evil Count Waxamillion, El Mustachio's nemesis. The scene ended as the bus arrived and they were off to school. After seeing the kids get on the bus Samuel went back to the house and started his to do list. This day it would be a little easier with no interviews. Samuel edited his to do list in order to be home before Marcus. While he took items off the list, Samuel started to have the conservation in his mind he would initiate with Marcus. He did this to try to orchestrate the conversation with his son that would take place later, planning it all out this way so Samuel could avoid any missteps when talking with Marcus. Samuel's day consisted of shopping, dry cleaning, fueling and searching for more jobs. *I'll make Marcus' favorite tonight in hopes that it will make the medicine go down a little easier. I've taken a couple of items off my list let me add one; call Mary Patricia.* With that Samuel stopped at the butcher shop to get the special ingredients of his spaghetti, fresh ground beef and Italian sausage. Then to the grocery store for the more usual ingredients. The rest of the day went by pretty quickly. Samuel noted the time and raced home in order to get the sauce started as well as attempt to beat Marcus home so he could butter him up a bit. Pulling into the drive and checking the car's clock, he was making good time and started to unload the groceries. Samuel went to work on the meats, which were browned and drained, added tomato sauces and paste and finally tomato puree. After an hour the sauce was at a steady simmer. Samuel added spices and left the kitchen, heading upstairs, to put the dry cleaning away when he noticed Marcus' door was cracked. Samuel remembered closing it before taking the kids to the bus. They were with him until everyone left the house for the bus, so they couldn't have opened Marcus' door. Barely touching the door, it inched open slowly and quietly. Inside the room Marcus lay on his stomach sleeping soundly with one arm draped over the side. Confused, Samuel looked at the clock on Marcus's nightstand; according to it, Marcus has five more minutes left till school let out. *What is he doing home so early?* Not quite sure what to do, Samuel gently put his son's arm on the bed knowing that Marcus wouldn't wake or stir at all. Testing how deeply Marcus slept, Samuel lifted Marcus' arm and dropped it, *typical,* Samuel thought. Marcus didn't resist, but that move would at least cause his breathing to change or cause him to move some way. *Oh my god he's ...* Samuel stopped himself as he noticed his son's breathing continued, rhythmic and even. Making sure, Samuel felt for a pulse at Marcus' wrist. *Sigh.* Closing the door Samuel, walked downstairs when he almost tripped over Marcus' school bag with an out of place piece of paper sticking out of an open pocket.

"I can't go through his stuff, but taking a closer look isn't over the line," Samuel said softly getting on one knee to examine the paper without removing it. The paper, folded in half, had Marcus' name and the address of the house. After that all he could see was that it was Marcus' report card, but with the paper folded he couldn't see any grades.

"Well, that's…mmmm," Samuel looked around feeling guilty and dishonest. He trusted Marcus but he was asleep and wanted to know if grades were the reason for the change in his son's behavior. Slowly, carefully, not pulling the paper all the way out, Samuel gave it a quick glance. Samuel saw all A's and B's. Then he returned it quickly to the position it had been, rising even quicker as he dusted his hands. In the kitchen, stirring the sauce, Samuel went back to trying to resolve the issue of his aloof son. The rest of the time before the family came home went by without a hitch. Samuel wasn't a big fan of spaghetti per se. The pasta shape wasn't conducive to holding the sauce, so Samuel pulled out the rigatoni; *this holds the sauce the best*.

Dinner was ready and Samuel couldn't wait to wake his son and see that sleepy smile and have Marcus ask "Is that spaghetti I smell?" Samuel jogged up the stairs excited to see that expression. Cracking the door and looking in on Marcus as the family assembled, Samuel was confused when looked at the bed and especially his son. Marcus had not moved, not an inch from the spot that Samuel left him when he found him earlier. His breathing was still rhythmic and deep, "Marcus, dinner is ready, it's spaghetti your favorite" Samuel stated bending over to touch his son, but stopped seeing him so peaceful and serene. It contradicted all that Samuel had seen since Marcus stopped being Marcus, especially last night. Second-guessing himself Samuel gave Marcus a gentle shake and still nothing changed. Marcus was still sleeping the sleep of the dead, the likes of which Samuel had never seen from his son.

"Son," raising his voice and shaking him harder, Samuel confused and concerned wanted to run to the phone and call the doctor right away. Lifting his son's arm and dropping it again,

Samuel knew his son was alive but in some kind of sleep coma. *Maybe he is just that tired. I'll give him till after dinner, and then I'll call the doctor.* Samuel returned to the dinner table, where his family waited.

"He's still sleeping," Samuel said as he sat with a shrug and joined hands with the family to say grace. Spaghetti night was special, everyone looked forward not just to the meal but the leftovers. The Willis family would go through all the leftovers in three short days. Even Maggie, who would make excuses to work through dinner, didn't skip out on this meal. The kids slurped the extra sauce off of their forks. At one point they tried to lift their plates to lick the sauce, but a sideways look from Samuel and Maggie stopped the kids as they giggled and put down their plates. Maggie and Samuel exchanged weak smiles each knowing the others concern for their oldest son. Putting aside a large plate after dinner for Marcus and cleaning the dishes in a trance, Samuel made sure the twins were ready for bed with more tales of El Mustachio. Then he would check on his son. As Samuel exited the twins room he found Marcus coming out of his room, pulling on a clean shirt. Taking in a breath, "I missed spaghetti didn't I?" Marcus said walking to meet Samuel at the top of the stairs. Marcus looked as if he had just woken up with evidence of long deep sleep still on his face, eyes barely open and not standing quite up straight. From Samuel and Maggie's bedroom, Maggie poked her head out to see her son was up and about.

"There is a plate down on the stove. After you've finished eating I think we should talk, what do you think," asked Samuel as Marcus shrugged and brushed slightly against his Dad and headed down stairs. Maggie intercepted Marcus and gave him a kiss on the cheek before he went two steps.

"Thanks Mom," said Marcus as he descended the stairs rounding the corner on the intermediate landing walking down the rest of the way he headed into the kitchen. Maggie kissed Samuel and went back to work, throwing him a wink for good measure. After checking on the kids and then Maggie once more, Samuel joined his son who had finished most of the plate already. Cracking a soda, Samuel slid it in front of Marcus and sat in silence except for the odd slurp or scrape from the plate to get all the sauce he could. Samuel got up without Marcus noticing, then returned with two pieces of buttered bread setting them on the edge of Marcus' plate. Samuel had done it all his life, they both enjoyed the bread and it was really good at getting the last of the sauce, as opposed to the twin's method.

"How is school?"

"Ok. Nothing unusual." Marcus said tracing the bread through the leftover sauce.

"Report cards come out soon don't they?" Samuel probed, feigning ignorance.

"I got mine. It's in my bag." Marcus got up, licking his fingers and went to the hall and retrieved the previewed report card and presented it to his father. Samuel looked it over, knowing the gist of the report card, just verifying A's and B's across the board.

"Good work," Samuel said sliding the report card back and taking the plate as well as the empty can and replacing it with a full one, before talking his seat again.

"Thanks," murmured Marcus taking a couple swigs of the soda that was followed by a stifled burp.

"Son, talk to me. I know something is going on. I can tell; I've known you all your life."

"Why the fifth degree Dad?" Marcus asked as he glanced up from this hands, going past the third and fourth degrees. "I get good grades and do my chores, haven't we agreed that is the deal?"

"Yes, but home earlier than school has let out, sleeping all afternoon and where were you last night? Your mother and I haven't set a curfew for you the last couple years, but last night was pushing it a bit don't you think," Samuel pressed as he noticed Marcus again looking at this hands. "You seem distracted, almost like you're not even here. I know you and your mother have had rough patches, but you and I have always been able to talk," Samuel said rising to retrieve the cookie dough ice cream he and Marcus would share over tough talks. At the fridge Samuel heard Marcus gasp and then a muted slap. Turning with the ice cream, Marcus had transformed. Fear was in his eyes and his face displayed despair and regret. As Samuel's confused look fell on Marcus it seemed that the colors in his clothing were fading; he was wearing the same face he wore last night.

"Marcus, son what's wrong?" Samuel's tone was strong, his face sympathetic. Before he could finish his thought, his son pulled his long sleeves down over his hands and then bolted for the stairs. The ice cream thumped on the floor as Samuel's foot hit the first stair. Samuel was at the turn for the stairs when he heard, SLAM! *Don't do this son I want to help you. Don't run away from me again please.* As Samuel reached the door and tried the knob stopping as Marcus started to speak. "I don't want to talk anymore." Samuel normally respected his son's space, but something very basic, almost instinctual urged Samuel to finish his turn of the door knob and push open the door without asking. The dim light of Marcus' reading lamp cast barely enough light in the room. Marcus was facing the window with his back to Samuel

"Son, what's wrong? You don't have to hide whatever your dealing with from me, don't pull away please, I want to help," Samuel pleaded reaching for his son and trying to slowly close the distance. Watching every move Marcus made, Samuel saw Marcus, even though his back was turned, wringing his wrist. "What's wrong with your wrist..." Samuel asked. As the "t" in wrist left his mouth his son went again through another transformation. Rage turned to face Samuel, not his son. Rage that Samuel had never thought possible from his son started in Marcus' stomach and spit froth from his mouth as if it had been fire.

"GET AWAY FROM ME!" Marcus pushed Samuel across the

room with amazing strength. Knocked back to the threshold of Marcus' door, Samuel was about to yell when he heard quick footsteps behind him. Samuel glanced back over his shoulder and saw Maggie head into the twin's room to check on the kids. Samuel was surprised by the shove as their house had never been a violet one. Marcus was spanked once in his entire life and the twins never. Samuel was into Marcus' room as his focus came back to Marcus but stopped as something glittering caught his eye. Suddenly Samuel was hypnotized by a band of gold encircling his son's wrist.

"Where did you get that? You didn't have that downstairs," Samuel, still shocked asked and stated barely audibly. The fear swept back in and Marcus started to cry, silent sobs as he turned his back to Samuel. Approaching his son with feathery footsteps the floorboard creaked under Samuels's weight. Samuel was about to grab his son's shoulders to comfort him when Marcus' fear took over and he unexpectedly spun into his father's arms. Marcus who was now in Samuel's arms, started to thrash and try and free himself of his father's loving embrace. "I love you Marcus." With a few shakes and twists, Marcus had worked out of the embrace. Samuel reached out and now had both of Marcus' wrists to try and contain him so he could look his son in the eyes and let him know it was going to be alright that he would help him through anything that happened. Marcus managed to get one wrist free as he increased his efforts, his desperate struggle to be away from his father. Marcus shook and thrashed as Samuel held on with every ounce of strength he could muster. Marcus kept up the movements, a crazy dance of jumping and trying to circle his father, yanking his arm every way imaginable wanting only to free himself from the grip his father had on him. Marcus pulled and leaned away as Samuels's hand rested against the watch. Marcus stopped his efforts for just a moment and stared into his father's eyes. Samuel saw fresh panic and fear wade into Marcus' face producing more tears, not believing his son expressions could be more hopeless.

The color was all but gone from Marcus who was pale as a sheet, standing still as his eyes went from the watch on his wrist to his father's astounded face. Marcus pleaded one last time, "Dad, no, please no. Just let this go. You can't help me, not with this."

That was the source, the watch. A simple gold band had sent Marcus into such a frenzy of emotions that Samuel knew he had to relieve Marcus of the watch. Samuel's love for his son overwhelmed him at this critical juncture. He maintained his grip, firmed his resolve and kept repeating, "I love you Marcus. I love you, son." Samuel repeated the words aloud like a prayer as Marcus started his sporadic movements again throwing himself to the floor, doing anything to be liberated of his father's grip. Marcus stood up as fast as he had fallen, jerked once, twice more, straightened and then called upon the strength he used to push his father before. Samuel could not hold on and took two steps back. Marcus with tears in his eyes smiled ever so slightly at his father. The smile disappeared in a blank stare. Samuel stood before Marcus and opened his hand. There was the watch, glittering just barely in the faint light of Marcus' reading lamp. Samuel looked up from his hand, his eyes came upon his distraught son as he held the watch. One moment later Samuel was gone and Marcus was alone in his bedroom. "NOOOOOOO!"

CHAPTER 5

Grayland

A foreign sensation enveloped Samuels's body, it was a chill from head to toe as if he wanted to shiver but couldn't. This covered an ache that stretched from his toes.... As Samuel looked down at his feet they were white. Not only that but they had no flesh, muscle, tendons or anything else that would cover the bones in his feet. The rest of his legs, bony as well, were covered by black or faded black. It could have been dark gray fabric. Samuel reached down to pull up the material that felt like heavy canvas and noticed his white hands as he looked at his white feet. Bony, no skin or blood, just bone. He lifted the cloth covering his legs and bits fell off the edges of the material like ash from a fire. Dropping the cloth and now focusing on his hands, something he could see up close, he slowly flexed his hands right in front of his face. Hypnotized by each flex and reflex, Samuel wasn't sure what to make of this change or how long it would last.

"What is going on?" Samuel asked out loud, now looking around to see if anyone was there to hear his question. The four stone walls surrounding him certainly couldn't answer his question. Moving closer to the wall to study his surroundings, each stone was built upon another. Mortar or cement, he didn't know which, held the stones in place. The floor like the walls were made of stone. Reaching out to touch the wall to make sure he wasn't dreaming or hallucinating, he heard bone scrape on stone. He barely felt the surface of the stone under his fingers as well as the vibrations from running his fingers over the surface, but the stone itself he could not feel; not how rough it was or any temperature either. Pushing on the wall with his right hand he felt only the faintest pressure as he lent all his strength to that one spot. Looking up with his hand still on the wall, Samuel stepped back as he gazed up at red storm clouds as they flew by. A sky light, or really the lack of a top to this box, was a window showing fast moving clouds giving way to spears of black, blue, yellow and green lightning. Focusing back on his hand, Samuel went to move away from the wall only to find his hand stuck to the wall. Looking closely, his bony hand had sunk into the stone and mortar, ever so slightly, as if a bond had been formed.

"Great, what do I do now?" Throwing his other bony hand on his hip, he faced the wall. Putting his foot on the wall to get more leverage, he pulled with all the force he could muster trying to get his hand free of this mess. Feeling a slight give from the wall he leaned back and looked at the driving clouds and angry sky hoping to free himself from the wall. After he felt a couple inches of movement, like his hand was being slowly release from the stone, he looked. The scene had changed to his amazement. Learning something new every minute in this stone box, six inches out from the wall his hand was still attached, but not to the wall. His hand rested on a mirror framed in weathered wood, the frame had come out of the wall along with his hand. The mirror wasn't as remarkable as was the image that Samuel viewed in the mirror.

He had seen enough movies and had enough of an imagination to know that Death was staring back at him in the mirror. The image was classic, white skull hooded in the black garment he now wore. Fixed staring at the image in the mirror, Death moved closer to the reflection. At six inches from the mirror he removed his hood and ran his hands, bone on bone, across the bleached surface of the skull…his skull. It was only then that he realized that his hand, the hand that retrieved the mirror, was his once again freed from its bond. Taking a moment, he flexed his right hand a couple times making sure that it was his to command. *I don't feel cold, I don't feel the stone, I can barely feel my bony hand on my bony skull. So this is me, I'm Death.*

"Weird," Death whispered as he put a bony finger where his eye should be. The bony extremity stopped at the second knuckle with an almost inaudible click, as it reached a barrier. He didn't feel a thing, he didn't see his finger, just a blurred spot in his vision. Witnessing the spectacle, he suppressed his gag reflex, and began to wonder could he even throw up being Death? Stepping back, he took the whole reflection in; "Aren't I supposed to have a scythe or something," he questioned his counterpart.

"In time Samuel Gerard Willis, in time," a voice spoke.

"Who said that?" Death asked looking all around and stepping away from the mirror. That kind of surprise normally would have had Samuel jumping out of his skin. He was shocked, yet he didn't feel fear, like the fear he felt in the parking garage. Life in the garage a couple days ago was at volume ten, here, now, everything was a three. *Does being Death mean that I'm not afraid, that I don't have to be fearful, that I can stop running?* Looking back to the mirror, his reflection faded and was replaced with his family. Maggie, Marcus, Denise and Robert dressed there in their Sunday best. Maggie was seated in an old fashioned chair with green velvet cushions. Marcus was behind, his arm resting on the back of the chair and the twins were at her sides. Again he looked around and found that he was alone except for the mirror and its reflection. Looking at the mirror the family was almost picture perfect, except for two features, their eyes and smiles. He could close his eyes and see every detail of his family from the minute lines at the corner of Maggie's mouth to the freckles on his kids. What he saw was not his family, but some perversion of what his family should be. The eyes were red, no maroon, with no pupils and their smiles fake, forced and strained to the limits their faces could endure. The image made him want to shiver again but all that seemed to be suppressed, like his feelings were unreachable.

"What is this?" Death asked.

"This is your family," each of their mouths moved combining all their voices and some voices that didn't belong to them. There were so many voices that Death couldn't identify all of them. "I ...am Regus Argent. I have chosen these forms to enlighten you to the happenings here and now." *Is that my voice I heard, how could that be? I think I even heard...no that couldn't have been my mom and dad's voice, could it?*

"You Samuel Willis have done something no other being has ever done; removed the summoning watch. In doing so, you have now relieved your son of his obligations. The guise of Death is now yours. It was passed from Richard Stanley Williams to Marcus Christopher Williams and you have taken that responsibility onto yourself," Regus finished. *That is why Marcus was out of sorts, that's why he...What does Richard have to do with this?* "What have you done to my son?" he said feeling the power of Death from the pit of his stomach that manifested in a growling, guttural question.

"Your family had been made unaware of your journey and the circumstances involving Marcus that was done by removing the watch. Ease yourself. He and the rest of your family are safe." the family faces answered. "You are not. Removing the summoning watch comes at a price. Follow the path that is presented, loving Samuel, and you will take your son's place. Fail and you will go back oblivious. Marcus will then have to fulfill his obligations." The image of his counterfeit family faded. "The choice is yours Samuel." As the words echoed within Samuel the mirror merged with the stone wall. Death had not the first clue what was going on. He didn't know who

Regus was or what this responsibility meant. His mind drifted back over the years to Christmases and baseball games, to funny gestures, even funnier expressions and school plays, all of which came easily to his mind, because he could see his son's face. Seeing that perversion, that mockery which was supposed to be Marcus and the rest of the family firmed his resolve. He loved Marcus so much and would do anything for him, as a good father should. *Where did this all come from? I mean I have ideas on how to deal with bad grades, drugs and even if my son got a girl pregnant... Maybe. This is beyond our world. This is not the time to run, this is the time to stand and take action, for Marcus, for the entire family. Can I do this? I have to do this!*

He knew when Marcus was born his life had changed forever, just as his old man had told him it would. Being a good father and husband meant more to him than life itself. Death called that disturbing image to mind, the mirror's image of his family with those maroon eyes and forced smiles that so unsettled him. "Nothing will stop me from doing right by Marcus and the rest of my family. I am ready." As if the four walls and floor could understand his proclamation, Death could feel as the stone box started to move. After the initial movement, the box was like an elevator, but he couldn't feel the box's motion. The room moved, Death couldn't feel the acceleration, but he knew he was moving fast as the robes covering his body were moving, telling him that the room was picking up speed.

There was no sound. Suddenly wind rushed by and his robes whipped around his arms, legs and body, almost obscuring his vision. *I must really be moving.* The small stone room seemed to be a vehicle of some kind whisking him towards another larger stone structure. Banking to the right, he could look down and see the vastness of a wasteland of stone riddled with pathways flying by, almost like a maze. The room turned and took him around to the opposite side of the structure. The box was now banking on a low eye line; he could see that nothing supported this gray wasteland. The entire structure was wrapped in the chaotic storm of lightning flashes and vicious buffeting winds. Death could tell that the room was picking up speed as the clouds and lighting flashes in the window above were like polaroid pictures suspended over his head.

The room, the box in which he was being transported ascended slightly. All of a sudden the floor of this room disappeared and Death fell to the grey structure below. The distance to the ground wasn't far at all, but even in that short distance he felt as if he was picking up speed as if he was being pulled to the ground. He hit the solid rock ground barely registering the shock of the landing through the bones of his body as bits of rock and dust flew up into Deaths vision. Dust settled and on the floor there were several cracks in the shape of a spider's webs, tight in the center and more spaced as the cracks went to the edge touching the walls. As the dust settled to the ground it then started to move, crawling across the ground and then up the wall. It climbed and changed color looking much like an army of black ants. They marched, then settled into a pattern on the wall just at eye level.

Choose your path

He looked left to see that there weren't any turns off the corridor. There was only a straight path that ended at some point in the distance that looked to be obscured by clouds of dust that clung to the walls. This fog started at about sixty feet away from his current position. The only light source was a sky light some fifty feet over head. The ambient light that came from the clouds and the lightning flashes did little to reveal anything in this direction, it simply looked to go on forever. To the right exactly the same. Death approached the lettering on the wall and wiped it with his bony hand. The dust fell away from the wall as remnants of the dust clung to his hand, then the message simply faded, blending into the grey stones as it fell. Looking around once more, the sky crackled with energy as clouds tossed and tumbled over themselves. The ground where he landed showed no evidence of his landing as the spider web pattern cracks were gone, left and right still looked the same, a never ending straight path. He turned to the left and started walking; *west is best, well it worked when I played D&D in college.*

The only sound that Death heard was the scraping of bone on stone as he walked, which was broken up by the occasional crack of lighting. The skylight, the same size as the room he began in, followed Death. The sky raged through the portal and provided light, just not enough to see very far while the fog that hung in the corridors didn't help his vision either. *Is this how Regus keeps tabs on me, this sky light? If he can do all this, I'm sure a few inches of stone aren't going to stop him from seeing me.* There was no smell, not that of new stone or damp wet stone, nothing. Stopping, he took time to examine everything about his physical being which wasn't much. The cloth that covered his body seemed to flake off and fall to the floor. There was no trail of ash from his colorless shroud, nothing to follow or represent he was even here. *Is this what it is like to be totally alone? Wait! I almost felt like I could have been sad, but it's gone. Just like the other emotions I should be feeling. They are there one second, and gone the next.* Death took an even closer look and watched the bits of cloth as they floated to the ground. The ash didn't come to rest on the ground it simply faded from sight. It didn't dissolve. There was simply less of it the closer it got to the ground, almost as if it had shrunk into nothing. Moving on, Death found, hidden within the layers of black canvas, a simple length of rope. The rope was white, it looked sturdy despite some of it fraying along the length, the ends were crimped with some kind of metal. The length was tied around his waist and the loose ends dangled at his side. As he examined the rope a simple knot kept the rope in place. He tapped the metal ends together and found it intriguing that the tapping of the ends made no noise.

Death examined his physical form by rubbing his bone white hands together and then over his face and the back of his head, wishing and hoping to feel something, but then if he did would he be able to withstand the emotional onslaught of all these new experiences? Probably not. He replaced his hood being slightly satisfied with the inspection and began to move again. As he walked, Death noticed through the overhead portal that the lightning strikes were coming quicker and the clouds rolled on, faster than earlier, now they moved like a hurricane. The winds were pushing and pulling the black cloth that covered him as violent lightning crashes were shaking gray land. Moving towards one of the walls Death put a bony hand onto the wall. Worried that it might stick again, he pulled it off quickly only to find that he had the freedom he didn't before when encountering the walls of the room in which started. His hand went back up to the wall trying to see, as well as feel, if the walls were going to shake themselves apart. *Is this place going to hold up to these storms? I sure hope so. If I believe Regus and what he said earlier I can't believe it would end like this. It sounded like I have to pass some kind of trial or test. Did Marcus have to go through this? I guess I do believe Regus otherwise why ...belief in Regus has nothing to do with why... my family is all the why I need. Is this storm going to shake this place apart and sweep me away like Dorothy? Is that my first test, survival?*

  The vibrations were coming stronger and faster rocking the walls and shaking the ground. Concentrating for a moment, Death could feel the vibrations were strongest when his hand was resting on the left wall. Moving across the hall and checking the right wall the vibrations weren't nearly as strong. *Wait, that tremor wasn't caused by a lightning strike.* The wall in front of him started to buckle under some force. Something was trying to get through the wall and Samuel didn't want to find out what. The storm overhead, the buckling wall and all of these new experiences were too much for Death to take in. He was frozen in place unsure of what to do or what not to do. This felt like fear, like the fear he felt in the garage, only this time it wasn't so debilitating. He was afraid, but this was different, he was different, so why would he be feeling things on the level that Samuel would.

Stones flew, as the wall couldn't take any more of the assault. Stones large and small pelted Death who covered his eyes with his arms as he came out of the stupor. Dust rolled up to Death and prevented him from seeing clearly. Something was moving in the rubble, something large and powerful. He felt a slight twinge of fear in his lower back like fear may take over and cause him to run or hide, and then it was gone. The hole in the wall was easily twelve feet high. The large form stood tall as the stones rolled off it's back. The dusty gold body moved with ease despite being covered with large remnants of the wall. Two horns, towering height and glowing eyes bore into Death. It had the head of a massive bull; *a Minotaur?* It moved cinder block size stones, as a child would kick a pebble in the street. The Minotaur stepped forward clearing the rest of the rubble. It carried a large pole with a cruel looking axe blade on one end and other end had a spear point, which was smaller but not any less intimidating. The beast brought the weapon to bear, holding it with both of its huge hands, pointing it at Death who slid along the wall trying to understand what was happening. The weapon was presented in some kind of challenge.

How could this be? What am I doing here? I'm going to die aren't I? Death could have stood there and kept asking these kinds of questions but he had to do something other than just ask rhetorical questions. He willed his limbs to move, but they offered no significant assistance as he was walking and looking over his shoulder, uncertain of what would come next. He desperately wanted to put distance between himself and the Minotaur. The dust had cleared and a large metallic Minotaur lumbered towards Death, and that finally prompted him to at least take his first real steps away from the huge axe-wielding brute. He had no weapons and this creature, attaching its weapon to its back, started charging. Looking around for something, anything, was costly, as the Minotaur closed the distance faster than Death anticipated. He turned to face the creature and was slammed in the chest by the Minotaur's head. Sliding back some fifty feet Death tried to think. *This isn't the time for thought. This is the time for action. This is so new to me; I don't want to fail. I'm not afraid, I don't feel fear like before. I have to do something. I can't let Marcus and the family down.* This whole situation was twenty-thirty minutes old to him, gray land, being Death as well as fighting for his family. What could he possibly do to hurt this juggernaut? He remembered the rope at his waist and started to try and untie it when the walls around him again started to shake. Death looked to see the Minotaur still a good forty feet away. The wall to his right exploded inward just like when the first Minotaur came through the wall. Another Minotaur came through the wall, immediately attacking with a backhand that sent Death sliding and then slamming into the opposite wall. Still dazed, Death saw that this one carried an axe with blades at both ends. *If they start using those axes on me I'm through. One chop and I'm dead, done, no happy ending here.* The closest Minotaur picked up its foot, Death reacted and moved just as one hoofed foot crashed into the wall where he'd been standing a moment ago. His legs seemed to be moving better, faster than before. Death was still trying to free the rope while the nearest Minotaur readied its axe for a massive downward swing that would surely cleave Death in two. The swing came and all Death could do was put his arms up to block his view. CLANG! Death looked as metal rang against metal, his hands had changed. Where only bony digits were before, now two curved metal blades resided. The blades looked much like scythes, only smaller. The blades absorbed the incoming blow. Halfway up his wrists, white bone, gave way to brown carved wood that made up the handles of the weapons.

Whew, I thought this was going to be my shortest trip ever. Thanks Regus, these blades did come 'in time'. With a twist, Death let the deflected blow slip to the ground. The huge monster's strength embedded the axe deep in the stone. Death moved towards the first Minotaur as the second worked to free its weapon. Turning his back on the second monster, Death faced the first Minotaur. The gold-bodied monster stepped up and swept its weapon horizontally. Ducking the blow, Death came up swinging. The blow didn't have much strength behind it as he wanted to slow the Minotaur down and prevent the next series of attacks, somehow. With almost no effort, Death swung down on the creature's exposed elbow and was astonished. The arm from the elbow down was completely severed. *YEAAAAAAAAAAAAAAAAAAAAAAA!!!!*

    The elation, the thrill that Death felt was uncharacteristic for this form, Death really felt nothing, it was simply as if the world's volume was down low regardless of fear or exhilaration. As fast as he felt the fear or excitement, was as fast as it left. Samuel might have felt excitement like this and jumped up and down pumping his fist in celebration, but actually he would have probably soiled himself and curled into a ball, if he Samuel, not Death, had been attacked by these mechanized creatures. The high of striking a blow didn't last long. Gears, wires and actuators were exposed inside the metal shell. The creature's axe now stuck in the wall from its powerful blow forgot the weapon and brought it's fist down to crush Death. That blow again was easily dodged, but another attack, this from the double bladed axe of the second minotaur caught Death by surprise. The axe bit into Death's upper arm. It didn't hurt too bad he realized, but the pressure and the fact that the axe was being pressed in his arm as the Minotaur leaned into the weapon was posing a problem. Death's other hand came up and snapped the haft of the double axe and the blade fell to the floor. The one armed Minotaur went back to trying to free its weapon while the other turned its weapon presenting the second axe blade as it stalked Death. *I wonder if this one will try another downswing, I might be able to take him out quickly if he does.* Death readied his weapons and saw that a small bit of black dust, not unlike the dust on the wall earlier, was covering one of his bladed hands. *Am I bleeding dust? Can't focus on that now.* The Minotaur was closing the distance with a charge and started to raise the axe again. *Only one shot at this, gotta make it count.* Quicker than he had ever moved before Death stepped within six inches of his foe, shortening the distance as the heavy attack landed behind Death. He stood in between the arms of the Minotaur and in the blink of an eye he brought both blades down taking both arms and, for good measure, he then cut his antagonist in half across the waist. Amazed at his speed and precision Death turned and started to back away from the one armed Minotaur. It had freed its weapon and now moved slowly, cautiously. Behind the Minotaur that stalked Death, the pile of black dust started to collect and take shape. *That black dust, my blood, what's going on?* In the pile of dust, a skull formed, opening its mouth slowly and then closing it again as if it trying to call out. *Is the pile going to form another Death? That would be sweet, some help in all this chaos?* Watching, Death hoped that his wounds produced help. The skull disappeared in the dust and on cue a scythe like Death's reached up from the pile of dust and hooked on to the creature's foot. As the balance of the metallic creatures was taken when its foot fell away, Death moved in and finished the creature with a quick slice across the midsection sending it crashing to the ground. Moving, so Death could keep an eye on the downed foes and the pile of dust, the weapon that severed the Minotaur's foot returned to the dust. Another face started to form in the soot, a skull almost identical to Deaths visage. No it was identical in every way. This left an uneasy feeling in the absent stomach of Death. *Wait something is wrong. I haven't felt a lot since I came here but this is wrong.* Death couldn't feel much but could feel the conflict, the sense that something was amiss as the other death formed. Arms started to reach out of the churning, living dust and almost got a hold of Death's two legs. Death wanted no part of this and drove both blades into the pile of dust. With a hiss it faded just like the black cloth he wore. Looking around at his handy work Death wasn't sure what had just happened. The first Minotaur he had defeated, which had no arms and was cut in half, now fell in a heap of metal limbs and parts, startling him.

There was no sound after the crash. He was used to at least the beat of his own heart but as Death there was none. There was no flesh to injure, no lunch to throw up and no one to save or look after. Death wouldn't even know where to start, with no feelings to sort through he paused to think about what just happened. Standing there not doing anything, Death slowly took a step and then another. Checking his arm, the wound seemed to close on its own. The cloth that covered his arms showed no evidence of the wound. Death surveyed the area after the carnage. Of the two holes produced by the giant golden attackers only one remained, the first Minotaur's entrance was gone. Somehow, someway, it had been patched, like it had never been. There was no evidence that there was ever a hole there in the first place. The large and small stones that littered the ground from before were gone as well. Continuing his look around, the Minotaur had started to rust almost instantaneously. The reddish brown dust faded to gray just like everything else in gray land, and then faded from sight. *I am in a strange place. I have just destroyed two robotic Minotaur. I have done this to spare my son the fate of a station from who knows where. I can remember the emotions on his face, particularly the extremes in which they changed and the severity in which he felt them. Marcus didn't even have to go through these trials, yet I do. Or did he have to go through something else? Almost everything I touch turns to dust, how long can I last against these tasks? All I know is that I must. Marcus will never endure this or anything that has to do with Death.* With new resolve, *ashes to ashes, dust to dust* and Death strode to the opening. Wary and tired already of these events, Death walked to the only opening left. He stood there trying to take in all that he saw through this portal. It was something that he never would have expected and still he took the first step through, half in and half out.

CHAPTER 6

Felicia

England mid 1300's

The sound of rushing wind through the trees was interrupted by the sound of the wheat being cut. Several sheaves lay scattered as the workers went about collecting the wheat and binding it with a single stalk of wheat. Felicia went about her work, working slightly quicker than most. The cold carried on the wind brought a rosy color out in her cheeks and kept the sweat from dotting her brow. Dark hair danced across her face as her bonnet was unable to keep all her hair back. She kept her distance from the rest of the workers, this was her time. Time to think, to wonder how much life would be different if Peter were still alive. She could conjure the image of her husband's face, not the sickly face that was there at the end, but the pleasant soft smile that he would give her. That smile spoke the words "I love you", more than Peter had ever vocalized. The way he would touch her gently, just patting her rump, or a rub on her back when she would clean up after supper.

"You're off the pace young miss," said Ralph with a hint of sarcasm bringing Felicia Willis back to the moment as she stood up straight, pausing for a moment, all while the other workers around her kept their pace. He was in charge of keeping an eye on the workers. Felicia went back to work not wanting to be distracted and resumed her normal pace not realizing that she had gone too far into her thoughts. Ralph strode over full of confidence. He always dressed better than he needed, as if trying to impress upon the workers that they were below him. Standing in Felicia's way she stopped again, sighed and stood to face him. "Yes sir," Felicia answered wanting to get back to work. Ralph stopped her in mid-bend by putting his finger under her chin. He then raised his other hand and wiped the dirt off her cheek. When he pulled both his hands back, Felicia knew it was safe to return to work.

"Tonight?" turning back curtly Ralph asked just so Felicia could hear. Looking around to make sure no one was within ear shot, "Michael is sick," Felicia replied, tired of Ralph, but knowing he still had his uses. Ralph frowned then left her to work addressing the next worker who wasn't keeping pace. Binding another sheave, Felicia looked at the sky and then the land around her. A deep sigh put her right back into the rhythm of work. *How could I be so foolish to drift off that far not to notice Ralph.* She sighed again and kept working. *I could do better than this farm work. Peter taught me to read and I keep working on my letters for writing. Will I be free of this? Peter left me to this; no Peter didn't have a say in what happened when he became sick or after his death. I know that he would rather be here. He would never have chosen to leave me and the children. He swept me up from my low station and showed me a good life only to leave me back where I belong. WHY DID THIS HAVE TO HAPPEN?* Felicia stopped, running into another worker.

"Beggin your pardon," Felicia said as her eyes met the gaze of the young man she bumped into. The young man looked not too much older than her oldest son. He nodded, tipped his hat and went back to his work. After a deep breath Felicia steadied her mind and her hands and settled into a normal pace. How long until her son was out here, two, three years? She knew she could use the help with supporting her two youngest children. The rest of the afternoon was uneventful, just thoughts of Peter and how she was going to make life work without him. If she was lucky she would be able to catch a ride back to the Foster's farm where she had a room that she paid for. The Fosters were decent to her and her family in not charging them much for the room. Her oldest son John helped at the farm and that kept money on an even keel. Even Mary, her middle child was able to help out a little. The space at the farm was cramped for the family. Three children John, Mary and Michael and then Felicia totaled four people all in a single room just off the Foster's barn. The day was coming to a close, at least for the harvesting. Some stayed on longer gleaning, while a few more walked off finding their way home. There was probably an hour of daylight left and she would need most of that to get back to the farm. Felicia noticed the wagon on the other side of the field, which meant she was walking. Felicia paused before starting the walk home. Looking over the fields, she knew that once this field was done there were at least two others to work. She was able to save up most of her money thanks to the Fosters. It was Peter's generosity that made all this possible. Peter had taught the elder Fosters to read which then enabled them to teach their children. Learning was like the warmth from a fire. Knowledge needed to be fed like the fire to provide warmth and light, knowledge would be a fire in anyone willing to feed that hunger. As Felicia walked she thought of when Peter was teaching her to read, spreading the warmth of knowledge. She smiled as warmth grew inside her thinking of all that Peter had taught her.

    He was a gentle man, taking his time, not being vicious or cruel to her, he was always patient in his teachings. That patience waivered when he got sick. He would grow frustrated of debilitating headaches which took time away from the end of the reading lessons and the beginning of the writing. If the illness had been caught sooner Peter might have had a better chance, but he pushed himself and Felicia could see sickness taking over. The Black Death is what they called it, horrifying is what Felicia thought of it.

The clouds lingered like Felicia's thoughts of Peter as the sun set which made the last of her walk towards the farm a little challenging. Felicia knew the way but had to make sure not to step in any gopher holes or trip over any ground clutter. Breaking through a small grove of trees the farm was a light spot in the darkness. The Fosters home was just large enough and they needed all that room to fit all their family together. Off the main house, 150 feet, there a small room located just off the barn; this is where her family waited for her. She walked in with a smile and that quickly changed, when Felicia noticed Ralph sitting at the table playing with Michael.

"Good evening Felicia, I hope you don't mind. Since you said that Michael was sick and I was able to catch the wagon, thought I should be a gentleman and check on the children. Michael was telling me that he was ill yesterday. He seems to be feeling better today, right Michael?" Ralph asked ruffling Michael's crop. The child nodded and then smiled at Ralph and then at his mother. Mary was sitting on the bed that the children all shared playing quietly with a doll that Felicia managed to sew together with a few scraps of cloth the Fosters had laying around. John was busy stacking wood close to the fire as well as retrieving more hay to stuff in the oversized sack that made up their bed. John and Mary knew better and would avoid Ralph at all chances as Felicia had explained to them that Ralph, who seemed nice, could also be a wolf. Michael was looking for a man to learn from and to love. *Michael, I wish you would learn this from John. He sees John as an older brother, a pest, keeping him in line and telling him what to do. Not as the man of the house looking out for me and the rest of the family. John is only ten, yet he is the man of the house; Mary is starting to see this but Michael hasn't yet.*

"I didn't want to take chances on you getting sick sir," Felicia answered going quickly to her the other children and kissing them each on the head. John winked at his mother as they both knew Ralph was trying to close the space between himself and Felicia. *John is a good boy and wouldn't confront Ralph knowing it might make things more difficult for me.* Felicia smiled at her son and then her daughter, who had the look that she might be starting to catch on to the subtlety of nonverbal communication between her mother and brother. Inadvertently, Michael helped the cause and started to cough. Ralph held Michael away from himself, turning his head, and trying not to breathe the same air Michael was coughing.

"Michael's coughs could easily turn into a fit of vomiting. Even a weak cough like that can have little Michael there throwing up," Felicia finished and rushed to Michael to kiss his forehead. "He might be a little warm," Felicia said looking at Michael's face to see if there were any other signs that his sickness had not passed, then she turned to hang up her wrap.

"Well Michael I hope you feel better. Felicia I'll see you tomorrow," Ralph finished from the door, leaving Michael sitting on the bench at the table. Felicia had to do a double-take from the table to the door, thinking that Ralph was still seated. With that he shut the door. Looking back to the table, Ralph hadn't left anything to eat this evening. *Oh well.* Felicia went to Michael and cuddled her youngest hoping that he was really done with being sick. *Your father died from the Black Death. I can't lose my little one as well. Peter would die all over again if he knew that he had passed it onto his son, but that was a couple years ago. Without Peter we seem to be just barely making this work, get well my son prove me wrong, be strong. Rest so that the family doesn't lose another.* It was tough on Michael, even something as trivial as eating breakfast could upset his stomach and trigger him to get sick. As her thoughts drifted to those mornings when Michael was sick, it didn't seem like the black death. Felicia moved Michael's hair aside and left a lingering kiss on his forehead to check his temperature. Felicia then got up and looked to the small fireplace and the evening's meal which was contained in a small iron pot just off the fire keeping warm.

"It isn't as much as usual. Mr. Foster had someone at the house tonight," John said. He retrieved the cracked bowl and two plates that the family used to eat with. They were given to the Willis's from the Fosters when they bought a new set. The stew wasn't much, three or four mouthfuls. Felicia took one of the plates and Michael to the bed and fed him slowly as not to make him throw up the valuable bits of food. John and Mary finished each saving a mouthful for their mother.

"You both finish up. I'll take what is left in the pot," Felicia said as the kids finished their last bites chewing slowly, savoring the last of the meal. She went to the shelf that housed the plates and took the last bit of bread left from last week's loaf. Felicia picked off a couple of bad spots and ran the bread inside the dish getting a few small bits of meat and a couple bites of potato. Felicia looked back to Michael who was finishing his last mouthful and then to John and Mary, all were then licking the plates and bowls clean, not leaving anything. John collected all the dishes including the one that housed the meal and took them to the bucket and used a little water to wipe them clean. The routine continued as John walked to the Foster's house to take back the iron cook pot. While John was gone, Felicia felt the cold chill at her wrist. She didn't even have to look down to know it was there; it was a feeling she had been getting used to. Felicia embraced her daughter and put her in bed with her feet facing Michael's head. His breathing told her that he was asleep and that he might actually be getting better since he wasn't coughing. Michael stirred slightly and then pulled the blanket close. John walked in just as Mary was settling in.

"Straight to bed with you John. I need to talk with the Fosters," Felicia commanded and John knew not to question his mother and started for bed. John climbed in, Felicia was about to leave when she went back to the bed and kissed John. "Thank you, you're a good boy, growing to be a fine man" and another kiss was planted and she walked to the door. As soon as the door was shut, she let out a sigh and looked at her wrist as the solid piece of metal there caught the faint light from the Foster's house. Felicia started to walk and then she was gone.

CHAPTER 7

Garden

 Death saw a garden. He was unsure of why it would be here in the middle of gray land. The skylight still hovered above his head as a grim reminder of the harshness and severity of what he was going through. Lightning continued to strike the sky making the clouds look as if they were bleeding, being rent by claws formed of electricity. The mixing red with the different colored lighting made for a techno color nightmare in the sky. Yet the sky through the portal was blue, blue like he had never seen in his life. Death cautiously bent forward, one foot still in gray land in case he had to escape, wanting a glimpse of the either side of the opening to see if anything was lurking just inside the wall to the garden. He didn't want to stumble into another ambush or trap. Leaning into the garden, he could see there was a portion of a stone wall which supported the portal Death used to stand in between the two places. This small section of the stone wall was planted in the garden. This portion of the wall was slightly bigger than the gate Death viewed the garden through.

 The beauty of the landscape was enough to lure him, but learning the hard way with a few lumps and a notch in his arm, he didn't want to get surprised. On either side Death saw no assailants, no traps just a manicured lawn. The grass was such an earthly emerald green; each blade was perfect with no yellow or brown blades mixed with the perfect grass. Shaking off the green trance, Death looked further into the garden. This landscape seemed to have no walls. Inside, a couple hundred feet away, was a gray box of some kind. Afraid to move, Death didn't want anything to change. The view was perfect. Trees manicured to perfection with not a leaf out of place. He couldn't get over just how perfect this place was. Then it came to him, could this be Eden? Samuel was a good Christian, reading his bible and had been active in the church more so in the last couple years then all his life, this gave him faith that it could just be Eden.

I could be wrong, who knows if this is in fact Eden. It is so beautiful. I'd rather go here than stay in gray land that for sure. After what had happened with the Minotaurs, he wasn't sure why he was given the option to go to this place. As he looked closer he noticed that life was here. Birds and animals of various shapes and sizes roamed the picture-perfect landscape. Squirrels black, brown and red chased each other; a pair of foxes walked right next to a couple ducks. The portal suddenly went dark. Large sticks seemed to sweep by the opening. Death stepped back no longer straddling the entry to the garden, his hand had made the transformation to weapons on reflex. The obscurant moved right to left past the portal a couple more times, then moved on all together. Death leaned in trying to make sense of what just happened. His head was just past the threshold witnessing a very strange scene, a giant was sweeping the manicured lawn. Shaking his head to make sure he wasn't hallucinating, Samuel rubbed the bony sockets which would have contained his eyes and looked again. This man had to be at least forty feet tall. Looking through the portal, the giant was bald with glasses actually they were a kind of goggles, open on the side, he guessed letting the eyes breathe. He had on a stained apron that covered a black pair of shorts and a black tank top. Short, black boots finished the giants outfit. Dressed like that the giant looked out of place, like he shouldn't be there. Death scanned the area again. A small child was well off to the side sitting with her legs crossed working with her hands. Not as out of place as the giant, Death could not make out what she was doing at this distance. She would work using her hands for a while then turn and put something in the ground. No trees, vegetation or tilled earth was left behind where the child worked, Death thought she must have been planting what the grounds keeper would eventually tend, but nothing was disturbed as she left perfect grass in her wake as she worked. As he watched the scene, the child would stop occasionally to watch the animals. Besides the occasional distraction, she was diligent about her work. This giant seemed gentle enough. He didn't make a move towards the animals that scurried and scampered around his feet; *maybe I can get some answers from him.* Again checking for impending doom, Death crept slowly, walking through the portal with all his senses on alert. Putting both his feet on the grass, he was aware that he was no longer Death.

His bare feet walked on grass so soft that he had to bend down to take a closer look and make sure that it was in fact grass he stepped on. It could have been cotton balls for as soft as it was. The air was warm. Feelings flooded back to him now; feelings that he was flesh and not just bone. Then he doubled over and fell. Samuel burst into tears, he was suddenly so afraid. It settled on him like a blanket of bricks. He was having a hard time breathing, the worry of what if he had failed, what if he had died, all hovered about as he coughed again and again struggling for air. It was just like the garage, only a hundred times worse. His heart ached at the grand scope of events as the emotions smothered his perception. He felt and imagined he was cornered with fear, trapped in a pit with no way out, even surrounded by all the good things in his life, he just wanted out. That there was no way out of this pit of despair only compounded his feelings of hopelessness. The pit of despair Samuel found himself in started to close, so that there could be no escape. As it reached the point where there was only a pinhole of light left, the hole enlarged again, the pit became more shallow and the feelings that were gripping his chest and crushing the life out of him lifted and then rebounded in an entirely new direction. He was feeling neutral, indifferent. The feelings of dread were gone and then he was starting to feel better. He was feeling good, now it was joy, growing, swelling, he had defeated the Minotaurs and survived. He stood raising his hands over his head drawing in deep cleansing breaths, his head held high. Then he was jumping like Rocky Balboa at the top of the stairs, feeling the fight, a feeling he had never felt in his life being a runner. Everything was better right then. The feelings calmed taking a turn back down again. With one last deep breath he felt equanimity. The ups and downs had passed. This reminded Samuel of the up and down moment in his life, the moment Susan became his sister.

Samuel was eight years old when his father came to him to tell him that the family was adopting Susan Elaine Burstein. Susan came to the family from Samuel's dad's best friend, Jacob Burstein. His dad and Mr. Burstein were working a construction job when a terrible accident left Samuel's dad injured and Mr. Burstein dead. Susan's mother had killed herself soon after Susan was born. There wasn't a name back then but today it would be called post-partum depression. The day Susan came to live with the family was a black day for Samuel. He had enough to contend with having an older brother, and he didn't want to have an older sister trying to act like his mother and boss him around like Karl. What Samuel didn't know was that his dad and Mr. Burstein had talked over the years as they worked together. They had bonded and in that bond they decided to be there should anything happen to the other. This fellowship happened in days long past, when a friend would become more like a brother or sister and less like a friend. They would care for each other through a choice of friendship and love. It was like an uncelebrated union, it was understood through handshakes, kinship and a common message; take care of your family. Neither man dreamed anything bad would happen, they talked and shared the dreams they had about their families becoming like brothers. Samuel's dad made a promise to take care of Susan should anything happen to him and on the flip side Mr. Burstein would look in on Samuel, his brother and mother should anything happen to his dad. The adoption had been a long time coming, but that was neither here nor there the day that Samuel met Susan. His dad had pulled up in the family car, walked around back and pulled a large suitcase from the trunk, then walked to the passenger side and opened the door for Susan. Samuel was told of the situation and acted the part of an eight-year-old. He resisted, he rejected the idea of a new sibling. Susan handed Mr. Willis a small suitcase, got out of the car and thanked Samuel's dad. As she cleared the car door, she smiled. That smile defused Samuel, it made him think, *she had lost her mom years ago and just recently lost her dad, why would she be smiling? She didn't have anyone except maybe us.* As Samuel's father introduced each of the family members Susan hugged and then talked to them in turn. She talked with Samuel's mother for a couple minutes then she retrieved her case and moved to Karl. Susan repeated the process with Karl. Samuel again was taken back by this new person in his life. She was smiling, happy to be here, and he couldn't understand it. She came to stand before Samuel, bent down and let go of her suitcase, then went further down on one knee and embraced Samuel. As Samuel thought back, he remembered that hug, that hug transformed his family, as each member got the same hug from Susan. Affection was rarely given in his household, a sideways shoulder-squeeze as a hug or a pat on the back was normal before Susan. This stranger, who was now Samuel's sister taught the Willis' how to show love and affection. Samuel learned how to hug that day. It wasn't some fake shoulder hug, Susan wrapped her arms around her adopted brother and pulled him close. The hug lasted for a while, but not longer than a minute. After that she let him go as well as let him know that she was grateful for being here and that she loved Samuel. The day wasn't black anymore it was beautiful, even if he didn't have the mind to see it before Susan arrived. The blue skies and sweet smells of flowers in the front yard cemented that moment in Samuels mind forever.

As Samuel opened his eyes he thought he was still there in his front yard, smelling those sweet flowers and remembering a beautiful day. He still smelled those sweet scents, but he wasn't in his yard. He was in a garden of sweet aromas that floated by his nose. Samuel smiled a crooked little smile and after an easy breath, gentle breezes tickled his arm hair. No longer in the past Samuel checked himself. He was dressed just the same as when he last saw Marcus, minus shoes and socks. He looked back to see that gray land was no more. There was no opening there was no wall, it faded just like everything else, including his feelings. Samuel felt surprisingly relaxed given gray land and the ups and downs he had just experienced, so he started a casual stroll taking in the sights. Now he saw large animals, lions, bears and even moose walked about this pristine garden. Each of their coats shined with unnatural luster. The animals mingled not paying any real attention to the others. A look yes, a snort maybe but nothing that would make Samuel believe that these were predator and prey, more like roommates. Turning around Samuel fell back being taken completely by surprise.

Invading his personal space was a teenage girl with flowing long blond hair. Slowly, delicately she floated back giving Samuel a little room to breathe. That was not as remarkable as the fact that she had wings and was carrying a flaming sword. She was beautiful, the wings, the sword and her presence was stunning. The cloth that wrapped her was very nearly transparent. Samuel wanted to look away, and did for a minute, but the beauty and innocence of her face caught him in such rapture, he couldn't help but keep his eyes on her eyes. Her gaze intensified, eyes of blue bore into Samuel and he could feel a probe on his soul. If she were an angel her wings were smaller than he would have imagined. The sword she carried was broad, broader than her body but she handled it as if it were a twig shifting it from her left to right hand. Flames danced on the edges of the blade, but Samuel felt no heat from it. She made no threatening move towards Samuel who remained absolutely still. *Well I'm not Death. So am I going to be killed here and now or is this a part of the trial process?*

"No Samuel Willis. I am not here to kill you. I just protect this land in which you now dwell." Her voice was honey-coated with sugar on top of a candy bar, but there was something underneath it, a power that Samuel felt in the pit of his stomach. It was respect with a bit more fear than was normal considering this very alien situation; like you respect the ocean, or the edge of a cliff, you don't take it for granted. As soon as you do you will be swept away. Fear of the unknown, the unreal, was right behind respect ready to jump out and run the other way.

"How did you…"

"Read your thoughts Samuel? I will use terms you will understand so to facilitate your exodus. I am not an angel; I am a cherub. I have not achieved such an honored position, not yet and this is not Eden but a trial version of the garden. Man is not permitted there or here, you are only permitted here because of the station you hold. This land will serve as an intermediary to the next."

With his mouth wide open, he wasn't sure what would happen next. Putting the sword behind her back, so that the blade disappeared and only the handle was showing, she pointed across the way. "There will a door appear. It will only remain for so long and you must go through it to continue. I have other stations to watch over. I can answer no more questions Samuel. All I can say is you are doing the right thing for Marcus." When she finished there was sympathy in her eyes and concern in her voice. With that she turned her back. The wings, small, appeared to be woven from clouds, on the edges lightning and fire danced and intermingled with the wings. The handle of the sword rested on top of them, but not truly atop them. It floated just so she could reach back and unsheathe the weapon if need be, but now the blade was nowhere to be seen.

"Wait," Samuel started walking after her, he blinked and she was gone, no fading this time just gone, blinking out of existence. *What is going on? I have only begun and this is all too large for me. These feelings are slinging me back and forth. A station? Was she talking about me being Death? I don't know how much more I can take.* Not even the beauty of such a place could take the weight off Samuel shoulders. He walked forward slowly, as if in a trance. That trance brought him before the block he had seen earlier as he nearly tripped over it. Samuel walked laps around the block to try to ease his mind and work through how he was going to overcome all this. It was three feet square, except it had a trapezoid on top even though it was a single piece of charcoal black marble. The top was thin, an inch wide, and the slopes that connected to the three-foot square base were long and gradual. As he walked in front of the block he noticed dates. There were two numbers on the long gradual side he was facing that hadn't been visible when he first found himself in the block's presence. The numbers looked to be raised and printed on crypt plaques, yet there was a coating, or film that prevented Samuel from actually touching the numbers. Looking closely at the marble Samuel searched for some hinge or mechanism that might have hidden the now visible panels. The numbers started at 4241 which was on the left and went all the way to the current year, on the right. *These numbers…well wait…could these be dates? If they are they go back all the way to before Christ, well before Christ.* He slid his hand over the first date and a man appeared on the box. It was some sort of projected image out of the inch-wide top of the block. The man wasn't too tall. His long brown hair came over his shoulders. He was dressed only in simple loose-fitting earth colored linens. He carried a stick and a wooden plate of some kind. Samuel's gaze finished taking in the last of the image when his eyes came to rest on his dirty, calloused feet. Samuel slid his hand just a fraction of an inch towards the current year and the image changed. The next was another man, or a young man perhaps. He was younger than the first but his dress was similar to the first man except for the fact that the clothing did seem better constructed, as well as fit better. Each time Samuel slid his hand over a different portion of the plaque a new person appeared. Some old and young, male and female, as well as the rich and the poor, happy and sad took a turn projected above the gray block. As Samuel went over each inch of the slide, it was like watching a fashion show mixed with the History Channel, only he had a remote, really a slider. A knight followed a little girl dressed in rags. Samuel looked in the direction that would show the way to continue his tasks. The portal still hadn't appeared so Samuel returned his attention to the block. His hand stopped at the image of a Native American man dressed in boots that were made from some animal skins. His pants were the same, only more worn, and a simple shirt completed his clothes. The man had an intense look about him, a purpose driven demeanor. There was a particularly nasty looking scar on the back of his right hand that started at the fingers and stopped before his wrist, almost like he was burned somehow.

It was an interesting show until Samuel got to the last date. There Marcus stood before Samuel. Samuel tried to climb the gray box and look at his son's face, but when he did the projection went to where his foot had touched the slider. Climbing down and moving his hand to the current year he found Marcus' image again. It was just as he would have envisioned his son. Samuel could close his eyes and see that face, each freckle, his smile lines and even the small scar under his nose. The eyes on Marcus, when Samuel looked into them, were nothing like Marcus' hazel eyes. This caused Samuel to stumble losing his balance and falling over backwards. Quick to his feet Samuel looked again at Marcus' eyes. They were completely black. They weren't glassy and didn't reflect light, but absorbed and swallowed the light as well as the very warmth from Samuel's body. Samuel sat down and curled into a ball holding his knees, rocking to try and soothe himself. He cried softly thinking about his son. Seeing him immortalized, with no eyes, it was as if his son didn't exist. Every night for many years, Marcus would give Samuel a hug, like the ones he learned how to give from Susan, a kiss (on the cheek) and a handshake before bed. Then Samuel would pull away from Marcus before he tucked him in and say 'the day is done, I love you and I will no matter what'. Samuel's body convulsed at the thought of those moments stretched out over years. He didn't know if he would ever be able to get back to that. Marcus these days hadn't done it, in fact as Samuel stretched his mind, it had been a year or two since the last hug, kiss and handshake. Samuel wiped his face and looked back at the image of his son. "I will get back to you my son," Samuel declared, hoping for at least one more hug, kiss and handshake.

"He is in between places now. His eyes will remain that way until you have succeeded or failed," said a calm and smooth voice. The volume and tone seemed to calm Samuel immediately, but he wasn't sure how or why. Samuel turned, using his sleeve on his face to see that the giant had addressed him, but wasn't looking at him. The giant finished what he had to say, and went back to tending the garden. Samuel turned to look again at his son's face hoping that he was dreaming those soulless eyes but the image was gone as well as the dates. "The door will appear for you soon. I hope you endure Samuel," said the giant not even turning around, he then walked into a wooded area, left of the marble block. *Everything happens for a reason, I have to try and keep my head and focus. I swore that I would see this through to the end to help Marcus and I must. These feelings are so strong; they feel like a detriment at times. If this keeps happening I won't have the emotional strength to carry on.* Samuel let go of his knees and fell back looking up at the blue sky. He took a few breaths just to breathe. It did him some good. He pulled himself back up to sitting and wrapped his arms around his knees again to sort through all the happenings, then of course his mind drifted to his family. *Have I shown Maggie enough of a commitment? Have I given her everything I can? Only I can answer that, only I can say enough. Maggie would say 'don't be so tough on my husband'. I hope I get through this in one piece so I can tell her how much I love her. To tell the kids that I'm here for them no matter what happens. To be that better husband and father and push for that goal every day that I have left.* A single tear escaped Samuel's eye. Wiping the tear and straightening himself, he took a deep breath, stood and then started on his way. Samuel didn't look back to the garden keeper as each stride took him closer to where the door would appear; to his goal and the freedom of his son. *Maggie, kids I hope you know I love you I hope that somehow you know how important you all are to me. I'll be home soon.* As Samuel made his way to where the giant had motioned and the guardian pointed, Samuel arrived fired up ready to do whatever was necessary to free his son and take on this burden. Then he noticed the little girl who sat on the ground working with her hands. She had made her way around to where Samuel had been instructed to wait. With all the new information and feelings to sort through Samuel had all but forgotten the girl. She was sitting with her legs crossed knitting. That she was knitting wasn't as significant as what she was producing. With a single thread from her own hair, she fed the needles in her hands, she knitted a miniature tree. This was no fabric tree this was a bark and sap and leaves tree, only smaller. The roots and base were completed and she now started on the trunk and quickly produced the branches. She worked fast, but Samuel saw that there were no leaves to speak of on the trees.

"Not to worry Death, some things are beyond our comprehension, but we do what we know is right. I know that you can relate to that," the girl said as she finished the tree. Doubt crept into Samuel for a moment as he thought about the garage. Samuel was pulled away from his thoughts as the ground opened. Starting as a small hole and growing to encompass the branches of the tree she had just finished. The girl put the tree in the hole branches first, then ground started to close around the trunk of the tree. As soon as the ground surrounded the trunk the roots sunk into the soil, leaving no evidence that anything had been planted. The tree didn't disturb the surface, it just merged with the ground. *All her work disappears but she keeps on going, knowing that this is what she must do.* As Samuel was in mid thought she was already working on the trunk of another tree. Samuel took a breath as to ask a question, but he noticed the door had appeared.

There wasn't just one door but double doors. Nothing supported the doors; they hung in existence like a picture painted on air. Samuel inspected the doors, both sides. The metal doors, brass or copper, looked exactly the same on each side. Completing his circuit, Samuel waited at the front of the doors or what would have been the side that appeared to him. Samuel jumped as they slid to the side, one left and the other right, like elevator doors. Once they reached what would have been the frame of the door, the doors disappeared, swallowed by an invisible frame. The portal hung as if it were cut in the fabric of space, into the next world. It was as if someone painted a portrait of a beautiful landscape and then someone had cut through the canvas. This canvas led to another world. The portal's view offered only a single copper colored door. Peeking out through the portal, Samuel could see the way continued to the left and right. The way left and right were marked with doors, all looking the same in appearance. The hole in space that led to the next part of Samuel's journey looked like a hotel floor. Samuel had been in enough hotels to recognize the format. It was as if he was stepping out of an elevator onto one of the hotel floors, not the lobby, but one of the upper floors. Samuel walked into this other place. He felt nothing, smelled nothing, tasted nothing and looked at the shiny door ahead of him and Death stared back. A buzzing noise behind him took him away from his reflection only to see the elevator doors behind him close. The garden in all it splendor and grace was left only in the mind of Samuel Willis. A small part of Samuel died as he thought he would never see such a beautiful landscape again. As soon as the elevator doors closed they opened again immediately. Behind the parting doors an old couple looked at Death, "why are you holding up the elevator?" the man asked shuffling towards the opening, but not exiting the elevator. He moved to the controls and he tapped a button on the inside of the elevator. The lady simply smiled and shrugged as the elevators doors closed again. With the path behind him closed and only leading to an empty elevator, he looked to the closed door that was his path and the door across from him opened.

Death knew from the red clouds that filled a sky with multi-colored lightning bolts cutting across the nightmarish landscape that he had come back to gray land. There were no walls this time just a path of gray cinder blocks as wide as the door laid straight out in a path as far as he could see. The lightning flashed but there was no crashing thunder. Death was starting to get accustomed to the strange workings of the worlds that swept by him so fast. Death really didn't want to take more time than necessary. As he stepped through the threshold, lightning and the crashes of thunder filled his skull. The world shook and stone scraping on stone echoed as the entire world and the sky turned as if it were on a single axis that started at his feet. It seemed like God was turning a dial on this world as simply as we might turn over a game board. The world spinning again showed he knew next to nothing of what these worlds could be or do. Death stood there watching the spectacle. In just one moment he saw both worlds, split right down the middle. There was gray world on one page and a dark misty world that dawned to show Death his new path. *One step at a time.*

CHAPTER 8

Regus

The stairs were tall and steep, and wound slightly to the left. The assistant took the steps at a pace slightly faster than walking trying to reach his master to answer the urgent call. His footfalls were silent, padded by the espadrilles covering his feet. With all the recent activity he was dressed in the ceremonial robes in order to be prepared to act on his master's will, should the need arise. The robes were made of a heavy cream-colored material that he and all his associates were accustomed to. A silver and black stripe went from the posterior hem at the bottom of the robe and ended at the top of the circular opening where the assistant's face emerged. His face was cast in the heavy shadows of a deep hood as he lifted his garb so he wouldn't trip as he ascended.

The assistant knew, therefore the master knew. The assistant's ascent took him through the gray mist where he would seek counsel with the master. Once past the mist, light reflected off the stone all around, the assistant knew he was close to the top. Planets, celestial bodies and distant stars lit the spiraling stairs and the platform in which his master was seated.

As soon as the assistant's foot hit the platform, "Yes?" came a powerful commanding voice that stopped the assistant for just a moment. Shaking off the question the assistant made his way to the dais which was a large stone chair carved into the rock stand that faced away from the top of the stairs. The assistant closed the distance fast but dared not step in front of his master to disturb his focus. The assistant kneeled, "We have lost sight of him master."

"As have I. It is trivial. From what we have seen he will follow the course. Samuel wants to free his son from his duties as Death. He has done so not knowing what he has truly set in motion. The others made the rules, I am simply going to oblige them as well as the path set before me. The first point is revealed, the others will fall into place, more or less, and then the resting place of the scroll will be known."

"Do you think that he is getting help from the others? One might assist, but the first doesn't interfere," the assistant finished, standing and gazing into the vast beyond hoping that he and his master had just momentarily lost track of Death.

"I agree with the answers to your question. Fear not, where or when, how or why, Samuel goes, he will always have to come back. It is that anchor that ties him to who he is. He doesn't realize but his greatest weakness is also his greatest strength. To be more accurate, his greatest weakness will lead to his greatest strength. We have waited billions of years and are prepared to wait more. Samuel has put a light at the end of a very long tunnel for us. So our wait is almost up." The master concluded with a confidence that the assistant hadn't noticed in thousands of years. "I cannot see him either, so maybe the others are interfering. Samuel we can control to a certain extent. To control the others would be folly." The assistant could hear the finality in his master's voice. He paused for just a moment longer taking advantage of this point of view before turning and heading for the stairs. The assistant was on the first step down when, "assemble as many of the others that are not occupied. They may be necessary to forward the plans or flush Samuel from his shelter."

CHAPTER 9

Emergence

Death felt odd. That he could feel anything in this form was unusual. Samuel hadn't been Death for long, but, as Death, everything was dulled down especially his sense of touch, and the other senses he was still figuring out. The blunt trauma of a large metal ax which struck his arm he hardly felt. It was as if he were straining to feel the ax cutting into his arm. Being Death meant having the volume turned down on what he could feel, physically. Even the emotional pieces seemed to be turned down, yet in this place emotion was different. *Could this be some kind of defense as to not be overwhelmed? Feeling what I felt coming into the garden was just too much. I wonder if this will get any easier as it goes on. I'm guessing no.* But the physical part had changed strangely. Now there was a sensation, a feeling as if there was something that reverberated from his center. Death's center, his bones, since there was no flesh, no organs, felt like they were going to explode with some charged energy since arriving in this place. Death looked around as the feelings, both physical and emotional, clung to him, tugged at him, leaving him unsure again.

Can I just explode? If I go to a particular place will I just explode? What happens after that? Duh, nothing does, you've just exploded. Am I like a zombie, will I explode or melt if I go to holy ground? Or are those vampires? This nervous, excited feeling motivated Death to start walking. The trees that he could see were covered with water droplets as fog blanketed the area in a quiet and moist embrace. *It feels like I'm ready to jump out of my bones. I can feel the moisture of fog; I feel unsure with a hint of fear.* He reached out wiping his hand in the cool gray blankets of mist as little droplets of water collected on his hand, which also collected on the fabric of his shroud.

Death had been walking for a while now. He left behind not even the copper-covered doors that led him to this place, for they had faded from existence as soon as they weren't useful, just like everything else. He had no idea where he was going but the surge of power radiating from his being, his bones, compelled him to motion. With his vision limited to just ten feet, he could just see enough to make sure that he wasn't walking into any trees. The light that he used to see with came from an unknown source that reflected in the mist, which was of no consolation because there wasn't much to see in mist this thick. Something splashed to his right. Death tried to focus, prepare for what might come his way. He tracked movement out of the corner of his right eye and could only see a small fish fly across his field of vision just at eye level and land somewhere off to his left with another splash. Walking over to approximately the spot the fish should have landed, Death stopped and saw nothing. No fish, no creek or other body of water, only grass along with some bare patches of ground. *Strange. This has to be a dream. Marcus is ok in his bedroom and I'm sleeping next to Maggie. That has to be what's going on. This isn't real; the world doesn't work like this, angels and giants or disappearing doors.* Death looked around to make sure that he wasn't going to be ambushed and then crouched at the spot looking for the fish that had disappeared. Knowing and feeling that he had to move on to whatever this location brought, Death lost interest and wasn't sure of what he was doing. Death started just picking at the grass and bits of rock occupying the dry patch where he knelt. *What am*

I doing here? I know I am supposed to help someone or do something I just can't figure it out... What was I just looking at? Something just flew by and I was looking ...mmm... but I can't remember what that was either... Something is making me ...oh this is a nice patch of grass. Unable to focus on anything but what was right in front of him, Death started to count the blades of grass and sort the rocks into different size piles. As he counted the grass he could see faces form in the blades he counted. It was simply mesmerizing. Several beads of moisture danced a little dance and then bowed to Death in appreciation. They began again with a spin and danced about on the blades of grass, hopping from one blade to another.

There was a sound that should have taken Death's focus off the patch of ground, but the spot had him. He was now taking out the brown blades so that the green would stand out more. The brown blades simply weren't highlighting the moisture bead dances as well as the green blades were. The sound circled him and was getting ever closer; *footsteps?* Death didn't care and couldn't take himself away from the simple task, couldn't remember what he was doing here or why he should do anything else other than what he did now.

"You're not the first you know," a gravelly voice announced as it circled Death. The voice was right around Death but his sorting took precedence so he went on with tending his patch not even acknowledging the newcomer's presence. Its voice sounded like that lizard from the insurance commercials but mixed with gravel and glue.

"It's forgetting fog. If you stop within the fog you will forget everything and focus on what you were doing when you stopped." Death half looked up, clicking and gnashing his teeth as kind of a warning. "I know that you don't want to go on doing this Death, so I'll help you out. Actually I was told to expect you and help you out of this jam" the voice proclaimed as it walked away from Death. The voice irritated him and he was relieved that it stopped. There was order and contentment right here within six inches, Death's order was right here. The chaos of the world drifted by as he sorted the grasses and watched the performing water beads. The footsteps came back and Death knew that the annoying voice would start again as well. Something accompanied the footsteps; it was a low hum and a sharp cracking. Death never took his bony sockets off the patch. He felt something draped over his back and briefly interrupt the moisture's performance.

"Oh I missed the mark," the voice said. "Until I put this in your field of vision you'll never stop pickin' at the grass." A hand adjusted the moss, putting it directly in Death's field of vision. Obscured by a cloudy mess of weeds, Death's focus went to what was now hung before his face. He was about to sweep it away when he noticed the intricate pattern of vegetation that hung before his beloved grass and dancers, those patterns now held his attention. Energy, crackled and surged through the tiny branches of the vegetation adding to the strangeness of the moment. Small blue arcs of electricity began to weave itself within the tiny branches, as if the electricity was responsible for its growth. Death's complete focus was utterly on these electric reactions, the movement of the current and the boogie of the electricity. It moved closer and closer to his eyes. Now Death felt as if he were flying, shrinking into the mossy vegetation seeing the reactions and growth on a cellular level. Suddenly prickles of pain took him back from those smallest levels; suddenly a pain so great, flooded in causing the black walls of Death's peripheral vision to slam his regular field of vision. He moved but not under his own control. The current had him now as Death danced a strange spastic routine that started to uproot the enthralled Death. Rising from his crouched position. He stumbled and shook as the electricity was controlling his arms, legs and body. Where before there was an energy that propelled Death, that energy had escaped him when he started sorting the grasses in his little patch. Now there was too much energy and Death knew he couldn't take much more. BAM!

Occupational Death

Death was sliding backwards propelled by the force of the energy from the strange plant. Bouncing off a tree, Death shook his head and limped along a step every couple second.

"That's better now," the voice said as Death felt something under his arm helping him keep his feet and propel him forward. The Spanish moss rolled off his back and disappeared after a few steps forward. Death looked to the arm that supported him and saw rotted flesh. Holes of various sizes barely covered bones that Death could see moving under gray, blue and brown flesh. Then he heard the clank of metal on metal. The one who helped him was wearing armor that was in great disrepair. Sections of the armor were missing altogether and some hung attached at a single precarious point. As he looked at the face of the person helping him, he didn't notice that there was no flesh covering muscle and sinew and he didn't notice that the side of his head was caved in. All he saw was the determination and kindness in his eyes. Taking in the entire picture, the one who was helping him looked like he could have been a knight or soldier of the medieval times. Death looked back down to the arm that lifted him and helped him keep walking forward, then he noted the strangeness of the situation; the arm barely supported by flesh was supporting Death's fleshless arm.

That didn't hit Death as hard as the fact that he could have failed his family. Samuel had worked so hard to keep his family together and far from harm but the gravity of the encounter was too great. After the shocking assistance that freed him, he thought his physical form couldn't feel, but these physical feelings were too great. With everything that he had experienced thus far, he just had his emotional feet swept right out from under him. Death shuddered and he thought he could have lost it all. Death shuddered again and started to weep. In this form he thought it impossible. The tears welled in the sockets of bone and fell off of his cheek into his fleshless hand. The tears fell like drops and turned to dust and faded as soon as they hit his outstretched hand. The stranger, no his savior said nothing. This person who walked beside him supported him in what could have been the end of his task and damnation of his son; he was grateful and wondered if he could ever convey that gratitude. It was good to know that there were people who would aid Death and that he didn't have to do it alone. After the garden he thought cryptic answers and one-way conversations were all he could expect on this journey. Death felt less and less support on his arm and found that he needed less as he found his feet, and eventually the newcomer let him walk on his own.

"Thanks…"

"No need to thank me. Just keep moving." the stranger with the accent said. "I've come across a few who don't know the particulars of this place. Once I got closer to see who you were I knew I had to help."

"Forgetting fog? Where …," Samuel started to question further.

"First let me say this Death, you can't ask me any questions. As soon as you do, my services are voided. Since the first was rhetorical and the second you didn't finish I'll continue to lend a hand. Besides they are pretty standard questions and it has been a long while since I've talked to anyone. These lands are misplaced. Pockets of places collected from all over the universe as well as gaggles of spaces that can no longer be used. Is this the first one you came upon?" he asked sounding unsure, but also wanting to hear the conversation continue. The guide pointed in a new direction as they changed course slightly.

"No I was in a type of gray structure. Then I was in a kind of garden," Death wanted to tell more but something was stopping him from telling a complete tale. He wanted to explain his battle with the Minotaurs and the strange encounter with the cherub. He felt that he shouldn't mention Regus at all. *He knows about Death. I wonder what else he knows, but then I'll never know because I can't question him.* Letting his mind not be trouble by the obstacles or rules, Death took in the landscape. As he and his companion walked, the fog started to fade and Death saw what he had meant by misplaced places. They walked by what looked like a normal street corner, like one you would find in any major city, fire hydrant, stop sign, even brick walls and asphalt streets. The difference was the fleshless skeleton, looking much like Death except it still had its clothes. It was a human skeleton, or so Death thought, that was laid out with its hand touching the fire hydrant. The clothes looked fairly new and showed little signs of decay. Death didn't dare stop to take a closer look at any of it. As they walked by the scene, Death could see the edge of the wall and the piece of street were perfectly smooth. In the background of the street corner was a building like nothing Death had ever seen before. It was tall, bright and shinning like polished aluminum. There were people, creatures within the structure. They didn't move but to organize or look closer at whatever they were doing when the last remnants of the forgetting fog captured them.

"The fog is lighter here yet they are still slightly enthralled. Not stuck, but certainly not going anywhere fast" stated the guide. "You weren't kidding this place has a little of it all," said Death, as he looked all around and noticed that his walking companion had slowed after his statement.

"This is as far as I travel Death. The fog is lifting and I hope that you find your way. Keep walking until you are completely free of the fog." The fog dissipated slightly as the medieval soldier offered some parting instructions, then the man that helped him turned and walked back where they had come from, fading back into the fog. *Just like everything else in this world as soon as something seems to become clear it is obscured by time or the lack there of.* The pieces of other places continued as Death walked leaving the fog behind. Each was unique, some were beautiful as to take Death's non-existent breath away, and others were so alien that comprehension seemed impossible. Death walked turning this way and that as if he were walking by the world's longest electronics store that displayed all varieties of comedy or tragedy; Death was trying to catch a snippet of each channel.

All of a sudden Death felt alone. Even with the happenings of so many other worlds, he wanted to see his family. It was a thirst that could only be quenched by being home, by squeezing Maggie's hand, by holding the twins close or watching a little TV with Marcus. He knew that he should want to be home with his family but suddenly he was missing the emotionlessness of Death from before. It was a fleeting moment, but it was there. Samuel had been a slave to his emotions for years, fear of losing his family, fear of losing his job, all these fears gnawed at his spirit and it was taking its toll. Was it the fear or was it his lack of confidence in himself?

He tried to let those feelings slip aside as the next world or station came into view, this one put a smile on his face, but lack of flesh prevented it. Small beings, about the size of children, chased their companions around as they tried to build something with hardly any building materials at all. There was a scrap piece of metal and three boards these creatures were trying to manipulate. These creatures were wearing white space suits that made them look like earth astronauts. The white suits were equipped with visors which gave way to blue fields, which could have been their skin, because behind the faceplate of blue skin there were only the black circles that could have, should have been their eyes that continually blinked while they worked. They planned and discussed, and then would pull tools way too big right out of their pockets as one produced a wrench that was two times its own size. One would take charge mumbling orders as the others would comply for a while and then one of the other white suited creatures would get an idea, stop working, walk up to the current leader and slap it in the head, taking charge. The current construction project would fall to the ground and then the process would start all over again with that new leader directing the others.

Another "station" had an orange being, with several

limbs, sitting quite calmly in a comfortable chair smoking what could have been a hookah while it read its newspaper. It was probably the creature's Sunday morning. Alien notes of music that drifted towards Death, produced by a music player just beside the orange being. He could actually see the notes as well as hear them. These tangible forms were like snowflakes floating into his life only they too were alien to comprehend since Death couldn't recognize a single note. A single note floated to Death and dissolved as it came to rest on his shoulder. The orange paper reader folded his paper to another page, noticed Death was walking by, nodded and went back to reading. Death nodded and continued walking. Station after station, step after step, Death walked with nothing in sight but more stations. On he walked. The stations gave way to nothing, just rolling hills of sand and gray skies.

"I really don't know what I'm supposed to do. Oh great! Now I'm talking to myself. Well let's see, I've met what seems to be a power that has yet to be defined, Regus. I've fought metal Minotaurs and what could have been duplicates of me in gray world. I've seen a trial version of Eden, maybe, and met what will soon be an angel, excuse me, angel in training, who could say. I've passed through a couple worlds that I'm not even sure of and now I've got these pockets of other places. I really don't know how much more I can take," Death finished. He cursed himself silently, if only he could put aside these feelings, then he could get down to business. As if on cue the last pocket world, a room with three walls, a floor and a celling that constantly changed color, was gone as well. Death walked for what felt like an eternity.

"You will endure more unless you want Marcus to take your place again," a voice said from behind Death. Without stopping, Death looked over his shoulder to see who was speaking and saw the last thing he expected. As if he were looking at a mirror reflected in another mirror, a line of Deaths followed his footsteps that stretched as far as he could see. If his feet weren't firmly planted on the ground, Death would have surely fallen over at the sight of hundreds, if not thousands, of Deaths all in a line. Not caring what he could stumble into, he walked looking over his shoulder. Death didn't know if he were going to be attacked or have conversation with his other selves. Like a child first discovering a mirror, Death stopped and waved his right arm. The line of Deaths complied as if he were a puppeteer and these were his marionettes. The line of Deaths, spaced just so he couldn't reach the next, lowered their arms following his movements.

"Did you say that?" Samuel asked not expecting an answer, "as if it couldn't get any stranger," Samuel with an idea, did an impromptu about-face so now he was looking at the line of Deaths, their backs, all moving back in the direction he had come from.

Well let's have fun with this. He turned so he was shoulder to shoulder to the Death on his left. *Start spreading the news;* with that Death started to kick one foot after another while watching the line of Deaths follow suit. *Death meets the Rockettes! Hehe.* He stopped. Death enjoyed the moment, it was just what he needed right then. *What is this Regus and the 1000 Deaths? Sorry I didn't see that movie. I guess I should enjoy the moment and the laugh. That was a moment for me, no one else was around, and it was fun.*

He turned again so that he could see the back of the next Death and tried to reach out and grab the shoulder of the Death that was now in front of him. It moved just as he did. Picking up his feet a little faster, Death suddenly was running down all the line of Deaths. His feet were moving so fast that he couldn't see them. The line of Deaths ran, though they weren't running fast enough to outpace him. Each step took him not closer but into the next Death in the line, absorbing each of the other Deaths as he ran. He looked back. Nothing remained as he let this new-found speed lead him to the next part of this world. The world around and the pocket worlds were nothing but a blur. Death was not even trying to move so fast but each step over took another Death in the line. The sandy soil and gray sky blurred as Death ran faster and faster. As Death ran, his eyesight seemed to stretch and everything seemed to come into focus. The pockets he had passed were clear now and his eyes could track even the finest details from rocks on the ground, to the tools the little white and blue suited men left lying around. It was exhilarating. He felt the wind whip around him as the fabric that clothed him tickled at his bones. He put his head back and looked at the sky. It blurred as he ran on and on, taking another moment for himself. The garb he wore moved, protested under the speed at which he ran; it felt as if it the black cloth might just rip away at any moment. Death was on the move with such purpose and power driven by the lifting of his feet. He brought his head back to level and saw the last Death. Before he overtook the last Death, it moved to the right as Death stopped, instantly with his toes on the edge of a precipice. The pockets were gone, and the landscape in front of him changed dramatically.

Looking out, Death's bony jaw slacked and fell open at the sight of a vast churning body of black water. The inky liquid rolled and slammed into itself causing large blobs of inky blackness to hover and then fall back into the mass of itself. As the blackness rolled, Death thought he could see rough edges of animals that might be trying to form or escape from the blackness. There was no wind but the sea of inky liquid that fought the rocky coast, battering it wave after pounding wave. The coast and the surrounding land was colored like jasper. The inky liquid didn't approach the top of the cliff where he had come to rest while Death watched this ocean as if it were a living thing.

"Marcus needs his father," the Death to his right uttered bringing him back to the here and now. He had forgotten about the last Death. Death reached out to put his hand on the last Death. This one didn't follow his movement, it remained still. Death paused, then continued his movement grabbing on to the shoulder of the last Death. All the life that was in this last

Death left the moment the current Death grabbed him. Death now held the empty black garb that resembled his. There was no bone frame, nothing was left to support the empty garment. The garment took on a new form as he held it. Its length increased and it stiffened. A pole formed and atop the pole, a blade. The blade was a larger version of the ones his hands changed into. Falling out of thin air, a rope belt like his own fell to the ground just below the bottom of the pole. Death looked at the rope on the ground after noting the ropes fall, his eyes came up and the pole and blade were no more. It transformed back to a piece of heavy black canvas as he searched the garment hoping for answers. After a minute he discarded the cloth so that it rested atop the rope belt.

 Looking around to check the landscape, Death saw it was all reds and oranges in different shades that made up the sandy, rocky ground, grays and blues the sky and the sea of black was now completely still. It looked like black ice. The waves were gone and everything was eerily quiet. Spinning in a circle to check to see if he was in fact alone, he noticed that the sea was starting to rise. It wasn't thrashing as it was before but the volume of liquid crept up the cliff walls. Uncertain if he should run, Death was hypnotized by the movement of such a body of liquid. For as far as his eyes could see, up and down the coast, the sea climbed slowly. He couldn't see any rivers or tributaries adding to the volume of the blackness, just the steady creep of liquid towards him and the cliff top. From his position on the cliff, Death witnessed these events and was frozen. He could not have moved if he wanted to. All the speed he had just produced couldn't compare to the silent majesty; that silence was broken by a loud whoosh in the sky above his head. Death looked all round for the source of the noise and could find none. His hands had changed without a thought, ready to meet any threat. Something above reflected in the bright metal of his blades. Looking up, Death's hand fell to his sides reverting from blade to hand as a black form appeared in the sky. He then checked the black sea which stopped just before reaching the edge of the cliff.

It was as if someone had taken a pencil and drawn a line in the sky. The line then separated as if being pushed apart and a new blackness was introduced to this strange spectacle. It squeezed and came from this opening as if it were growing through the devised line. Its movement was a growth, almost like the inky black liquid of the sea before it became rigid. The floating blackness was less chaotic though it looked to be a living thing. Death couldn't quite be sure of the size of this thing as it grew, there was no scale with which to compare the growth. Despite the lack of perspective, he could feel it in his bones that it was large, no enormous. Death looked around hoping that he wasn't the only one to see this awesome sight; *pity.* In the moment he looked away it had moved and grown quickly trying to get above the black sea. The entirety of this floating black mass hadn't yet come completely out of the line in the sky. The leading part of it had formed a semicircle. With that formation, the last of it finally cleared the line that birthed this anomaly. It heaved and stretched, and two extremities started to form at the same point on either side of its mass. It kept heading further out over the sea and yet it didn't get any smaller. Wings formed on the sides of the flying black mass and the wings began to beat the air. The wings changed from feathered, to bony, to insect and kept changing, each new form a surprise. Even with the massive wings beating the air, Death couldn't feel the air moving. It turned and appeared to be making its way back to the land, back to its destination. Then it corrected its course and flew lower, flying over Death. The size of this thing and the force it produced just occupying a space this close to Death pushed Death to his knees as it flew over and slowed. Death stood slowly, carefully and stretched, straining his hand as he reached out, fingers wiggling desperately, wanting to touch the great mass. He wanted to feel it, to be a part of its wonder and its grandeur. Six squares on each side of its body opened. Blinding light poured out of the openings followed by clouds of steam that drifted down to envelop Death as he shielded his eyes for an instant. He fought the bright light because he had to see and he didn't know why, but knew he had to witness everything. Liquid light combined with steam ran down and all around Death, then faded quickly. The winged mass started to take a more proper form after that. It looked like a massive serpent, sometimes it had legs and arms, other times it didn't, but each time it changed the appendages were swallowed, vanishing within the bulk of its body.

The beast was close, Death could feel its presence, it greatness, its enormity and all this was in some way connected to him. He wanted to remember all of this. It was something that he felt he would never see again. It circled over Death. Two eyes formed and they were nothing but light, the same light as before from the six squares on its underbelly but nothing poured from the beast's eyes. A mouth opened and the beast roared as he started its journey back out over the black sea. The sound was high pitched at first, then it changed to a dull roar that made his bones vibrate as it poured over him and knocked Death from his feet. Sitting with his hands propping him up, Death watched as it continued its flight and ceased its roar. It flew now to a particular spot and began a slow circle. Each lap it took, its form changed. Sometimes it was a serpent, sometimes a lizard other times a dinosaur. Its wings would leave and come back in various forms. Death sitting, watched the event as he felt the land start to shake. He got to his feet to see cracks starting to tear through the solid black sea. As the land shook, a large angry crack grew, reaching for the land. As it extended, it threw up solid pieces of the blackness. The blackness rained down in chunks, mostly on the hard black surface, with occasionally a piece that would make land and be embraced by the jasper colored sand.

Right in the middle of where the beast was flying, a blinding column of light reached the blue gray clouds splitting them and the heavens beyond. A night sky filled with stars grew as the beam pushed the clouds back further, shaking the heavens and the land. The creature circling, increased its altitude as something was growing out of the cracked black sea. The solid parts of the sea were crashing closer to the cliff. Death was unable to move or stop watching. He stood in his place and was enthralled, having to witness this and accept what happened, even if that meant being crushed by the huge black debris. The light stopped its journey to the heavens and the large object was breaking through enough that Death could see it now. The serpent slowed its pace but kept circling, guiding an immense egg to the night sky. The rumbling finally ceased as the egg ascended out of the blackness. It wasn't perfect white; it might have been in a different light or a different situation but here it was a dingy white. It stopped for just a moment as it cleared the bonds of the black sea. The winged black beast that had been circling the egg's assent, completed one final lap, then it shot off and was gone piercing the layer of clouds and flew on into the heavenly sky. The egg resumed its slow steady climb as the clouds seemed to be closing around the egg as it just barely made it through the opening the light had produced. The clouds then matched pace with the egg, closing as fast as the egg ascended. The egg drifted up and the clouds closed behind it. The spectacle was complete. Death was shocked to see such a display of power, and he felt privileged to be a part of something so immense, so breathtakingly beautiful. It was unlike anything he had ever seen in life. Staring at the spot where the egg disappeared, Death wanted to feel more of this. He didn't want to go on like Death as before unfeeling. He would try to feel while in Death's form, not forgetting what it was that he was fighting for, his family. Death brought his head down and noticed that he was about to be overtaken by the black sea that had now reverted to is original viscous liquid form. It was already touching his bony toes. It rose unnaturally quick, like a pouncing animal, as he felt the pressure of the liquid on his bones. He wanted to run but the thick black liquid prevented it. It was cold and it was about to overtake his head. Death instinctively tried to take a deep breath as the blackness swept over his eyes.

Death could see nothing. It was pitch black. He couldn't see his hand in front of his face. He knew he was moving, he could feel the light flapping of the heavy material, the canvas that robed him as Death. He felt like a feather falling. A single point of light erupted below him, sending out a wave of light in all directions. He was sinking slowly towards the light and he watched as it continued past him. Death noticed that there were small bits, rock, maybe sand, floating and moving all around him, bouncing off his body and the bits started to collect. The bits were attracted to each other, forming larger and even larger fragments. Death pulled himself away not wanting to focus on any one event; he vaguely remembered the point of the lights origin and turned his focus back to that spot. The black patches, the empty spaces between the light started to collect into a mass and it moved on the light, probing, trying to take pieces of the light. The blackness succeeded. The light backed away and protected itself, it fortified the light with light. The dark shot out tentacles attacking the light and tried to wrap the light in a dark embrace. Huge arms formed and swept at the darkness, through the bits of forming matter, and went at the darkness, fighting it back. Death continue to drift, through the light and the dark. The fighting stopped eventually. It was calm. Death continued to float down and saw the darkness moving on the light again. The light and the dark fought again and then, stopped shortly after. The light formed into a gigantic humanoid, as did the dark. They seemed to shake hands and be at peace with each other. Death noticed that he had stopped floating down. Looking down, he was standing on one of the collections of debris. It resembled a small rock, with smaller cavities, it was just large enough for him to stand on. Death then noticed bits of light and dark were floating down and all around as a result of the battles. The rock that Death was standing on had bits of the light and the dark resting and collecting all around. He also noticed the rock on which he stood was getting larger, about the size of a dining room table. Death looked around again, wondering what this was all about, why was he shown this? The rock, suddenly, swallowed Death.

CHAPTER 10

Lineage

Felicia gently shut the door. Just leaving Ralph, Felicia tried to move past the last half hours' events. She never really liked these episodes but saw them as necessary. Her children were her world and everything went out the window when it came to their care, even her body. She gently set a couple pieces of wood close to the fire to warm. Later they would be thrown on the fire after Felicia did a few chores. Ralph's offering was slightly more generous than the last few. The cheese was a nice treat she would share with the kids. She unfolded it from her apron and placed it on the top shelf. She went to the bucket and washed her hands. Wiping her hands, she gathered her wrap, then went to look in on the children. Each of them were breathing the heavy sleep breath, none were feigning sleep. She stood there for a moment basking in their peacefulness, absolute stillness, that was completely absent when they were awake. Felicia didn't think herself lucky, not after losing Peter, but she considered herself better off than some. Even in his death, Peter had made sure that Felicia was taken care of to the best he could manage before the sickness truly took him. In this moment of quiet she allowed herself to think of Peter, his touch, his gentle smile that said 'love you' more than he ever did verbally. She closed her eyes and went back to one of hundreds of happy moments she remembered with her husband. His smile, easy and endlessly pleasant, flashed through her mind taking her back to a better time. It had taken Felicia a while to get to a place where she could see the smiles of her late husband. Just after he had died all she could see was the sickness, a frail Peter, a man she loved who was stripped of all he had or ever would have. She squeezed her eyes shut, banishing the haunting images of her dead husband. With a deep breath, she could see Peter smiling at her as he would leave for work. She wiped the single tear off her cheek as she opened her eyes and remembered where she was. She allowed Ralph but wouldn't, couldn't love another like Peter. He was her soulmate.

She left the children to their dreams and straightened a bit. After cleaning she allowed herself some of the cheese she had earned, and then she put the warmed wood on the fire. After that she went to where the children were sleeping. She went to the end of the children's bed that supported Mary's head and gently lifted the straw filled sack. Under that corner of the sack was a small box. Felicia reached down, retrieved the box and put that end of the sack where it had been. This was the one thing she allowed herself to keep after her life with Peter, that was a life of working on the children and the house, not the fields. Toiling in the fields she rarely had time for the contents of the box, but the more she thought about her time and what had happened after Peter passed, she knew she had to make it known to others. She placed it on the table and opened it like a book. Inside there were sheets of paper. This gift from Peter, which he bought from a Spanish sailor, was acquired in order to let Felicia practice her writing. Reading and writing were treasures that Peter gave her that no one could take from her. Peter said that she could make a life of writing, but being a woman trying to do a man's job would make writing a struggle Felicia didn't have time for. From the box she pulled a quill, the ink and a single sheet of paper and closed the lid. She looked at her children and knew that in time she would make sure that they knew how to read and write as well. She began writing:

Ralph is a decent man, though he wants me to send my children away. I cannot. Never to see their smiles or tears would finish me and send me to Peter's side. The children mostly look like me and my family. Every now and then, I see Peter in them. As long as they are alive, a small part of Peter is as well. How I would love for Peter to be at my side now, to rub my back or brush my cheek with the back of his hand. Those touches still echo on my body, but I long for more of Peter than echoes. As time passes I fear that even those echoes will fade. Nothing will change the fact that Peter is gone and my life is forever different. Different in ways I will try to explain now.

I, Felicia Willis, write to tell of what I have seen, where I have been and who I have met. Shortly after my husband Peter died, a metal band appeared on my wrist. A short time later, I was sent to another place and after that different places at different times. These places could come right out of story books. I've seen creatures that could be made of nightmares. On each of these journeys I was different from myself. I was dressed in all black fabric that covers a white skeleton. I have read stories and seen pictures that describe how I looked and in those stories it was Death. With the black death disease, that form is being made popular by drawings and tales. Our benefactor, a being of watery, shiny metal in the form of a giant told me that he is from God. He told all of us. He said that he would direct us on what we were to do when summoned. The tasks are performed and then we are sent back. The band has come to my wrist several times and each time the location is different, the task as well. Fear for my children keeps me from asking too many questions. I think the shiny being could destroy any of us with no effort. There is a power about him that makes my stomach churn. So I do as I am told and keep moving forward. I know not if Regus could harm my children. Those worries aside, I feel free when I am doing that job. It fills me with a sense that the world is right and I am where I need to be. That freedom comes most when I run. While I am Death I can run faster than I could imagine. There is nothing that I cannot chase down. This freedom comes at a price as I cannot jump. Both my feet cannot leave the ground at the same time. As Death, I feel a pull to the ground that I can never escape it. My hands can change into scythes and cut through anything I have come up against. There is some greater purpose at hand, I just do not know what that is now and I may never know. If someone else is to read this, they may think me mad, I am not. This has come to me, though I do not know why. I will see this through. I will see my kids age and find lives of their own. This is the first time I have written about these events. I think it helps to unburden my soul and so I will continue. As I continue and think of each time I am summoned, it is a comfort that the tasks change but hardly anything else. When called for the most recent task I was truly frightened. Something happened that was not normal.

Felicia paused to check to make sure that she was alone in the room, even though she knew that she and the sleeping children were the only people around. Her hands were shaking as she dipped the quill into the ink well and continued her account.

When I was injured performing tasks in the past, ash would flow from the wound. On this task I was wounded by a tree-like club with spikes as long as swords. Before when this would happen another Death would appear from the ash that came from my bones, the Death from the ashes would help. It happened just like that this time as well, only the Death born this time attacked me. I wasn't sure what to make of the other Death's attack and I am worried it will happen again. It worries me that maybe this work may not be so fixed, that it may be changing not just for me but the others as well.

Felicia laid down the writing quill and took a deep breath to steady herself. She got up and went to the bucket and splashed water on her face. She didn't know why but when the other Death attacked her it shook her to the core. She expected it to aid her on the task, but then was ambushed and this didn't set well with Felicia. After she wiped her face she went back to the table to finish her writing, even her body was telling her it was late. Noting that this wasn't her best handwriting she continued none the less.

Occupational Death

I also want to speak of what affects me day to day. I do the job of reaping so that I can care and provide for my children so they are not taken away from me. I do the job for Ralph so that we can have a little more. Men doing the same work I do make more. I work just as hard if not harder than some of the men and am paid only five pence, while they receive eight. I could try and make something more of myself. The fact that I have been taught to read and am working on writing, I probably could find a different job. Fear, my perception of what the children would think of me, keeps me from that. Will that fear drive me to press on and try a new trade? Although, if I am to teach them, they will have to know eventually. Would other children make fun of my own just because of what I can do? Someday I hope I get over this fear, someday I will teach my children as Peter taught me. My children behave and listen, for that I am thankful. I don't sleep well. I don't find peace and contentment in my sleep like my children. I sleep, then wake. This process repeats three to five times in the night, sleeping, waking and sleeping again, it has been this way since Peter died. I think this is a good start and will do this from time to time, only if it does not interfere with my responsibilities, here or elsewhere.

Felicia put the materials back in the box and walked to the bed where her children were sleeping. With the box hidden again, she sat at the table. As she sat her stomach growled. Her gaze went to the shelf where she had put the cheese. With a sigh, she went and pulled off another small hunk, leaving the majority for the kids. She chewed slowly, enjoying the rich flavor compared to the mostly bland stew and bread she was accustomed to. She took her seat again at the table and rested her head on her arms. Looking at her children, she drifted off to sleep.

CHAPTER 11

Points of Light

Lit by spiraling celestial bodies and nearby stars, the large platform buzzed with anticipation and was hushed in secretive tones. Many creatures dressed in black and silver robes huddled in small groups sharing with each other secrets, desires and hopes for the future. A new future promised by their master. At the far end of the platform, an expansive dais supported a large, thick stone throne that was carved in all sharp angles. The master, seated in the throne, gazed out, waiting.

"He has reappeared sir," said one of the assistants hovering at the side of the large dais. The figure in the throne didn't move, didn't speak for many minutes. As the master addressed his gathering, a hush fell over all who collected in the master's presence. "Again it doesn't matter. The prophecy has been set in motion. Now that it is started we can start to move other pieces into place so that we have the desired result. Contact our man and have him start to prepare the lady for her journey. It will take some time for her to be ready for the journey after so much time has passed. No matter the outcome, we will have our time and neither of them can stop that."

"Now Samuel Willis. Where have you been?" the master queried, leaning forward in his chair resting his chin on his hand. He focused his gaze, knowing it didn't matter. Now that it had started it couldn't be stopped. His gaze fell on the first point that had been revealed when Samuel removed the watch.

CHAPTER 12

Many Rivers

There was darkness. Then the lights were turned up as if on a dimmer switch. The sky rolled by with colors varying from bright orange to deep red. Death took a moment to take in the environment. The journey, so far, had been long and he had seen much. Thunder rumbled off in the distance, then closer. Lightning split the sky, leaving him startled and shaken, only for a moment. Death laid prone with his knees bent at ninety degrees. As he propped himself up on his elbows, he saw the lands around were barren. Broken rocky terrain was colored in shades ranging from ash to pitch black which made up all the landscape as he looked left and right. Rock mounds, some small and some larger, were the only topographical break to the seemingly uninhabitable land. Death noticed that he was laying on a hill facing down a gentle slope. *Down it is, cause down is easier.* So he rose to his feet and started the long trek to another unknown location, to do some unknown thing. While he walked, awe, wonder and amazement from the last world he visited swirled in his mind. The last grains of the emotion he had felt in the previous realm fell through an hour glass with no bottom and slowly he felt nothing, the normal for Death. With only his thoughts, thoughts of how to free Marcus from this burden, Death kept an even walking pace downhill.

Trying to keep his spirits up he thought of home and of holding his children's hands and skipping with them in the grocery store parking lot, but even that was a strain. He stopped and recounted what he had been feeling on this journey. In the grayland, nothing, in the garden everything from all-time lows to superficial highs. Now the nothing he felt in grayland was back. Not wanting to let go of these feelings just yet, Death let his mind slip back to his thoughts before of skipping with the kids. Skipping with his kids had always brought a smile to his face, but in this form, this place, the feelings were prevented as was the smile that skipping could bring. So Death skipped, or at least he tried. One foot would come off the ground, but as he would bring the other up to hop, completing the skip, it wouldn't come off the ground. So he tried simply to hop with both feet, and wasn't able to do that either. *So I can cut through solid forms of metal, but I can't hop.* It felt as if his feet were connected to the ground in some strange attraction. He could walk, he had been walking since his journey had started, so he pushed the pace of his speed walking. Each step taken was pulled to the ground before the other foot could come free from the ground. This allowed him to walk faster and faster. Stopping, he lifted both of his bony feet one at a time. Resuming the speed walking, his pace seemed to increase the longer he kept at it. Soon the fast walk turned into a run. Death was fast, covering great distance in just a few seconds. He tested this weaving in and out of the larger and smaller mounds of rock with ease. Soon he was running at the speed he used to run down the line of Deaths, it took him a while to get to that speed, but eventually he got there.

Then he stopped as he came upon a major change in topography. The ground leveled and just ahead of him a river of sorts stopped him in his tracks. Still getting the hang of "speed walking", Death took his time to approach the change in scene. The last couple of venues he had toured had taken him by surprise and this one he didn't want to take for granted. Death climbed to one of the smaller mounds close to the river and was amazed. The river itself wasn't whole, but many rivers running together, not unlike a delta, but one river would then drop off and be taken over by another. Death looked up and down the collection of rivers trying to make sense of where one would end and the other would begin. A river running red would be up stream and another part of the river would surface again later as he attempted to follow the maze of rivers. The only reason Death could keep track of it all was that this was no ordinary river. One river steamed by channeling hot lava. Then another river whisked by carrying large chunks of ice. Several of these different types of rivers flowed in and out, up and down of one another, and there was one that just poured out of the sky. One such river just seemed like calm water. The perfect surface was broken by a huge shark like creature, which disappeared as quickly as it appeared. A cry for help brought Death's gaze to the shore line. Someone was trying to escape the clutches of the rancid water that made up a different stretch of the river. Death moved with care not wanting to run into a river of lava or be eaten by a large predator. He reached for the man, or what was left of him as hundreds of tiny golden fish latched on to his flesh and clothes.

"Help me, please. It hurts....it hurts," the man doubling his efforts trying to reach for Deaths boney hand.

"I wouldn't do that, even if I were you," said a voice off to the right of Death. He took his attention off the shoreline to see a boat long and shallow with a single figure manning the stick oar at the stern of the vessel. The figure in the shallow boat was rough looking, unshaved and uncombed. With a simple brown robe covering much of his tanned body, simple sandals kept him balanced as he brought the boat to rest on shore with the long wooden pole.

"Why not?" Death asked looking back down to see that the form was lifeless. The currents washed up and took what was left of the man as well as the tiny golden fish into the currents of that river.

"There is a balance to be held here. Do you know what this is?", the boatman asked with a thick Indian accent. Death thought that the accent he had heard first was a British accent.

"This is the river Styx," Death replied pleased with himself. After seeing the boatman, it all became clear. Thinking back to the mythology classes he had taken in his years of primary school and some of the college courses as well.

"Well don't look too pleased with yourself. If I hadn't come along and stopped you, you might have done something stupid and upset the balance. This place has rules, and it would take me the rest of my term as boatman to tell you. Yes, this is the river Styx and yes I am the boatman. I hate being called the ferryman, I don't really have wings do I," the boatman said chortling offering another accent, Scottish now, at the play on words trying to have Death laugh along. "Well aren't you just a warm ray of sunshine. I'm not here to help you I'm just here to make sure that you don't screw it up either. The man, or whatever was left of that man was on his way to the next stop in his journey. He made his choices and now has to live with them." The boatman's accent was changed again, this time with heavy Russian inflections.

"Does that mean he's is going to hell?" Death questioned. "Am I not supposed to ask you questions either?"

"Oh no, ask away, just remember that you will have to live with the knowledge revealed here. Anyone you ever knew or will know could be put on this path. Would you really like to know the outcome? The suffering they have to endure, that you might have to endure one day? I don't say this to scare you, quite the contrary. You see, even seeing what you have seen has altered your reality...maybe" the boatman continued with a half shrug and a thick New York accent.

"No it hasn't. The reality is that I am here to protect the ones I love, and there is nothing more to my reality than that,"

Death said standing defiantly.

"Easy big guy, easy. You say that now, but endure what they have endured. We aren't talking just a one-way trip. We are talking once you get to the bottom and endure what has been set out for you, your trip most likely will start again as they send you back to the top to get a whole new perspective on pain, suffering and abandonment. They will show you a sliver of hope then snatch it away and replace it with your worst fears or even worse make that hope into your fear" the boatman said leaning in to drive the point home with a German accent.

"You sound like someone who has seen a few things, experienced even more. Tell me. Did they pluck you from the river on your journey down?" inquired Death.

"I've seen quite a bit. Including my own family drift on this river. The only ones we can see are those that are connected to us somehow someway. That poor soul, that is someone you knew, know or will know. Oh but don't strain that pretty head of yours, you won't be able to recognize them, that's how this place stabs it in and breaks it off. Again a warning about knowledge is that it can certainly unnerve you. You think to yourself, 'I want to know', but really what does it get you? More thinking, who was that? Or what could I have done to prevent that outcome?" said the boatman with no accent at all, winking at Death. Death stared at the boatman for a minute and then looked further up river past the boatman and then down river, for souls he might know. The rivers continued to flow, putrid rivers of slime and dead animals, a river of rocks that would crush anything that dared to tempt those waters rolled on by. Death looked back to the boatman, who shrugged, rubbed his head and offered nothing but a matter of fact smirk.

"Mind your step" said the boatman "but don't fear these paths, they can't do anything to you physically, only bring you heartache, doubt and misery, if you go looking too long or deep in the waters of this place. You have much to do Death, don't dwell too long. Marcus is waiting for you to save him. Or was it as you said 'your family is waiting for you to save them'" finished the boatman with a draw to his accent that would put that distinct twang from the southern United States as he pushed back into the currents. Using the stick oar the boatman pushed off of the shore as certain currents took him further down river faster than others. Death felt a finality about the boatman's last words. The statement resonated with him 'your family is waiting for you to save them' as his mind drifted from Marcus to Maggie to Robert to Denise; *family*. It was strange. The longer he talked to the boatman the more he could feel, know and understand what was happening to him. *Maybe he did me a favor leaving, not giving me too much to fear or hope for. Although, was he giving me clues that I'm not just here to save Marcus? Maybe completing these tasks with save the entire family. Could this be passed on to the kids? God no please, they should not have to be subject to all this. If I fail will Robert or Denise have to take my place? That isn't an option.*

Death looked for a way across the river and the feelings faded again as he wanted nothing more than to get on with saving his son, possibly the rest of the family. He ran along the banks of the river for a moment picking up speed, practicing starting and stopping, as he was now able to cover great distances with ease and in a short time. He could find no way, bridge or path, to cross the river. *The boatman told me 'don't fear these paths', so maybe I can just cross.* Looking for the safest looking part of the river, he came upon a small stretch of river close to shore that was covered with ice. With tentative steps, Death made his way across. With no warning the ice gave way and Death fell for an instant and then stood on the icy water. Death made his way across the water to the next section and then over that. Over lava and a river that ran red, Death slowly crossed being careful where he put each foot. Standing on a different section of the rock-river, a wave rolled fast towards him. Thinking he was about to be crushed, Death braced for the worst and was amazed as the wave just rolled over him submerging him completely in the rocky, watery substance. There in that rock-river, it was peaceful for just a moment. There were no sounds in the rock-river just a feeling of being surrounded comfortably, like the inky black fluid that took him to the battles between light and dark. A couple more steps brought him across the river. Death looked back along his path and it had all changed. Different rivers were flowing in different directions and he even saw a pirate ship on the waters just before it was dragged under by large tentacles which belonged to who knows what. Turning back around, Death shrugged and sensed he had reached his destination.

The land went downhill rolling with an easy slope and leveled off. On the level ground below, a large sandy brown stone structure stood in contrast to the shades of black sand and rock that surrounded the monuments base. If was five times larger than any of the other black knolls in this barren waste. It was its size and color, and something else he couldn't quite make out, that made this structure feel like a monument or a place of reverence. Death picked a path that would take him to the structure and started down. He made his way to the top of one of the larger mounds when he reached the bottom of the slope. *I think there are doors on that thing and something is glittering on the top of it.* It had two equal angled sides that supported a small roof. The base was five times the size of the roof. Testing his speed out further, he made it to the flat surface in a couple seconds. *I'm getting better at that.* A large mound was in between Death and the structure. *This wasn't here before.*

Before he could move, a long black tendril unwrapped itself from the base of the mound. It undulated gently, hypnotically for a moment. Death noticed that there was a smooth portion to the tendril that gave way to fur, which seemed to be attached to the mound. The tip of the tendril pointed at Death and started to change. Eyes opened on either side as a mouth formed and a tongue flickered as it tested the air. It looked like a large snake of some kind. Needle like teeth appeared in its open mouth as it hissed. The mound moved, it trembled and shook, not like rock, but more like flesh and started to hover. It almost looked like it was going to start to fly. The mound wasn't flying. It was supported by even larger tendrils, no not tendrils but legs, as muscle and sinew pushed a body off the ground. Bits of rock fell from the mound as it stopped its growth; it was easily forty feet tall. The legs started moving the enormous body. The tail, which was tipped with a large snakes head, hissed and bared its teeth as it drifted away from him. Death caught the silhouette of the creature. Thick hairs danced and swayed on its back, yet there was no breeze to push the black manes. The head came to bear. Black fires danced in its yellow eyes as they narrowed and came to focus on Death. Drool oozed from its mouth over the sinister, long sharp teeth. Following the line of drool, he thought he heard it pop like water hitting hot grease when it dropped to the ground. Then another head, that looked identical to the first only slightly larger came around, snipping at the first head. The creature finished its turn, fully facing Death. Three heads gazed at him. The central mouth biting at other two heads, keeping them in check. Six eyes, blazing full of hatred and rage fixed on Death and each mouth issued its own low growl. *Cerberus!*

CHAPTER 13

Hope

Maggie woke just as the alarm clock went off. Shocked, she looked at the clock and knew she had to get up, Samuel and his alarm usually helped her wake up. Looking to his side of the bed, it was empty, and after rubbing the sleep from her eyes she noticed it hadn't been slept in. *That's right I got that text from Samuel telling me he was still at the job fair. I miss him, I know it hasn't been too long, but there is something incomplete about the house when Samuel isn't here.* Maggie looked at her phone and saw she had a text from an unknown number which usually meant that a potential client was contacting her. She looked at it briefly and noticed that it was a sales pitch. A new website, findyourwayback.com, was just a startup company and allowing a few select customers access to their database of family history. Wondering if this was some kind of gag she put her phone down and started her morning routine. She stopped halfway to the bathroom turned back to her phone and deleted the text. *Probably some kind of phishing attempt.* She went to the bathroom, after that, brushed her teeth and grabbed her housecoat as she went down to the kitchen to find Marcus dressed ready for school eating cereal. She grabbed her chest and started to act like she was having a heart attack when she hit the last stair.

"Well isn't this something? Did the house get hit by an airplane? My son is up with no assistance before noon! How can this be?" Maggie said, grabbing a cup and filling it with coffee as she smiled and winked at her son

"Ha-Ha mother. Maybe you should pinch yourself because ...you might be dreaming" Marcus said to his mother throwing her a forced toothy grin.

"So did your Dad talk with you?"

"Yes."

"How did it go?"

"Fine." Maggie just sipped her coffee and watched her son. Then she threw her hand on her hip, "Is this going be a one worded conversation?"

"No," Marcus quipped with a smirk seeing his mother was starting to get agitated. "Alright, alright. Yes, we talked." Marcus got up from his seat to clean up after finishing his breakfast.

"So tell me about the conversation," Maggie pushed a little, full well knowing that this could go nuclear at any moment. Marcus put the cereal back in the pantry and the milk in the fridge. "Dad asked me about my grades so I showed them to him, we ate ice cream and talked awhile. He said he had an early interview or job fair today and would be home late cause he was having dinner with an old friend." Marcus walked to the sink and started to lay the bowl down. Stopping, seeing his mother's posture, he rinsed it and put it in the dishwasher. "Later, Nelson is picking me up at the bus stop." Marcus grabbed his bag and left through the front door. Maggie looked around and nothing was out of place. Adding more coffee to her cup and some cream she walked past the trashcan back to the stairs. Stopping for a moment she went back and lifted the lid of the trash can. On top, rested of the empty ice cream container. Maggie had to get ready for work and also get the kids ready. *Why do I have the feeling that all isn't right between Marcus and Samuel? There is an empty ice cream carton is in the trash, which does support Marcus' story.* Maggie shrugged and hurried up the stairs.

Maggie put the twins on the bus and headed to the garage. She would have to step on it if she was going to make the next meeting. As she was starting on her way the phone rang. It was Shirley Osborne. She knew she had to pick up the phone.

"Hey sweetie, how are you?"

"Can I watch Hope tomorrow? Sure that shouldn't be a problem, Samuel is at a job fair so an extra set of hands around to help keep the kids entertained would be great. No, no luck yet, but Samuel has been looking pretty hard. The substitute teaching is helping out, but I know teaching isn't where Samuel wants to be. Alright hon, talk to you tomorrow...mmm bye." *That poor woman. Her husband died six months back over in Afghanistan. He was good to her, but being in the military took its toll on their relationship. Don't I know about strain, well really I don't, particularly not the strain the Osbornes had and now Shirley has being on her own with a child. At least Samuel is going to come back from this job fair, James isn't coming back. That kind of loss is life shaking. One minute you are married and the next you're receiving word that your husband is dead. Once I heard and then discussed it with Samuel I knew we had to help. James took care of them, but Shirley still works and needs to be an adult away from Hope from time to time. Plus, it will be good for the twins.* It was then that Maggie thought about Richard, less than two months ago she had a brother, but that was the past. Losing a brother certainly wasn't like losing a husband, but it still hurt. She could feel the emotions coming on so down the window went and after a couple deep breaths she checked the clock. Maggie knew she was going to make her meeting and took that as a good sign that things were turning around.

****

Saturday morning was going swimmingly. *The kids are up and fed, except Marcus, but he could fend for himself. Shirley should be over shortly to drop off Hope, and that will keep the twins happy. I did have some work that I could get done to get a little ahead at work so long as Hope and the twins are playing nicely.* Maggie topped off her coffee when the doorbell rang. *That has to be them.* Answering the door, Maggie greeted Shirley and Hope. *These are good visits. I'm sure Shirley could use the break after what happened to James and Hope still needs to be a little girl.* Hope was dressed in blue jeans and a pink t-shirt with white raised letters on the front that said girlie girl. Shirley thanked Maggie again, gave Hope a quick peck then ran back to her car as Hope came in to start the fun. *Girlie girl, well that's half right. Hope could be just that, a "girlie-girl" but I've seen Hope the tomboy as well.* Maggie ushered Hope upstairs and played with the kids for about 30 minutes. Once the playing was well established Maggie excused herself. She went to the bedroom and started to work on a few work details that wouldn't take too long. Maggie paused at the door to the twin's room, watched for a few seconds more, then turned and heading for her bedroom.

The twins room was littered with all sorts of toys. The twins were building a house out of bristle blocks as Hope rummaged through the toy chest for some toy cars. Hope enjoyed playing with the twins, it was like having a little brother and sister. She wished that was all she had to do today, but there was business to attend to as well. Hope was smart and waited for the right time. When the twins started to become bored with the blocks and toy cars she suggested hide and seek. It started simply enough in their bedroom but the places to hide were exhausted quickly. She suggested opening the game to the house.

"Mom, we are going to play hide and seek in the house." The kids heard a murmur that sounded like ok and Hope volunteered to go first. The kids ran downstairs and hid while Hope counted to fifty. By the count of ten, the kids were downstairs. By twenty Hope was taking careful steps to make her way to Marcus' room. The door was cracked, she peeked. Marcus was sound asleep. His breathing was deep and steady. Hope could feel warmth come from Marcus' room as the sun was filling the room with its radiance. She had come to care about Marcus more than the others. Hope wasn't quite sure why, but when she was around him, she felt excited and scared. Happy and unconfident, clumsy and light as air. Hope wasn't quite sure why she felt this way. All that she knew was that she couldn't stop these feelings. A noise from the end of the hall brought her out of her thoughts. She continued her count at 40, changed directions walking away from Marcus' room and started down the stairs. After about thirty minutes of hide and seek, everyone, that included Maggie, took a break with a small glass of milk and a few cookies. The kids were being kids as Maggie watched over them in the kitchen. Using the cookies as wheels and flying saucers, the kids played and ate.

"Glad to see you joined the land of the living," Maggie said to Marcus. Hope was mid sip of milk when she snorted at the unexpected appearance of Marcus. Milk splashed her face as she raced to put the milk down. A hard swallow sent that milk and cookie remnants on their way.

"Sorry went down the wrong tube" Hope said with a strained voice trying to clean up quickly. Marcus yawned and gave his mom the "ok" sign with his fingers. Marcus walked by the table, "Hope you missed a spot of milk." She quickly grabbed a napkin and wiped the spot. Marcus had messy hair and even messier clothes. Hope followed him with her eyes as he went to the cupboard grabbed a bowl, then the cereal, and plopped down next to Hope. Her focus went back to her milk as her stomach did a back and forth and made a sound that alerted the entire kitchen. "You must be hungry Hope." Maggie chuckled putting out a couple more cookies. "Or would you prefer some fruit?"

Hope smiled, "fruit please."

"We just got the last of the peaches, the season is over but these seemed to ripen just a bit later than the rest," Maggie finished slicing the peach. Hope seemed to be sinking in her seat as Marcus went about the business of breakfast while the twins teased their brother by making zombie groans with arms extended mocking their brother. He just smiled and shook his head. Hope stuffed the quartered peach in her mouth two slices at a time, chewed fast and when she finished with another hard swallow she looked at the twins. "Hide and seek?" The twins got out of the booth and Hope started to slide across the long way out of the booth to avoid going past Marcus, but Marcus got up from his seat so she didn't have to go the long way around. With a sheepish smile, "I'm ok" she said and when her feet hit the floor she took off after the twins. The games continued and on one of the times that Hope was it, she again snuck to Marcus' room while he was listening to music. He was about to pick up a book and start reading. "Hey Hope. I promise the twins aren't in my room" Marcus said with a little smile. Hope had a blank look on her face. She was nervous, she hadn't quite understood why she was feeling the way she was downstairs. Her initial intention was to ask Marcus where he had been the last few times, but that went out the window. The light from behind him seemed to cast him in an angelic glow. Hope didn't want to disturb that even if Mary Patricia wanted answers. "We haven't seen you in a long time. It's been tough. Did something happen between you and..."

"Hope, honey, your mom's here to pick up" Maggie called from the bottom of the stairs. Hope remained for a few seconds just taking in the expressions of Marcus. His hair was just over his eyebrows and he had an awkward smile that looked like he was happy and slightly confused all at the same time. Hope didn't want to leave on a bad note considering she didn't get the answers Mary Patricia was asking for. She smiled and said "Thanks." Then she turned, never finishing her conversation with Marcus. On the way downstairs Hope forced her face from confused and sad, to an easy smile so that her mother wouldn't be concerned, just like her Dad taught her. She jumped into her mother's arms and gave her a loving hug.

CHAPTER 14

Smiths

The room was dark, lit by torch and the glowing light of many forges. Oranges and reds dominated the lighter colors, grays and blacks embraced the shadows. The walls were made of stone that resonated the orange and red that reflected the flicker of the fire light. Dialects old and long forgotten echoed through the halls and shadows of this dusky place. The ringing and pounding of hammer on iron broke up the conversations. Each part of the conversation sounded different. The men that occupied this space spoke in ancient long forgotten dialects to each other with the questions, conversation and replies that were understood as if each were hearing their native tongue.

"At least I didn't die by my own sword," answered Creidhne. Creidhne, Goibinu and Luchtaine sat to one side as Creidhne laughed, Goibinu smiled and Luchtaine shook his head. Creidhne rested easy, almost reclining, his brown hair and bronzed skin were covered by his leggings, a simple linen shirt and soft boots. A large belt adorned with several bright bronze plates that reflected the ambient light as well his flashy demeanor also kept his sword in place. He wasn't the strongest and knew it, but he did try to make merry with the serious crowd. His eyes, a brilliant blue, looked to the others to help him out with his attempted jesting and merriment. His brother

Goibinu stood with his fingers interlaced in front of him resting at his waist line. He smiled to let anyone else know that his brother was joking, as well as to try to defuse the possibly ill received joke, hoping to keep a ruckus from breaking out. Goibinu was dressed finer than his brother and was ready to help anyone should the need arise, even if that meant gagging Creidhne. He smoothed his light brown hair and shrugged at the others, as if trying to make them understand his brother could be off-putting at times. He winked his soft blue eyes at his brother Luchtaine and patted him on the shoulder. Luchtaine's hard features didn't relent at Creidhne's joke. Luchtaine was serious all the time. His chiseled features, hawkish eyes and pointed chin did nothing except look away from the ever annoying Creidhne. He used his spear to rise to his feet even though he didn't need it. He grabbed his shield and walked to the other side of the room. His body was well muscled except for his right leg just below the knee, that was something else entirely. It was wood, but it wasn't a prosthetic. His atypical toned flesh was knitted to the wooden appendage, which acted more like flesh than wood. The wood brown skin of his lower right leg was supple and obeyed all the movements Lutaine would command of it. This fixture wasn't something clunky and cumbersome, it was a work of art. His silent footsteps took him to find a new seat, away from his brothers.

These comments were directed at Ogun. He was a perfect specimen of corded muscle and balanced movements. His black skin reflected and absorbed the light of the room. His eyes penetrated the smoky haze of the room and dim light landing on Creidhne. Short cropped hair was present under a green bandana as the ties from the head-covering were extra-long and danced gently on his back as he rose. He smoothed the green fabric that went from his waist to just above his knees. The golden armband, wrapped around his arm above his bicep but just below the shoulder, protested as his arm flexed reaching for his sword. Every motion, even the slightest movement was a testament of his strength. Ogun was strong, strong of body, mind, spirit and faith. Even Goibinu's perpetual smile, for lack of better terms, ran for cover. The laughing stopped. Ogun sheathed his sword and walked closer to Creidhne.

"If that hadn't happened would I be here to see this creation done? Would my anvil, arms and faith be here to help in this endeavor? I am here to participate, to lend my energy to make sure that when the time comes these," shaking his arms "will be used and fulfill what is older than all of us," Ogun finished with his voice strong and sure. The rest of the group grumbled.

"We know Ogun, the joke was just to make light," finished the burly man closest to the forge who was covered in soot and carried a large blacksmith hammer. The hammer was easily as big as his barreled chest yet Hephaestus swung it as if it were nothing, working on a personal project. His face was disagreeable; he didn't have the chiseled features of his fellow smiths. His thinning black hair ran down and rested on his shoulders. His chin, looking like it had stolen all the curls from his head, was full of black hair that covered his mouth as he spoke. "Relax gentlemen, we all know how Creidhne acts out when he has nerves. We have known that fact for years and I wouldn't expect him to change anytime soon. Just like I wouldn't expect anyone to change Ogun either, correct?" With that he limped over to a cooling barrel carrying his work. His left leg, which was not nearly as capable or strong as his right leg or the whole of his body, walked from the forge to a barrel where he dipped the piece to cool it. The impairment, his left leg, was from ages ago. He crafted a brace, one of the true marvels of his work that was bound to his flesh and bone to support the crippled left leg. Without the brace his leg was useless.

This was the group's anniversary. Each year they met to discuss what each was doing and had done the past year. Every so often the smiths that made up the group would work together on a project; it was necessary sometimes. They each had work to do on their own as well. The group as a whole quieted and settled back into their places.

"Is it time Ikenga?" The three brothers asked in stereo. Each was working harder to avoid any more unpleasantness while changing the subject. The group was on edge as they were each year when the appointed time drew near. The banter, back and forth was their way, but all knew that they would have to work together when the time came.

"The hour is not upon us," both mouths spoke. The man with perfect posture faced the group. His body was strong and sure. Pride was in everything he did, even each breath. There was no doubting Ikenga. Horns tall and regal jutted from his bald head making him the largest of the group. The horns were black unlike his deep brown skin, making it difficult not to talk to the horns when speaking to the smith with two faces. One face was old, with eyes that were glazed over and skin that had lost its elasticity faced the group. The young face opposite the old, had bright hopeful eyes and the skin of a babe. A curved knife in his hand rested at the side of his leg, which was covered in a colorful checkered black, red and green fabric that went from his waist to knees. One voice sounding like a child and the other older, closer to death, "we have time to laugh and make light now. When the task is presented, and we all know the importance of the task, joking must be put aside. We cannot be six in a boat each rowing in their own direction. We must channel our strength and knowledge into the weapons. Each year we meet we exchange jokes, and sometimes drink, but in this endeavor we cannot fail, we will not fail, we will achieve greatness. The light and dark both are depending on us."

As if on cue, a table appeared a short distance from the group. At the table sat an older woman and an even older man. A light shone down from above to cast the only white light in the room. That white light reflected on a white table cloth and pearl dinnerware. Roast beef, mashed potatoes, peas and green beans were shared by both the diners. "Is it done?" the old woman asked. Her dress, black and blue seemed to be just a bit much for this dinner. The old man, neat and pressed, sported comfortable slacks, shirt, plaid vest and bow tie said nothing as he worked on a bite of roast beef, looking at the group, pausing in mid-chew for an answer to the woman's question. The group of smiths first looked at each other shocked, then at the pair eating dinner. As if shaking off the cob webs Hephaestus stepped forward to address the pair. "Ikenga is waiting for the appointed time. We did not expect a visit."

"Well...we have to make sure that you all are performing your duty don't we? This isn't something that we just want to hope happens correctly," the woman stated looking at the man, who nodded while dabbing his mouth with a napkin then placing in his lap. "Good, we finally have agreed on something. Someone should write this down, who knows when it will happen again," the woman finished the end of the sentence in a muted tone. "You all have all the materials that will you need?" Not waiting for an answer, she continued, "we may send one more even though he hasn't been a part of these...annuals. Well we each have pressing engagements so we will leave you to your jokes and drinks," the woman finished and they were gone just as suddenly as they appeared.

"This must be the year to draw out the likes of those two," one of the brothers said. "It is always something different with those two, keepin' us on our toes." After another minute the team shook off the shock and this time they all took a drink. Ikenga set his drink down after finishing it in a single swallow. "No, this is not the year. I do have to concur with you. That with them showing up, I would speculate we will be at our task sooner rather than later," Ikenga finished. "I wish you all the best and I will see you in just under a year." The room was left vacant, except for Hephaestus who shook his head again and went back to working on the wings of his latest project.

CHAPTER 15

Bloodlines

Mary Patricia Dooley had had a rough day. Two people in the office had the flu and that wasn't the worst of it. She knew she had to let that go as she got off the bus. If not, the evening would be ruined, then the rest of the week, so on and so forth. She had two blocks to walk and dinner to cook for herself and her brother Eric. It was getting late and she didn't want to have any mishaps on her way home. The apartment where Eric and she lived was all she could afford right now. It wasn't in the best neighborhood, but it would have to do when medical bills from her grandmother and the cost of tuition was on the rise. Eric helped out a little working at the school store, but the lion's share of the cost fell to her. The walk was hassle free and quiet, just what she needed to get the dysfunctions of the office off of her mind.

The second floor one-bedroom apartment was barely big enough for the both of them but she and Eric made it work. "I'm …home" Maggie said to an empty apartment. She had expected to find Eric at the small kitchen table doing homework, but all she got was a note that was resting on top of a postal service box.

Patty,

Went to grab a quick bite with a friend, sorry I didn't wait I was starving. This arrived for you. Don't be too upset with me. Love Eric

With a sigh, she left the note and the package as her head was starting to drift from a lack of food. She preheated the oven and threw the veggies in the microwave but didn't start them. With another sigh she unpacked the rest of the groceries, then went to the front door and slid the security chain into place as well as locked the deadbolt. She went to the cupboard over the fridge and reached way in the back. There, resting all the way in the back laying on its side was a mostly empty bottle of Ancient Age 10 Star. The oven beeped letting her know it was warm. She slid the fish in. Then went and got a glass down. She poured herself just enough knowing that Eric would be home sometime soon and didn't want him to smell it on her. She could have more later if she wanted since Eric had the bedroom and she slept on the pull out. She took a sip, it burned a little, but the smoky flavor lingered long enough for her to savor. The next sip was slightly bigger and then she went to the microwave to start the veggies. She took her comfy clothes into the bathroom and changed. She looked at herself in the mirror and knew she was taking a risk. She knew the bottle could lead to the dark one. Her mind went back remembering the troubles she'd had before she had reined it in previously, and she knew she could handle it. Mary took a moment to look at herself in the mirror. She looked good and long into her reflection's eyes, wanting that message, the message that she could handle it, sink in and take hold in her mind. Her hand went to the rosary that hung around her neck as she called prayers to mind, just then the microwave beeped, which brought her out of her own mind and back to the apartment, as the aromas of dinner drifted to meet her. After a quick wash of her face, her work clothes were put back on the hangers, then she dressed in a t-shirt, sweat shirt and sweat pants to keep warm. Eric had to have it cold so the air conditioner was turned down to sixty-eight. Her unmentionables went in the hamper and she walked out as the oven was letting her know dinner was ready. She finished her drink in one quick swallow. The dry smoky taste was just what she needed. She ate her dinner, put back the bottle, making sure that it was all the way to the back and then slid the security chain off the door.

Clean up was easy. The aluminum foil and the veggie bag went in the trash and the plate and utensils were rinsed, ready for the dishwasher. The warm feeling of her drink was settling in so she figured she should see who is sending her a package. *Almost forgot my glass.* Maggie washed this with soap and warm water and put it back in the cupboard. *Now let's see...Grace Williams? Richard's wife? Why would she be sending me a package?* The red, white and blue cardboard was pulled back revealing a stack of documents snuggly secured in bubble wrap. She pulled out a novel size stack of documents and an envelope. She set aside the stack of paper and went for the envelope.

Mary,

Richard said that you should have this information. He didn't know who the responsibility would past to next, but he knew you would be strong enough to last the longest. He also trusted it would be safe in your hands. Let me know if you have any questions or concerns. Richard respected you, you never led him or any of the others wrong. That's why he didn't balk at your leadership. Thank you for everything.

Sincerely,

Grace Williams

It must have been the booze and the reception of this parcel, but she wasn't ready for this. What would Richard want her to have? She went back to the cupboard above the fridge and retrieved her glass and poured more of the Ancient Age. It was gone in one swallow. She went back to the table and stood staring at the letter and then the pile of paper. She went to Eric's closet and retrieved the lock box. It took a couple of times to punch in the right code as she was shaken. Once the box took the code, she dropped the letter in there which also housed birth certificates, passports and the emergency cash Mary kept. Once the box was back in its place she sat down at the small table. The only noise was the buzz of the fluorescents as she looked over the pile of papers and peeled off the bubble wrap. The cover page simply said "bloodlines". Mary Patricia lifted the cover page and set it aside and started to read the first page.

Now why would Richard want me to have this?

CHAPTER 16

Learning Curve

Oh man! Death tried to take it all in, tried to grasp the situation, yet he couldn't. This huge mythical beast Cerberus, its hate filled eyes, all six of them, blazing with fire of damnation, were fixed on him. Cerberus leapt, its front paws diving hard, trying to crush Death with a single blow. He quickly accelerated running past the front legs, towards the rear legs, to just avoid the first attack. What he didn't anticipate was the tail. The large snake mouth, which formed at the end of the tail when Cerberus revealed itself, snapped twice trying to get a piece of him as he ran down the length of the beast. Still running, Death narrowly dodged two more strikes. He could hear the snapping maw just behind his head. *This thing moves too fast for something its size, how?* Death ran out towards the stone structure that Cerberus seemed to be guarding. As he approached it, he made out two doors barred by what might as well be a redwood tree. Carvings that decorated the doors went by in a blur. As Death paused for a moment to take in the structure to see if it offered any answers, Cerberus got around faster than Death had anticipated and swatted him with a paw. Sliding some distance away, as he stopped, his hands became his weapons. Death ran with all the speed he could muster, recovering the distance in a second or two. Cerberus, rearing, tried again to use its massive front paws to crush him. Death ran past, and expecting the tail strike, he veered left to avoid it. Dodging the tail, he now had an angle to one of Cerberus' back leg. With both hands, Death chopped as he ran past. The beast howled in pain. Death distanced himself to take a moment. Hearing the howl, he knew he could hurt Cerberus and wanted to see his handy work. There was nothing to see. The leg was whole. *I can hurt it, but none of the damage remained.* A couple moments past and neither opponent moved. *Wait did I smell something when I ran by it? I didn't think my senses could register anything significate in this form. The longer I've been Death the more I notice that I feel and smell less except in the swamp. Taste isn't an option, although sight and hearing have been unaffected.* Hearing Cerberus is what saved Death. The three-headed dog had closed the distance and was about to take a bite out of Death. Folding over backwards at his ankles, his feet still firmly planted, Death came back up taking an opportunistic slash at the front leg. Death stayed put to see his attack land on Cerberus' leg. The blade landed and cut the legs flesh as another howl split the air. The leg opened as the blade connected with the beast's flesh causing a nasty laceration as blood spilled out onto the ground. Death watched closely noticing the open flesh knitted itself back together almost as quickly has Death had opened the wound. From the blood that pooled on the ground, snakes slithered out and away from the two combatants. These snakes looked normal and were just trying to get out of the way. Distracted, another bite from Cerberus came. Death now inside its snapping maw, used the position to his advantage to cut the inside of its massive reeking mouth. *This stinks, the odor is awful.* The beast continued to try and chew through Death as he slashed and stabbed at the first vulnerable spot presented to him.

He noticed the shroud that covered his exterior fell away faster than normal and not just from the bottom of the garb. Open holes in the black garment revealed more of Death's bony white structure. He stabbed and twisted his blades causing the other heads to howl in pain. *What's that?* Death felt as if his bones were on fire. He could actually feel his bones getting weaker, as if they were supporting him less. *Oh no, I have to get out of here before I start bleeding again. I have my hands full now, I don't need any more challenges; this thing is quite enough right now.* With that, Death saw ash starting to leak from one of his rib bones. *Times up.* Death threw a couple of roundhouse slices cutting the inside of its mouth to the outside through its cheeks. The large mouth with its wounds to the muscles and skin could no longer keep Death in its mouth. With the jaw less taut, Death was able to fall out as his feet pulled him to the ground close to where the ash had landed. The entire front half of Cerberus came up off the ground, rearing on its back paws. Death stabbed the ground where the ash started to stir; *I must have missed with the first slash. One of me is enough, especially if they aren't teammates.* Now that he was free of Cerberus's mouth he set off again with hurried footfalls, out past the reach of the creature. Death's shroud went back to its normal length and he could see and feel that his bones were becoming more substantial, sturdier. Death ran at the beast again just avoiding the large mouth and bite. Instead of running past the leg, Death planted his foot on the creature and another and another up the beast's muscular front leg. Death was about to crest the back when a snake, planted in Cerberus's flesh directly in front of him, tried to bite. The snake was attached high on the beast's shoulder. Another attack came, this time the snakelike body ended with the head of a scaly dog. The creature's scales started at their heads and became fur halfway down the length of its body. Death avoided the first but couldn't get out of the way of the second. It bit his wrist. He didn't let the dog get very far with its bite as Death cut the head from the body. He continued his cut taking the snake head as well.

The massive head of Cerberus came around when a long sinister looking tongue whipped out of the closest mouth and wrapped around the waist of Death, beginning to drag him into the foul, noxious hole lined with oversized teeth. He dug in his blades as well as his feet trying to avoid the mouth's toxic environment. The beast screamed a horrible deafening scream and yanked Death off the top of its shoulder. Death turned to run back down only to be knocked for a loop as the head closest to him slammed and pinned Death for a moment. A wild slash cut the tongue around his waist. Now in a bad spot, Death ran right towards the ground. Stunned from the massive head slamming into him, his footwork wasn't steady and his feet pulled him down to the ground as much as he ran down. Cerberus took advantage of Death's shaken condition and stomped several times. He tried to roll out of the way only to have one of Cerberus's stomps land and pin Death. His feet still on the ground, this legs allowed for the impossible bend, but for how long? The rotting foul mouth kept coming down trying to get a hold of Death again. Many superficial wounds opened on the snout as the head came down again and again trying to snap up Death. *Gotta get out of here, this is not good. I don't want to end up in the mouth again. If only I could get to something more vulnerable...the eyes!* Death tried to reach the eyes, only his blades weren't long enough. Knowing that he couldn't fail now, he tried to wiggle from under the car sized paw. His blades started getting closer. Keeping up the effort to try and free himself as well as fend off the constant bites, Death reached out and finally got an attack close to the eye. Cerberus, stunned and angered as the pain from the wound forced it to close its eye, let up its paw just enough to retaliate with a weak paw attack to push Death along the ground. Death ran to gain perspective and consider his next move. As he ran he saw that it wasn't his efforts to free himself from the paw that bore fruit in attacking Cerberus' eye. This attack worked because his blades had changed shape, they were longer. Cerberus batted at its head with a free paw trying to wipe the pain away. The wound closed but slower than any other wound that Death had dealt before. Cerberus shook its head as spittle and blood rained on the ground, making the beast more hesitant than before, as it kept its distance. *Wait...I was able to sever the head of two of the serpents on its back and the eyes seemed to heal slower than the legs or body.* Death charged back in avoiding another bite from one of the massive heads and ran at the leg and up again. Not slowing or stopping, he crested the shoulder and then plunged into a sea of serpents. Hundreds of serpents were planted on Cerberus' back and swayed like hair in a gentle breeze. All the tresses had the body of a snake attached like hair on the back of Cerberus. Several different heads attacked, some snakes, some dogs like before. New attackers presented themselves goats, dragons and apes were what Death could see. With an easy swipe of his scythes a single head fell and the body was still when the head fell away. It changed back into a thick black hair as serpents crawled from the severed heads slithering for their lives off of the back of Cerberus. Death went on each step taking another head. Death neared the rump of Cerberus and was waiting for the larger snake head attached at the tail to take its shot. On cue, the large snake's head attached at the tail shot through the forest of writhing serpents just missing him. He pushed his speed greater and ran, leaving the sea of serpents, he willed the blades to extend again as he started down the rump. The blades, now longer, took the tail with Death's full momentum behind the cut. Death used his momentum down the back leg to run away and turn again to try and take another piece of Cerberus. Noticing the tail wasn't reforming, Death was glad for that. He circled about quickly, seeing his target which was the back leg he had just come down. Cerberus turned slightly and flopped down on its belly like a dog eager to play. Death avoided a vicious bite but was clipped by the back side of its front paw. His feet dragging across the ground slowed his momentum. Before the beast could rise again, Death ran at the flank of the beast trying to get on its back once more. As soon as Death was about to plant his first foot on the greasy matted coat of Cerberus the beast rolled atop Death. *This was a mistake!* The ground came up to meet him as he was crushed, pinned in between the side of Cerberus and the black sand and rocks that made up the ground.

Immobilized, Death shortened his scythes and kept slashing at one spot. Snakes spilled out as blood ran over him. He kept going making slow progress into the beast only to have molten lava come from the deepest wounds. Cerberus howled and thrashed with a frenzy that Death had yet to see. The lava spurted out of the deep wounds and landed on Death, going through his shroud and down to the bone as another wound opened on Death and ash slowly started to seep out. The beast rolled on to its belly, Death didn't want to waste an opportunity so he picked up speed and ran on the side of Cerberus' body towards the shoulders. Over the shoulder, he put out his weapon willing the blade closest to the nearby head to become longer, and kept running. The scythe bit deep into the neck as Death willed his legs faster, pouring on the speed hoping the blade would be long enough to sever the head. Death ran and then turned a short distance away to see a black blob fall to the ground and a vacant spot where the head used to be. Snakes erupted from the severed head, shooting out like confetti, and then scrambling for safety. Death stood for a second, horrified at the spectacle. *GROSS!* Cerberus wasted no time and lurched to its feet and pounced on the stationary Death again. Death with just enough speed, was out of the way and running up the leg again extending his blade. The creature rolled on its side again denying Death another shot at the second head. This time he was ready. With a stab, he anchored his blade in Cerberus' flesh, so that it would trail behind him biting and opening the flesh as he ran. Death ran along the creature's side at first, then Cerberus kept rolling so that the beast exposed its soft underside as Death was running on its belly. He made a curt turn, removed his blade and focused his attention as he was determined on taking another head. Faking left, then going right, the head on the right followed the fake. Death stood, blade resting on the throat of Cerberus. The massive creature still on his back didn't move. It wasn't even breathing hard as long slow labored puffs of noxious fumes came at short intervals. The huge creature that had given him such a difficult time seemed to submit, only for a moment. The head turned thrusting at Death for one last attempt. The scythe fell and took the second head before it got close to delivering another bite. Death ran out of reach and took the time to circle Cerberus, as if stalking it. The creature up now, was missing two heads. With empty spaces on either side of the central head, it looked down at the two severed heads laying on the ground with one just starting to erupt snakes, the other lifeless, done with its death throes. Death picked up his pace and ran pushing himself fast, much faster than before. Cerberus swiped at Death with its huge paw, but couldn't get a fix on him until Death stopped. Cerberus lunged low almost sliding, leading with his huge mouth lending all its weight to this attack. Death stepped to the side quicker than the creature could anticipate. Death's large blade waited on the back of the neck. Cerberus' body pushed him along the ground as the massive creature's momentum carried it and Death forward, then they stopped. Cerberus started to rise and Death let him up slightly as he rested one blade ready to come down on the back of the neck, the other blade slid in the gap between the ground and Cerberus' throat. There was no escape for the massive beast with blades above and below its neck. Death took a moments pause and then moved the blades where they met in the middle as the last head rolled off.

All was quiet. Death rested, leaning on the massive, lifeless body of Cerberus. Relaxing for a second his hands shifted back and the blades were gone. Looking at his hands he couldn't believe what he and just done. *I'm getting good at this...well better at this. Gaining strength, confidence and a stomach for the strange and unusual. I could get used to this.* Death watched the body of Cerberus as it started to shrink. Death stood, no longer leaning on the shrinking body, looking at the second head. Now that it was finished spitting out snakes, the lifeless blob simply disappeared. There were no more snakes, they were simply gone as well. The body stopped shrinking, it was now the size of a large mastiff. A rip broke the silence as a tear appeared in the carcass.

A small, seemingly normal puppy emerged from the remnants of Cerberus. The puppy trotted towards the stone structure. It looked back at Death and let out a small bark that could have been a threat or a challenge. Following the puppy's trail, it went to the structure. The timber barring the door was gone and the enormous door cracked. The puppy disappeared into the smoke and bright orange light that came from the opening. The door closed, shaking the ground and kicking up black and tan dust.

"Sam," came a cry from the top of the structure. He had almost forgotten about the glinting metal he had seen in the distance.

"MAGGIE!!" Death replied knowing that it was his wife calling him. He took a step to build up speed and then he was hit with pain that stopped his next footfall. A wound opened on his back as he fell on his hand and knees. *The ash...* Death knew that he had to get up quick. The new opening on his back pumped out the black ash and he knew that others would attack if he didn't get control of the situation. *Where did this ash come from?* He took a chance and threw a wild blind slash behind himself and started to run. Looking over his shoulder the other Death was there, keeping pace. The pursuing Death slashed wildly, savagely clawing with its scythes trying at all cost to get at Samuel-Death. Using the same curt turn he had used against Cerberus, he planted his foot, Death spun and slashed. The other Death was cleaved in half at the waist. The halves of the dismembered Death flew apart in a blast of black ash. Quickly Death ran to the spot where he was attacked and before they could form, stabbed and slashed the piles until nothing moved. He then circled the area making sure no others would attack him. *They must have been from when I was inside Cerberus. Maggie!?*

Death was on top of the structure surveying the scene. There she was, shackled at the wrist with her arms out at her sides. She was on her knees, bent over laying on her chest, hair fanned out in a disheveled mess. The shackles attached to chains, the chains attached to two squat, thick, heavy blocks of stone. Death was there freeing Maggie from the chains. She laid motionless on the ground except for her arms that came to rest on the ground after the chains were cut. Not the shock of her seeing him like this, not anything would stop him from this moment. It felt like forever since he had seen his wife. He rolled her over and brushed the hair away from her face with his bone white hands. The hair was right, but that was all. The eyes, nose, mouth and even ears weren't Maggie's. This wasn't his wife; was this some sick joke?

"Sam," the woman uttered again in exactly Maggie voice. The voice was right but hearing that voice, his wife's voice come from a different face, shook him to the core. Death didn't even notice as the body he was holding faded. Some of it sand but mostly air, faded and fell at his feet. He screamed, primal, deep and long. Rubbing the last bits of what he thought was Maggie over his face. Pounding his fist again and again, as he was swallowed by another opening in the ground.

CHAPTER 17

Cave

Northern Georgia early 1800's

The forest was quiet as green leaves whispered in the gentle breeze that caressed the branches of the summer trees. The creak of larger trees swaying filtered to the forest floor, but the gentle breeze didn't make it to the ground covered with decaying leaves or to Adahy. Breathing deeply the young man took more of his surroundings in with each breath. The warm air on his skin, the smells of the forest, the muted groan of the trees all let him know without opening his eyes he had returned. He was alone when he was summoned. He could have stayed with the tribe but this was his journey alone. Anytime the bracelet appeared the tribe would give thanks and praise to Adahy as they knew he would leave soon to perform his duties as Death. He opened his eyes and all was as he left it. Time passed differently with each summons, sometimes days, sometimes just an afternoon. Adahy always took time after his return to pray to the Gods and give thanks to them for his safe return and the honor he and his tribe had been given. The Cherokee tribe revered the young man and his position, looking at him as if he were a medicine man. The summons was considered a spiritual journey and Adahy would take the time after he returned to make sure that he was centered in this world, not bringing anything with him from those journeys that would hurt the tribe. The holy men of his tribe would cleanse the warriors after a campaign so that they could enter the tribe cleansed of the evils of war, Adahy did the same so not to endanger the tribe. He reached for his water skin and took a deep draw from the source and then another. Enjoying the quiet time, he put the skin away and rose to his feet stretching the slight stiffness from his back and legs. The horse he had used to come to this spot was gone, someone of the tribe must have come for the animal. That meant he was gone for at least a day. He collected his things and made for the village. He had expected to run into some children playing as he approached the village, but he encountered no one. Through the trees Adahy could see the first mud-covered huts of the village. Only a few of the tribe's buildings were made of logs, several were made using large sticks as a frame with mud completing the walls. All the dwellings surrounded the central fire pit, a large area where the tribe would collect to discuss the day to day of the tribe.

After walking through the tree line that surrounded the village, Adahy saw some of the villagers making their way toward the village center where other groups of village members had collected. He stopped, he could sense the tension in the air. The mob was speaking in raised voices and all at one time which made it difficult for Adahy to hear. At the center, close to the fire pit, Galegenoh was speaking to the village trying to keep them calm. After a couple minutes the crowd quieted. Galegenoh was the leader of the deer clan, this clans purpose was to deliver messages from village to village around the Cherokee nation. Galegenoh was delivering a message from Pathkiller, the chief of the Cherokees. Galegenoh continued relaying that Pathkiller had been speaking with the white man's government trying to have them understand that they had moved several times under the government's orders. This left Adahy with a sinking feeling in his stomach. He didn't want to hear anymore but was held captive by Galegenoh's words. Galegenoh continued. Pathkiller spoke to the red and the white governments and their leaders, Waya for the red and Gawonii for the white as well as Dustu the medicine chief. Adahy knew this was a serious matter as his mind drifted back to when Onacana taught Adahy about the white government, who were the tribal leaders in times of peace and the red government, who led them in times of war. Adahy knew the importance of the leaders and the messages that Galegenoh was conveying when he noticed Onacona. He was Adahy's uncle who had taught him the ways of the Cherokee since he arrived at the village several years ago. Onacona knew that Adahy was concerned about the developments between the white man and the Cherokee tribe. These were troubles that had followed Adahy for years. Onacona looked at Adahy and motioned for Adahy to join him. After waving to Adahy, Onacona was pulled back to the tumult as the leader of the deer clan started to speak again. Galegenoh was speaking that messages were coming in about the white man's government. Adahy had heard from other deer clan members before, word had come from the other villages from far and wide as whispers circulated that the Cherokee might have to leave this land, or fight for it. The anticipation had been hanging in the air for months like the stale, warm and sweet smell of a rotting carcass laying in the sun on a hot day. As the rumors, circulated Adahy and Onacona had spoken over the last couple weeks of the possibility that the government would try to take their lands. This would incite the Red Government, the faction of the tribe that led the tribe in war time as they chomped at the bit to drive the white man from their lands.

    That is all that Adahy had to hear as his anger and blood boiled. The discussions had been ongoing and he never expected that he would have to leave. He grew up in this village. He became a man here and he planned to take his permanent place among his tribe in the village. Not wanting to hear anymore he turned and headed back to the woods. Sliding the strap of his satchel over his head and securing it, he ran, disappearing into the line of trees at the edge of the village. The cool forest air was breathing gently on his bare chest as he ran to escape the announcement. He wasn't sure where he was going, but he had to run. First his mother, now this. Feeling betrayed he ran on, trying to run away the pain. Dried leaves crunched and shushed under his feet, as beads of sweat formed on his lip and forehead. He jumped onto a fallen log and ran halfway along its path, turning and jumping down, scaring a couple of squirrels. He ran trying to get distance from the situation to sort through the announcement. He didn't understand why the tribe wasn't going to fight this, why they would just accept the conditions of the government. He wasn't sure that would be the tribe's decision, but that is where his fear led him, surrendering without a fight. His breathing was fast as he pushed himself faster, trying to outrun the words he didn't want to accept. Adahy stopped. He stood straight and let his breath burn in his lungs. His heart thundered in his ears as he tried to slow his breathing. Even as his heart fell quiet in his ears the words that were spoken in the village echoed loud, reminding him that this is something that he might not outrun. Looking up, the green leaves wove a pattern letting the cloudy afternoon light down through the trees. Though a gentle breeze was still sliding through the trees making them murmur, there was another sound that brought Adahy back down to the forest floor.

Adahy heard water trickling nearby and with a few steps he was on top of some rocks looking down on a small tributary. He made his way down and sat beside the water. Watching the water flow over and around the rocks he focused on the sound, trying to let the sights and sounds take his mind away. Then he sniffed the air, there was something familiar about this place, like he had been here before. Looking around he saw a small area had been cleared of leaves and sticks. A small circle of rocks surrounded a small, shallow pit of ash. *Have I camped here?* Adahy put his hand over the ashes; the gray and black remnants were cool and the material was completely consumed. *Someone tended this fire to ensure nothing was left and I would have done the same thing… but this place…so strange and peaceful at the same time.* He continued to look all around when his eyes found the mound that he had just came down from, he rested in this spot by the fire pit, though he felt there was something strange about this place. He noticed there were deep shadows within the mound as the uncertainty of this place resonated in Adahy, questioning, had he been here before? The shadows hinted at the possibility of a small cave being nestled in the mound. *Half of me feels as if I have been here at least once before, the other half does not, but all of me feels …afraid.* He moved slowly, creeping, prowling slowly on his hands and feet. He stayed low and moved towards the shadow of the cave. Once he had passed the mouth of the cave, goose flesh crawled slowly up his wrist. He watched the tiny bumps as they moved past his elbow to his shoulder, the bumps moved like a ripple that had been started on still water. He sensed danger as he continued. His senses were telling him to respect the shadows, but his fear was starting to swell even more. A raven cawed in the distance startling him, taking his eyes from the shadows as he looked at the entrance of the cave which was highlighted in the light of the day. This was to make sure he wasn't being followed or he hadn't fallen into some trap. He turned back peering into the darkness, now he crawled on his hands and knees. There he stopped. In the shadows of the cave he could make out some kind of drawing on the back wall. He was afraid. He had felt fear before in his life, but Adahy had never felt fear like this. His whole body shook as if it were cold even though the day was warm. The goose flesh wrapped him from head to toe as it rippled along his body rebelling against this place, like his body knew of the power of this lightless space, and was trying to convey worry with horripilation. Cold sweat covered his body, yet he continued his crawl into this place. Then he caught a glimpse of the source of his fear. His body kept telling him to run, to flee this place to never look upon it again but he was a captive of his fear and had to see, he had to know what secret this dark place kept. Adahy's mind willed his hand to reach out to a picture on the cave's back wall. He adjusted his body so that more light could come from behind him to illuminate this depiction. There were two figures almost identically drawn on the back wall. They were drawings of two women. They looked like they could have been drawn by someone of the Cherokee tribe, but it had elements they wouldn't use as well. Each had small points coming off the top of their heads, as if it might be hair but more likely a headdress. The second one was in a box, which his tribe wouldn't use. Scribblings covered the box and the woman within the box. He was losing control of his muscles as he reached out and a single finger brushed across the drawings. As his hand touched the black lines of the drawing, his hand started to burn. There was no fire, no source of heat, yet the back of his hand was burning. The feeling increased as his hand started blistering and then blackening, in a matter of seconds.

 Adahy fell on his stomach in pain and all he could do was roll away and flee this place. He was flopping, clutching his hand as the searing pain started to subside. Then he was crawling on his hands and knees as the fear clutched him just as much as the pain of touching the drawing did. His eyes showed fear and felt as if they would leap from there sockets. The further away from the drawings, the more control he regained in his muscles. Now out of the shadows of the cave, he crawled on his belly back the way he came. Another crow cawed in the distance. He was able to get to his feet as he leapt over the brook and stumbled, as his hand went down to prevent him from falling on his face. Adahy was able to get his feet back under himself as he took off running faster than he had ever run in his life, away from the cave and away from the village.

 When the pain, his fear and the confusion of it all started to subside, he slowed. Walking, not running he found a place to sit and collect himself. He sat on a fallen log feeling as if he had just come back from his responsibilities as Death. He was drained of spirit. As his breathing slowed and he looked around making sure that nothing sinister was going to leap out and attack him, then he looked at his right hand. The burning he felt in the cave was gone. The skin was scarred, as if the burn had happened years ago. He touched the smooth pristine flesh and there was no pain, the hairs on the back of his hand were gone as well. Not sure of what had happen, he knew he had to center himself. He felt like he had just come back from a spirit journey as Death, so he closed his eyes, and breathed, bring himself back to the moment.

CHAPTER 18

Paperland

Death kept pounding his bony hands as sand flew up to meet his face each time his fist would fly. He kept screaming, shouting things that no one could understand. He lashed himself with curses, bombarding his already weak confidence with a tirade of insults while a couple of tentative jabs were directed at Maggie and Marcus and even fewer at Denise and Robert. The pendulum of blame that was a part of Samuels coping mechanism would do just that, it would swing out to those close to him and inevitably come back to his own failings. "WHY ME? WHY THEM? WHYYY?? DOES IT ALWAYS HAVE TO BE SO DIFFICULT? Am I cursed to constantly swim uphill? I've lost so much already. I barely have a family to rely on since mom and dad died. I would lose everything else, including myself, if I didn't have my family." He screamed as the energy, the venting of physical and emotional stress left him. The questions just kept coming, as did the uncertainty; could he continue? He slumped with exhaustion and silently berated himself for losing control. The pendulum of blame, an instrument of his own imagination, came to rest upon his actions. After a few more minutes he slowly lifted his head and noticed that he was no longer atop the stone structure. The brown traces of sand, remnants of the imposter Maggie, faded as he dug his hand deep in the black sand that surrounded him. Clutching the fine black granules Death pulled his hands up to his face and then let the grit drift though his fingers and collect in small piles. *How much more of this do I have to endure? Marcus, Maggie, Denise and Robert, that is your focus. I have to focus on them, but when I focus on them my inability surfaces and I want to blame them, but this is no fault of theirs. Wait...is it about them or is it about me? Or both? Do I finally want to finish something significant on my own? I know that I have accomplished things on my own, but this, this is something more. Saving Marcus, I'm doing this for him...but for me as well, proving I'm a good father. Maggie would tell me that I don't need to prove it; I have the entire lives of our children as proof. This experience, this journey...this will banish all the doubt and my lack of confidence. If I do this, when I finish this, I'll know without a doubt that I'm a good father.* He picked up his head, no longer focusing on the small black sand mounds produced from his hands dredging deep through the grains that drifted through his hands. These tiny bits of pitch that covered the ground as far as he could see giving way to a red sky. The air was still, and hung with the anticipation that there was still much to do. Death willed his hands into blades and then back to hands, flexing and reflexing several times between the two forms, examining the transformation up close. The alteration in his hand reminded him of all that he had been through up to this point and how he had changed even since the beginning of the journey. He pushed himself back to his feet and straightened to stand and see if he was missing anything.

  Death took in his vacant surroundings wanting to know that he was on the right track, wanting to know that it would be alright though the stark landscape offered nothing in the way of an avenue of promise. *I wish I still had that watch. I'd like to know how long I've been at this. Now that I come to think of it, the time spent here doesn't seem to be very long. Well I've wasted enough time with my tantrum. I do feel slightly better though.* With that Death took his first step forward ready to try and find the path, his path to the end of these turbulent events, when six inches in front of his foot, that he had just planted, the ground fell away. A line stretched left and right as far as Death could see with the red sky making up his entire view. It was as if an invisible barrier kept the sand Death was standing on from falling as a slice of existence directly in front of Death had vanished or had been consumed. The land to the left, right and behind him were unaffected. The sky below the level of the sand where Death stood seemed to swallow up the entire direction he had planned to walk. He bent over at the waist reaching down past the line of sand while he stared into the red sky that remained and felt nothing. Death stood back up straight still not quite sure what to make of this event. He bent over again reaching slightly further still, his hand went past the line and under what should have been the sand that he was standing on. He couldn't feel anything past the line of black sand. Death moved his trailing foot up to the first and kicked a little sand over the edge. As the sand went past the invisible barrier, past the other grains of sand on the ground, into the red sky, the sand disappeared. *Nothing. Gone.*

Sigh, "Wrong way?" Death asked the sand, the red sky and whoever else could be listening. Death just looked at the perfectly straight edge that could have been the edge of the world for all he knew. Not wanting to fall off the edge, Death took a step to his left. As soon as his foot hit, the sand fell away. From the first edge that was created when the sand fell away and to Death's left as far as he could see, the sand was gone. He stood at a corner, in mid step, as there was sand now to his left and behind him but nowhere else. It seemed that he was doing something wrong. *I hate this. I just don't know what to do. Again it's always difficult. Is the ground just going to keep falling away? If it does, can I run fast enough to propel myself on nothing?* Bending further at the waist, Death looked under the edge this time. *Nothing, no supports just a layer of sand a couple inches thick and the red sky that is now taking over the ground.* Playing along, Death pulled his right foot up to his left and again nothing happened. Looking to his left the sand appeared to be whole. He crouched and put his hand in the black sand. The hand disappeared beneath the sand. Pushing his hand deeper, up to his elbow, Death looked over the edge, past the line of sand, and his forearm was not there. *I feel like I'm in some cartoon or silly sitcom.* Death could feel the pressure of the sand, the grains between his bony digits but this was contrary to what his eyes told him. Death stood, shook the sand from his hand and looked left. *That field of sand is going to drop off as well. Am I trapped here? Is this another test for me to overcome to save Marcus? Of course it is, else why am I here?* Death concentrated on the floor just to his left, he could visualize where he was going to put his foot. *I really want to see where exactly the sand goes. Does it disappear, does it fall into nothingness or was it never there to begin with, a figment of my imagination?* Death readied himself, straining to put all his focus to what he would see transpire. Death stepped and it happened all over again. *The sand dropped six inches faster that I would expect and then just disappeared.* He marveled again at the scope of worlds he was seeing. Where once there were vast fields of black sand, only the red sky and a three-foot-wide path remained. There was no sound, no wind. It could have been a painting, but again Death reached down with his left hand and again it was swallowed and embraced by the black sand. *Well...I have to get out of this place otherwise I'll be going where the sand went and I'm not too anxious to find out where it went. One more step to take.* Death lifted and quickly planted his foot taking off at the best speed he could, trying not to fall from the path. Glancing behind, the sand was falling in five-foot sections just as fast as he ran. Letting his eyes focus on the path ahead, Death concentrated on the point in the path where it became nothing but a distant black dot in a sea of red sky and he ran. Death ran for Marcus, Maggie, the twins and now himself. He pulled a picture of his family into his mind and willed his legs faster, then he extended that will to the tips of his toes and pushed harder. Death pushed past all the limitations, all his uncertainty, feeling the faster he ran the closer he would come to joining his family. The scene changed drastically as the red sky gave way to a black canvas. He stopped his legs as he could no longer feel the sand beneath his feet, as he was swallowed by a colorless void. He couldn't see anything. He started to reach out his hands feeling for the sand that had showed him the way and felt nothing as he remained upright although he couldn't see or feel what he was standing on. His hand went out feeling in all directions, trying to find a way, a path. He felt a slight resistance at one point directly in front of him at knee level. He crouched fixing his eyes on one-point as Death pushed forward with his hand and felt a slight resistance again.

"Wait, what was that? I know I felt it," Death asked. His hands worked fast, at a blurred pace knowing the barrier was there and wanting to feel it again just once to know that there was something he was supposed to do, something other than just run.

Samuel had run all his life; he was good at running. He ran from Mitchell, the bully who rode Samuel's bus, not every day, but a couple times a week. He had loved the bookmobile so much that he would forgot about Mitchell when it would come to visit. When he would get off of the bus the bookmobile was the friend he needed, the friend that would make the world right. The space inside the portable library was small, the smell was slightly musty, but it wasn't over powering, it was comforting. Samuel loved Richard Scary books. In each of the books he would try and find the elusive gold beetle on each page. Then he would look at the pictures as they told a much funnier story than the words ever did. He would use his imagination and different voices for each of the characters coming up his is own stories. The bookmobile was a great place for young Samuel to be a boy. The day was bright and would have been perfect except Mitchell was waiting for him outside of the bookmobile. At least twelve inches and twenty pounds separated Samuel from his childhood tormentor. Samuel stepped off the bus.

Mitchell reached for Samuel's arm, Samuel swung his backpack, knocking Mitchell's arm off course and then Samuel ran. He ran under pine trees, across hot blacktop and around brick townhouses. Samuel dared to glance back and saw that Mitchell was letting up on his pursuit. Samuel ran into something hard that gave way slightly and then spoke, "watch it dork." Samuel coughed and waved his arm trying to send the dust cloud that encircled him on its way so that he could see who he had run into, as well as to see if Mitchell was getting any closer. Mitchell was gone or at least out of sight while his brother Carl stood over him. Carl reached through the cloud and retrieved his brother. "Such a spaz. What was it this time Stormtroopers, or the little pink muscle guys? No, I think it was the bully you are having trouble with." Samuel dusted himself off as he thought about why Carl would be here. Was it chance that his brother was there to save him from his own private thug or was there purpose in running into Carl, literally? "What are you doing here? Don't you have a date with Britney?" Samuel finished with an exaggerated finger to the mouth and several gagging noises. Carl was dressed in clean blue jeans; in those days they were worn tight which hid the bottom of his tucked in Rush t-shirt that was black with white sleeves and collar. What really tipped Samuel off to Carl's destination was the pristine feathered hair. Wheat colored and parted down the middle and as if on cue, Carl reached for the comb in his back pocket and made sure his Goldie-locks were just right. "One day you'll understand dork," Carl replaced his comb and went on his way, but not after roughing Samuel's hair. He thought it was a dig for being little, but Carl was actually removing the last of the dust from his little brother's hair. Samuel turned and headed the last 300 feet home. Carl was a fighter, Samuel would never know that Carl saw Mitchell lurking about and faked to run after him. Mitchell ran and then tripped off the curb skinning both of his knees. Samuel had always been running, running from Mitchell, running from the job possibilities, from the muggers in the garage and now from the possibility of failure. As Death he didn't want to run, he wanted to complete this for all the right reasons.

"Where is it? Where is it?" Death asked touching nothing but empty space. The faster he moved the faster his frustration began to rise. Lifting his head and his hands to an imaginary sky, Death yelled. There was a whisper of sound first and then a throat noise that turned into a yell as loud as a banshee losing her death keening, a cacophony of pain and remorse, then Death slumped. *After a yell like that anyone normal would have to take some deep breaths. I don't. I'm tired of not knowing what to do. I'm tired of the answers not being clear. I'm tired of this bony form and no eyelids or skin. This is pushing the limits of my sanity. What good is it if I succeed only to be a crazy person when I get back? When I get back...that means I will get back. It means that I have to keep trying, no more running, not from this, not from any of these ordeals. It means that I might have only started to be challenged, but when I get back home it will be worth it.* Death straightened himself, then crouched again trying to find the point of resistance. Slowly he put his hand out. *Nothing.* He kept at it and in an instant of searching there it was again, a resistance other than air. Looking at an angle below where he was looking before, Death saw a faint thin vertical line. Death adjusted his vision and got slightly lower, again to look directly at the spot he knew the line to be in. It disappeared. Moving back and rising slightly, he was able to see the line again. *It's big enough for me to fit in; I can just barely see the other side.* Death extended a hand through the opening then pulled it back again; his hand looked and felt the same as before he put it through. *I don't fear death.* Death laughed out loud. *This is really not funny but I can't help but laugh at the play on words. If we don't laugh, we cry. I just fear failing my son, dooming him to a life of dealing with experiences that are, for lack of a better terms, above his grade level. Everything is just so strange, so alien, with every step I feel smaller in reference to everything else I have seen.* The opening waited patiently. The light from the other side was only visible at a particular angle. Nothing was happening around Death as he stood in the void. Nothing on the other side was visible. It was as if there was simply a cut in reality. Death tried to look through to whatever lay on the other side, but all he could see was white, the purest white imaginable. Parting the threshold with his hands he then poked his head in through the gateway. Nothing lurked or schemed, nothing could. It was too bright and revealing as the white light filled a new path forward. Lifting one foot he stepped through and then followed with the other, when a switch was flipped. The plain white area gave way to a beautiful day on a sunny suburban street. The sky was blue, the sun shone yellow and there wasn't a cloud in the sky. It would have been the perfect day to take Maggie and the kids to the park, with a cookout later and then sit on the back deck and watch the evening drift by.

Death felt thin. He looked and he was thin, not skin and bones like before, but that really hadn't changed. What had changed was that he was two-dimensional. He was a tall, paper-thin picture of Death, and he wasn't the only one. As the streets seemed to come alive, like another switch being thrown, people of all shapes and sizes began walking the street, and they were two-dimensional as well. Moving about their day, families, businessmen, runners and even two-dimensional dog walkers didn't react to Death standing on a street corner. The buildings, however, were just as normal as any other street should be, of three dimensions.

"Hello," a middle age woman said to Death smiling and continued on her way.

"Wait, you can see me? How ...what," Death stammered.

"Of course I can see you, you're standing there plain as day and you're not invisible," the lady said still increasing the distance between Death and herself, perhaps a little quicker than before. Flipping his hand over was like twisting a sheet of paper, Death saw the same on the other side of the page, a paper image of bones and black canvas that moved. Looking down at the black robe, then looking at the faces of the passersby, Death noticed that they didn't cringe or cower as he expected they would. Passersby simply went about their day. Death took his first step and that too was an adventure. It was like walking through water with wide boards for legs, each step took a few seconds to begin and end. Looking around none of the other people on the street were struggling with this thin form. Death stood there shaking his head. *Ok I am thoroughly confused. They must be used to it. And why wouldn't they be? I'm the only one caught by surprise of these events. I guess being paper thin would offer some difficulty as each movement I take is an act of resistance.* Death struggled up the street hoping for answers, looking for answers. Walking past a glass front shop, Samuel finally knew what was going on. They perceived him as Samuel Willis, not Death. A reflection of a three-dimensional Samuel starred back at Death. *Well that was easy to sort out, I only wish the moving through this place was that easy as well!* Samuel just watched himself and enjoyed it. He had a spare tire, but not as bad as some of the people he knew. His thinning hair was combed straight and neat. Samuel caught a few looks from those who passed by, but one person caught his eye and then all of his attention.

"Marcus? Son is that you?" Death asked Marcus, who, unlike everyone else including himself, was not paper-thin; Marcus slowed slightly already well past Samuel and looked down as if just to catch a glance of who was speaking to him in his peripheral vision. He then lifted his head and continued at his original pace.

"Marcus?" Death asked again and then Marcus took off. "MARCUS, WAIT!" Death took off as fast as this paper body would permit him. Each footfall was a labor. Death ran on, not taking his eyes off his boy. *It's Marcus, I have to catch him. I hate this world. The one time I want to run, I can't move effectively, grrrrrr. Marcus just turned down that alley. The way he's moving I'll never catch him. Why can't I use my speed here? I'm guessing cause I'm myself.* Death finally reached the corner. Death somehow closed the distance on Marcus but he was just out of arms reach.

"NO, MARCUS WAIT IT'S YOUR OLD MAN!" Death screamed and lurched at Marcus who continued away from him. Death noticed homeless paper people just lying on the ground. Marcus outpaced Death, exiting the alley on the other end while Death was just barely a quarter the way through. *I have to be ready to lunge for him around the next corner if I catch that break again. Why is Marcus running from me? Is this some trick, and the way Marcus looked at me; was it to bait me or was he just letting me know that he saw me but didn't want to do anything about it?* Dumpsters and doors with graffiti were the only things to witness Death's long walk. *My god this is the cleanest alley I've ever been in.* The walls were painted with graffiti but there was really no trash or bad smells, giving this alley the feel of something completely alien. *I'll hopefully catch Marcus and get some answers.* The last ten feet of the alley had to be the longest for Death. He knew his son would be there at the corner somehow just as he was at the entrance to this alley. Samuel got close to the right corner hoping it would give him the edge he would need to grab Marcus. Death rounded the corner and lunged. No Marcus, just more casual walkers throwing concerned glances at Death. Scanning, hoping his son was in view, Samuel spotted Marcus a half a block away at the threshold of a building. Marcus locked eyes with Death. Samuel knew that face, it was the face that Marcus wore when he was in trouble and he knew it. The corners of his mouth were turned down just slightly and his eyes were glazed over. Samuel had seen this face many times in watching Marcus grow. Everything from bad grades to broken windows had been introduced with that exact face.

"Mar..." before Death could finish saying his son's name Marcus stepped into the building closing the door behind him. The street was suddenly vacant so Samuel could hear every whisper of sound. The door closed, latched and then the building collapsed. There was no explosion, just the sound of broken glass and the groan of bending steel being dragged down by gravity. Dust clouds enveloped Death. He felt the wind and had to steady himself so that he wasn't pushed back any further. The pieces of paper that were his arms covered his eyes. He wasn't sure if the dust would affect him. Before all the dust settled, Death was already moving towards the building or what was left of it. Moved by purpose Death didn't dare shout, as he diverted every bit of energy he had and channeled it, pushing his legs as fast as he could move them. *Marcus has to be alive, he has to be he's just trapped under rubble, I can make it to him. I can help him. This form won't stop me this can't be the end of Marcus.* Nothing made sense to Samuel. He just pushed himself on as his paper feet brushed past the first bits of rock from the building. He was breathing heavy. He could imagine Marcus' shocked expression when the building betrayed him, that image of Marcus stole Samuel's breath, imagining Marcus broken under stone and steel. Death saw the twisted metal frame with chunks of broken glass and wondered how he could reach his son. The door came into view as Death climbed the pile of rubble marking the way to where he would find his son, alive. Falling to his knees was easy for Death as his paper hands started to push the small stones from the top. Only then did he call, "Marcus, son can you hear me? I'm here," he whispered lowering his tone as if harsh words would be strong enough to push more wreckage on top of Marcus and finish his beaten and battered son. He kept digging even as little bits of rock tore through his paper form. As one stone rolled free from its place a hand was brought to light. It was scratched pretty badly and two of the fingers were misshapen.

"MARCUS, MARCUS CAN YOU HEAR ME, ITS DAD," he yelled now with the air from his shout making waves in his paper chest. Holes started to form all over his fragile paper-thin body and along his arms and legs, but Samuel kept digging. The shoulders were now visible and Samuel paused, unsure if he could or would want to see his son like this beaten, possibly broken. He started back to the slow task of moving stones to see if in fact it was Marcus. Thinking about the betrayal after the fight with Cerberus, he wasn't sure if it would be Marcus or some trick to tug at his heart strings. Holding his breath Death looked on the face of a dead boy that was not Marcus. He was still horrified at the damage this young man had suffered as he was able to slightly roll the boy to his side. The boy was about Marcus's age and again the resemblance was close, but it wasn't Marcus. The boy's nose was bloody and blood seeped from a couple of nasty cuts around his head. *What kind of sick joke is this? These tests, these experiences are too much. I know that I have to keep going but what am I going to run into next, another gut-wrenching scenario? Am I going to have to watch my parents die all over again? Or see the future of my children only to know that they aren't going to make it? Will I ever succeed?*

"You're going to be ok, I'm going to go and get some help, just stay still," Death said looking for help but the paper figures of this town were gone. "Now is not the time for sorrow Samuel," said the boy with red eyes. Eyes so red they took him back to the beginning of his journey, seeing those eyes in every member of his family. Frightened, Death let the boy slip back to his initial resting place and stood stumbling back a step. Then the eyes changed from red to black. Death had seen eyes like that in the garden when the image of Marcus stood on the pedestal. These eyes with no color, stole the color from the world around and warmth from his soul.

"This too shall pass," said the all voice that Death recognized as Regus. The boy finished his statement and fell lifeless and its body changed to that of a paper-thin form just like everyone else. Looking around desperately for help, he felt exhausted and had nothing left. He took a step, then back, two steps in another direction unsure where to go or what to do. He had set out to try and save his son from a life such as this but who was to say that he could, or even should be able to do it. *Just when I think I can't bear anymore, I have to. I have experienced loss. My parents have died, and as nature intended they died before me. Marcus should have the opportunities to live a long and healthy life. Mar-*

cus should have his triumphs and his tragedies. He should know the touch of a woman who truly loves him. I say should as if he isn't going to accomplish those things and more. I was just subjected to the possibility of saving my wife to only get duped. It hurts each time I go through something like this. Each place, episode, it takes a piece of me. Part of me wants to give up, but I can't, what kind of a parent gives up on their child.

Death rocked himself slowly trying to sooth himself, to take away his thoughts of just giving up. Giving up on the family and more importantly, himself. *I don't know if I can give up, I'm sure that Regus would just love that. Pushing on, taking that step forward even though I feel that I have reached my limit, that is the second choice. I remember one of the last things my father said to me as he was dying, 'A man walks his path, he doesn't talk about it, he just puts one foot in front of the other, quietly knowing that it's the right thing to do'.* Death stood up determined to keep going. He took one step and the paper land, the rock pile and everything else that was, suddenly fell away including his paper form. The world around him fell away fast as he drifted, at first like a piece of paper would fall, then the last shreds of paper ripped off leaving him in the original form of Death. When, as the last piece of paper detached from his body, he began to speed up, Death fell into blackness.

CHAPTER 19

Thomas

Marcus felt as if the entire building shook as he closed the door. He was going to be late for class if he didn't hurry. *That was weird. It felt like the earth shook as the door closed.* Not wanting to dwell on the oddity of a door closing he moved to class. A short distance down the hall he heard the door open and close again behind him. Marcus glanced over his shoulder and saw Thomas. Thomas Jackson was a friend of his and lived in the same neighborhood in which he lived. They played ball together and as of late had become closer due to circumstances out of their control. Thomas jogged to catch up to Marcus.

"Hey Marcus…it's been a long time, how's it going?" Thomas asked not wanting to just hammer him with questions right out of the gate about where he's been and why he hasn't shown up the last couple of times, but he decided to open the conversation with some light banter.

"I'm good, classes are really good. How have you been?" Marcus asked just continuing the small talk on the way to his class.

"You know, wrestling is good. We have a shot at states with the team we are looking to put together this year. It's a lotta pressure, but I'm doing my best. Haven't seen you at any of the workouts lately." Thomas was on the varsity team while Marcus was on the JV. Thomas switched to something personal to try and draw out the Marcus he knew, not the superficial Marcus he was talking to at the moment. "It hasn't been easy losing my brother, even if it has been a few months. My parents are still kinda lost since we lost Isaac but I try to keep it together for Keisha. How are the twins? I haven't seen them in months." Thomas said checking his watch. *I only have a minutes to get to class I have to cut this short.* Thomas stopped and put a hand gently on his friend's arm to stop him and look into his eyes as he knew he had to get answers. "Why haven't you been there the last couple times, we really could have used you. Mary is concerned, so am I as well as…"

Marcus stopped. His body posture changed, and went from the typical high school posture with his focus on the ground or not on who he was talking to but rather a focus straight ahead with his shoulders back, standing tall and erect. Thomas put his arm at his side not sure what was happening. Marcus displayed confidence and a posture that Thomas has rarely seen in his friend and teammate. It was this stance that stopped Thomas in mid-sentence and set him on guard to expect anything. "I have to go. Talk to you later." Marcus didn't even look at Thomas as he continued to speak, then turned right and walked away from Thomas who had no clue what just happened. "Well…later," Thomas watched Marcus walk away, confident that Marcus wasn't being himself. Thomas took a quick left hand turn and hurried upstairs to class with a distracted pace, replaying the past week's events and his last conversation with Marcus. *Last week he was scared as hell, not sure if he could hold up to the pressure. At the start of the conversation he was typical Marcus and then bam, the switch, it's like it wasn't Marcus at all.* Thomas hoped he could continue this conversation later with Marcus. Thomas quickened his pace to class thinking, *it hasn't gotten any easier. Just when I think I can let go of my brother's death the topic is brought back up and I can hardly believe he's gone*

Occupational Death

with dirt is still fresh on his grave and the pain that resounds in my chest. That isn't entirely true, it's been a couple mouths, but it still hurts. I've thought of talking to Marcus' mom about losing her brother, Richard, but they weren't close, not like Isaac and I were. The final bell rang just as Thomas walked into class, pushing his emotions and questions down like the urge to vomit. *One thing at a time, I have to take these things one at a time.*

****

Marcus felt that he hadn't talked to his Dad in years. He had called Samuel on his cell, only to get his voicemail as he was walking into school. Not reaching Samuel only amplified his feelings of absence when concerning his Dad. Marcus' mind drifted to a better, warmer place with himself and his Dad, Saturday mornings on the couch. This is when he and his dad would watch cartoons. It was something Samuel had done as a kid and he had passed it on to Marcus. Marcus remembered Samuel telling him that when he was growing up, cartoons were on every channel on Saturdays and even some on Sundays. A car with its muffler needing to be changed, rumbled by and brought him from those carefree easy days with his dad.

These streets were his. Marcus felt comfortable this close to the house, just slowly walking the sidewalks. He felt that he has lived here long enough to call them 'his streets'. He'd played manhunt with his friends in the summer, built piles of leaves to jump in during fall and built snow forts on snow days in the winter. Even as Marcus thought of the fun he had living in the neighborhood, he couldn't help as his mind drifted back to his dad. When he thought of his Dad, he felt unsure and reluctant of the future relationship. *Dad is great. I know Mom, Robert and Denise think so as well. Mom has her issues with Dad as well, if I can even call them issues. Their issues are theirs alone, I really can't know what goes on between them. Dad has been pressuring me to open up more, maybe I can try a little harder.* Marcus let his thoughts drift back to his walk and the neighborhood. It was Friday, no classes for two days, that was the good stuff. The houses were set well off the street with large front lawns and red brick fronts. Manicured lawns looked like cookie cutter templates, with only the slight variation in the horticulture. The sidewalks were old but in good shape. There were also small patches of grass between the sidewalk and the street, just wide enough to accommodate another jogger and the precisely spaced fire hydrant. Marcus had to hurry home and get the twins off the bus and watch them until his mom got home. His thoughts went to the voicemail Samuel had left him. *The old man really sounded excited about the conference, lotta job possibilities, I know Mom would breathe a little easier knowing he had some steady money coming into the house. I kind of like Dad at home, it's easier that way, but money does seem to be a universal lubricator.* Marcus hustled home and had just enough time to drop his bag, grab a soda, *I really wish Mom would stop buying these generic sodas, or is it dad? Hey at least I have a soda to drink.* He took himself and his soda out and sat on the front porch. Marcus heard the bus rumble up a parallel street so he walked out to meet the bus and his siblings. Marcus was halfway finished with his soda when he looked up and saw that Thomas was heading in his direction, still several houses away. Marcus had felt all of a sudden disquieted by Thomas and was not looking forward to the conversation. He wasn't sure why but talks with Thomas these days felt heavy, not like the good old days. Thomas was still a few blocks down. Marcus hoped the bus would speed up to avoid the potential uncomfortable conversation. That was when Thomas stopped suddenly even though there was nothing to stop Thomas. Marcus kept watching, curious as to what stopped his progress. Marcus looked up the street hearing the bus was rumbling around the corner up his street. The bus stopped and the mad scrabble of grade school kids ensued. Everything was normal, as kids, big, little and noisy got off, except the twins. Marcus felt a rush of perspiration under his arms.

"Where are my brother and sister?" he asked an unfamiliar looking bus driver.

"I don't know. I have an empty bus. Is it possible they stayed for some after school function?" the bus driver questioned with a shrug.

"No they're in kindergarten." Marcus said it so only he could hear. He set his soda down hastily and pulled out his phone. The phone rang. The pause between the rings seem to last forever. *Come on Mom pickup, pickup, pickup. Don't go to voicemail!* Each ring seemed to take longer and longer, until. *Click*, Marcus didn't wait for the formal greeting "Mom, do you have the twins?"

"Yes Marcus, your father called me and told me they had a doctor's appointment this afternoon, but it isn't until next week. Leave it to you father. Have you heard from him?" asked his Mother. Marcus gave the driver a thumbs up. The driver smiled and nodded just before closing the door and rumbling on his way.

"Yea, he said the convention is going well, few opportunities, but nothing concrete. Well if the twins are with you I'll be heading to the computer to relax. Oh one more thing Grace texted me asking me how I was doing. Weird huh? I've never really spoken with her except at the service. I know the two of you didn't talk much at the service but she seemed concerned about me. She asked me to text if I ever needed to talk. Anyways. Ok I can hear you're busy, love you. Bye."

Marcus pocketed his phone and *sigh*. He looked down and reached for his soda. The contents of his soda was running down the driveway to the closest run off drain. *I must have kicked it over when I was talking with Mom.* As his eyes focused on the grill he saw Thomas in the distance. Marcus and Thomas had a good relationship but Marcus questioned that relationship; *why has it been so strange lately? I mean when we do anything but talk its cool just like old times. When the conversations start they are about as awkward as talking to you parents about "life".* With that Marcus got a good case of the willies. *We have known each other since we were little, like when his brother would come over to babysit. Those were good times. He is my friend and I have to play this out.* Marcus picked up his soda can ready to try and talk to Thomas, to bridge that gap and put things right, things that weren't right for reasons that escaped him. The entire situation felt odd like he should just forget the past and move on. Marcus was ready to do just that. After the five second self-dialogue he looked to locate and make eye contact with Thomas, who suddenly, was nowhere in sight now. Even if Thomas crossed the empty street he should be in view. *Where did he go? If he was heading home, he still had to walk past here to get to his house. What's happening? Maybe he went back to school because he forgot something.* Taking that as a sign that it wasn't the time to talk with Thomas, Marcus went in ready for some gaming. One of his favorite old games was just waiting to be picked up in the middle, even though he had beat it thirty times before.

CHAPTER 20

Hard Day's Work

"When can we expect the last one? Are we at the appointed time?" Ogun asked pacing the floor, the twin green tails from his bandana whipping around at each turn. This was not the behavior of Ogun. He was tall and strong, yet he sensed something, as did the others. The six smiths hadn't seen each other in a year. The last time they met the mood started jovial, light with conversation that conveyed friendship and a cooperation. After the unexpected visit a year prior, a readiness to complete the project that they had all been tasked with years before, made the mood sober and pensive. They were all ready but there was an edge to the atmosphere that was tenable.

"No Ogun. We can expect Phat when he arrives, not any sooner. Would anyone else truly know the whereabouts of the others...no," Ikenga answered with both mouths in customary fashion. He maintained his proud, regal stance despite the misgivings of the others. These misgivings were hidden only slightly as the rest were quiet and went about their work collecting materials and making sure the forge was stoked, ready for the work ahead. The six of them waited until the appointed, time and as if on cue, Ikenga opened his mouth to proclaim that the appointed time had passed. He stopped his inhale and Ptah appeared. The god was tall, wrapped in perfect white linen layers, mummified. Atop his head was a helmet that was so blue, that even the orange of torch light and forge light couldn't diminish the smooth crafted and brilliant headpiece. His face carried no emotion even though his eyes were moving to each of the other smiths in the room. He nodded to each while his long, braided goatee bobbed up and down wrapped in silken gold. He carried with him a staff that had three separate heads. The first, the Was scepter, the second, the Ankh and last was the Djeds. His movements were slow and deliberate. This skin was slightly wrinkled under the wrapping that seemed to shed a faint white light. He bore his staff in one arm the other dragged a large stone box which looked like a sarcophagus behind him. The sarcophagus wasn't ornate at all, the clay sides were almost invisible in the light of the forge and work area. Ikenga let his breath out slowly and said, "it is time. Welcome Ptah." Hephaestus, not caring for ceremony, lowered his head as he shoveled charcoal into the fire. Creidhne grabbed the bellows pulling, coaxing the flames to rise. Goibniu went to the water pump and brought fresh water for the work. Luchtaine went to work selecting the wood for the handles. Ikenga strolled past all, overseeing the work that would forge a future world. Ogun was digging in the boxes looking for the best pieces of ore to use. Ptah walked over and helped his collaborator select the ore that was stacked on a metal rod. Each layer of ore was wrapped with cloth that Ptah pulled from his own wrappings. Goibniu soaked each layer with water and then the process started over again until several layers of ore and cloth waited for the flames that Hephaestus and Creidhne kept coaxing to their peak.

    Creidhne stopped at the bellows and the rest knew it was time to begin. Once the ore was in the fire each would take turns on the bellows make sure the flames would not diminish in the least. The small bits of conversation had everything to do with the work at hand, offering suggestions and help to anyone who needed because there was no time for jawing. Five stood ready as Goibniu pulled the rod and the glowing ore from the fire and placed it on the anvil. Immediately the five with their hammers went to work in rhythm hammering the material. As they worked sweat glistened and flew, hammers rang in rhythmic song and all were pleased to start the work on these magnificent weapons. Each of the gods adding a little something of their own to the process. Each took turns at the bellows and bringing water, and each knew that this was the pinnacle of their cooperative work. The blades started to take shape as did the handles that Luchtaine worked on. The others offered suggestions and compliments as the plain wood surrendered to the finely crafted handles of the weapons. As the glowing block was dipped into water, it hissed in protest then it was back to the fire, but not before more powdered ore was added to the mix. Some took rest, napping where they could, while some partook of the trivial amounts of food that were around. They would then wake, ready to get back to work.

Ikenga oversaw the work, lending a hand here or an idea there. He looked at Criedhe and nodded. Creidhne went back to the shelves containing the materials he would use and started setting another forge a light, this one not as hot as the other. He worked it alone, knowing that the silver/gold mixture had to be handled expertly. Not that his colleagues couldn't work the silver but this was what he excelled at. Ikenga walked to him and helped him with the pieces.

"We have to mix the silver/gold with the other two materials or it will never survive the heat that is needed to make the weapons whole," Creidhne suggested. "That is correct. Ogun take Phat and select the two best last materials," Ikenga finished pointing to a low cupboard. They followed Ikenga's suggestion and then worked with Creidhne to marry his work with the new materials they selected. This new combination of materials would put the final strength to the blades. Once Creidhne, Ogun and Ptah had finished joining all the materials, the blades and his work were taken to a third forge. There Creidhne's work was fixed to the blades over a fire that was strong enough to combine the blades with the new pieces, yet not weaken Cheidhne's delicate work.

"We need help here. We are starting to tire and need new arms on the bellows," Hephaestus called out keeping the main forge hot enough to have the reinforced blades in the hottest of fires once Cheidhne was finished. "You have what you need Creidhne. Keep working and I will help at the bellows. The achievement will be ours, just keep going. This work, this creation is something that no one will sing of or ever know happened. However, all that toiled and sweat and bled here will know the importance of this magnificent work," Ikenga finished with a pat on the shoulder of his fellow smith. As Ikenga walked away to the forge the young face on the back of his head winked and smiled. Creidhne nodded and went back to his work. Once Creidhne had completed his work the blades needed one last heating in the hottest fire. The bellows groaned under the strain as the strong arms of the gods pulled the bellows handle down over and over again. With the fires hot enough the blades were put in. Green and blue flames leapt from where the blade rested, and then the blades were pulled out, no longer glowing from the fire. The blades were tested once again, with a touch. Creidhne's flesh didn't burn or blister as the metal was cool to the touch.

Luchtaine announced that the handles were ready and moved to help Ptah who called for help. Each of the blades had taken shape under the careful work of the smiths. The short straight non-descript metal handles would be concealed expertly within the crafted wooden grips. The curved blades were sharpened, sharp enough to cut anything. Hephaestus raised one of his shields and pulled the blade through the finely crafted metal with no resistance. The curved blades were polished so that the sides reflected the light of Ptah. Ptah broke away from the work and walked to the sarcophagus. He then kneeled over the clay structure. The others watched for a moment as he started his prayers, nothing more than whispers, to ready the vessel for the blades. The others sipped water and watched as most of the work was done. The dirty sweaty group watched as there was little that they could do now that Ptah had to carry the load. Ikenga, inhaled softly, the others took notice and their demeanors brightened. "We are close," he said and all gathered around Ptah and the sarcophagus. Then some of the others joined in Ptah's soft prayers, the others sang verses of hymns closing their eyes. Others looking around at their fellow smiths, gaining strength from each other and the importance of the next several moments. Ikenga presented their achievement, the blades, polished and ready for Luchtaines work. Luchtaine walked to Ikenga and put the handles on. Ikenga held them fast, while each of the smiths took a single strand, produced from their various garments and wrapped it around the handles. The handles firmly in place, the others stopped their chant. Ptah continued and pushed the top off of the sarcophagus. All were surprised to see the contents.

A glowing cloud that roughly formed a skeleton floated in the clay structure. The skeleton was gaseous and glowed with vibrant reds, oranges, blues, purples and the faintest yellow. The smiths evenly distributed to each side of the clay box with Ikenga at the foot. Ptah finished his chant with a loud exhale. The polychromatic skeleton's eyes came open. Light spilled forth from the eyes that for a second was too bright to look at as the smiths shielded their eyes just for a breath. With everyone in place around the sarcophagus, the weapons were lowered on to the gaseous form. They stayed on top of the gas, resting on the wrists of the vaporous skeleton. "We have achieved what we have been asked to do and now....," Ikenga said looking at his fellow smiths then stopped, his face horrified, then his gaze fell to the skeleton. All the eyes of the smiths follow Ikenga's to study the skeleton. The weapons were supposed to stay, laid ready for use. Instead they were absorbed and disappeared into the arms of the skeleton.

"I did not foresee this," Ikenga stated, worried, even

shaken, which was not his posture at all. All in the room knew that Ikenga could see one year into the future. All here were hoping that Ikenga had the answer, really knew the answer with his ability to see a year into the future. The fact that he didn't foresee this unnerved the others. "The outcome I had seen was different. I can't explain it. We had done everything to the design right up to that point I stopped speaking," Ikenga said pleading with is collaborators. Everyone looked closer at the skeleton, the weapons were gone, a part of the gassy form that now started to close its eyes. "This is peculiar. This I saw, the only difference were the weapons. They shouldn't not have melded with the host."

"So is it done?" came a question from behind all the smiths. Two figures stood there. The man wore slacks and a tie, his appearance was groomed and well kept, just as if he had come from a saloon. The other, a woman was dirty and had the dress of a homeless person. "We have come to collect it," said the man. They all looked back to the sarcophagus and the lid was back in its place.

"All is as it should be but....," Ikenga started and the man interrupted. "Not to worry," he said looking back at the woman. She nodded meekly. The stone floor opened beneath the sarcophagus and accepted the box which held the skeleton and their finest achievement. The smiths watched it descend slowly as the floor built itself back as if the hole never had opened. The smiths looked back to the man and woman and they were gone.

"We have done what we set out to do. They have accepted our work. Now let us commemorate this great achievement with food and drink," said Goibniu. With that a table appeared from nothing. Goibniu produced a small piece of white cloth and started to unfold it. Once it was too big for him to hold he laid it on the table and opened the last fold. Within the folds of the cloth, a feast fit for gods and kings lay before the group.

"We have achieved our goal," said Ikenga picking up a glass and toasting his fellow gods.

CHAPTER 21

Vision Quest

"Have you spoken with Dustu?" Onacona asked speaking of the Medicine chief of the village. Since Adahy's spirit journeys began, he relied on Dustu's council about the journeys, the experiences on the jaunts and particularly about the importance of centering himself once the journey was through. Adahy had not spoken to Dustu yet about the cave, the feelings of a familiar place, even if he had not been, and the burn he suffered on his hand.

"I have sent word to him." Adahy replied. "He will speak with me when he is done speaking with the Red and White government." The two sat on a log by the fire that was located near the center of the village. Speaking Cherokee, the men continued their conversation. Onacona's soft eyes looked over at Adahy. He had seen him grow from a boy who was impatient and angry to the man who sat talking with him, talking about all the happenings of the village as an elder would, listening more than speaking. Onacona was proud of Adahy.

"That is good. Dustu will have answers. With all that is taking place between the Red and White governments and the white man's government, our people cannot forget the spirit parts of our lives and how that will help us. Have you spoken to Awenasa?" Onacona was Awenasa's brother, therefore Onacona was responsible for what Adahy learned in the village. Onacona had come to terms with Awenasa's decision, Adahy didn't want to understand.

"What could she have to offer? She is gone, made her choice to leave and nothing I can or have said to her can change that."

"Are you sure that she has nothing to offer? The one they call Gerald may have some information as well." Onacona let that information settle on Adahy's mind, still looking at the young man, he decided to move on to other news. "We have fought beside and against the whites for years. We might have to fight again. Pathkiller is talking with the government and there hasn't been word yet. Are you prepared for that?" Pathkiller, the chief of the Cherokee's, was talking to the white man's government.

"When Galegenoh was speaking with the village and you waved, I then ran deep into the woods to escape his Galegenoh's words. That is when I came upon the place that we spoke of. Do you think they are connected? My journeys and the government coming for our lands?"

"I cannot know. Raven was with you when you arrived and left that place. I take that as a good message. Your journeys have been a good for you and the village. We welcome you and what you bring to the tribe. Pathkiller has even expressed his approval. The deer clan has spread his words so that Pathkiller can be heard. I have heard that he is proud and that he is ready to take us to war. The fact that Raven found you on your journey might be that you have something greater to do than fight in this war over land. Have you thought of that?"

"I have. I want to be with the tribe where I belong."

"You belong in two worlds Adahy. You have known this for several years. It is hard for you to understand that, I know. I have watched you grow to the man that I am talking with now. You were named because we found you walking in the woods, you still walk in the woods, the woods of the forest and the woods of the spirit. Listen and the answers will come, either on the wings of Raven or from your own heart. You must be open to these answers, they may be difficult to hear."

"Thank you Onacona. These talks calm my heart from racing. They quiet my mind and help me see the path that is clear before me, even if it is a path that I do not wish to walk."

"Let us smoke. Then I have other people that I need to talk to." Onocona filled the clay pipe and lit it, sharing it with Adahy.

Adahy woke with his knees on the log that he sat with Onocona. He was on his back looking up into the black of night. He focused, there were no stars. He rubbed his eyes, still there were no stars. He looked around and Onocona was gone as fire light flickered and wavered, pushed by a gentle wind. Movement drew his attention away from the fire to where the shadows started to form. In the light of the fire many spiders moved from the firelight and disappeared in the shadows.

The first form he saw was that of a huge man that wasn't just man. There was something animal about this creature. Adahy saw this being that was twice as tall as any man he had ever seen and half again as wide. His large eyes were looking at Adahy, twitching fast, up and down and side to side as if it was catching any movement in his vision from all around. His beastly appearance continued as a single tooth was poking up from his bottom lip. A deer carcass hung about his shoulders. He was muscular, far more strength was in his arms than any other person he had ever seen, with thick arms and chest that was free of hair. The brown hair seemed to only be at his back. Adahy could see the hair or possibly fur as the large man-beast shifted his legs and body. His legs came to rest again and might as well have been tree trunks, large around and sturdy. He tapped a long spear on the ground adjusting his stance.

Atop the spear were two birds. To Adahy they were huge

eagle like birds but to the wielder of the spears the birds were proportionate. *How do both the birds fit?* The bird's colors were subtle, shifting colors that changed in the firelight from colors of browns and whites to gold and yellows. Both the birds shifted as did their wings which shot out, spread wide, and where the wings joined the body a rainbow of earth tones was revealed. Then the wings settled again against its feathered sides. The two birds were as one and yet separate from the other each fitting on the spear, almost overlapping each other. Adahy knew there were two from the stories he had been told. Four wings appeared at times and then only two, as the birds balanced on the tip of the spear. Talons, sharp and black, as big as his hand, fingers to palm, gripped the side of the spear's head.

An Indian warrior, who didn't look any different than he did, moved into view drawing Adahy's eyes. It rose from a crouch and walked in front of the larger snaggletooth man-beast. As soon as it passed in front of the huge grizzly man, he disappeared, only to reappear when he had finished walking past. He placed perfectly balanced footsteps as he continued his course. No sounds came from his footsteps and he shifted his bow from one hand to the next and crouched again. The warrior's gaze went through Adahy, making him feel more like prey than a man. The warrior's crouch placed him next to a woman.

The woman's delicate hands worked the dirt. His eyes drifted up her arms, where his eyes locked with hers. Her eyes held him, captivated him as he took in the entirety of her presence. This was the most beautiful woman he had ever seen. Her skin was dark; her hair was thick and black. That was until her hands pushed it aside. When the hair was moved it changed color to a yellow/white hair that was instantly as fair as corn silk. Once her hair came to rest again, it reverted again back to thick, black tresses. She was kneeling in the dirt, stroking the dirt, caring for the dirt around the fire with a tender touch, caressing it like the cheek of a child. As her hands moved, corn sprouted, full grown wherever her hand had passed. Another sweep of her hand and the corn was gone, collected in her basket which swung easily on her other arm. She rose and moved to another position around the fire and as she walked, each of her footsteps produced fully grown cornstalk as well.

She passed in front of a small group of people, which could have been members of the tribe that were huddled together and talking among themselves. The firelight could not penetrate the edge of group as the center was huddled in shadows. They moved together as a pack never going very far from each other. They could have been any one of a number of people from the tribe. Adahy thought he recognized a few of the faces but he was mistaken, or really distracted as another person would appear and remind him of someone else in the village. That too was not right, for as soon as he recognized someone, or thought he did, they weren't who he thought they were.

"Introductions," a voice said in Adahys ear as his shoulder length black hair was blown into his eyes. Adahy pulled his legs off the log and stood straight and tall, then moved his hair out of his eyes. He has seen a great many things in his travels as Death. He would have been afraid but he knew who this group was, well... most of them from the stories he had heard since he was a boy which struck a chord of familiarity.

"Tsul Kalu," he nodded to the hulk of a man with the snaggletooth, the spirit of the hunt. The god nodded back. "Kana'Ti," Adahy said looking at the hunter with the bow, the great hunter of the Cherokee. "That is Selu," the goddess smiled at Adahy as he looked her way, the corn woman. "That," he looked at the group milling about "is Nunne Hi, spirit people." Adahy turned his attention to the birds resting on Tsul Kalu spear, "and you are Tlanuwa," he finished with quite a bit confidence, to the huge raptor.

"I am Oonawieh Unggi," said a voice in is ear as his hair again began to dance. Adahy had also heard of the formless spirit of wind. "You are quite knowledgeable about the spirits of our people. Although you did forget Uktena." When the name was uttered Tlanuwa flapped their wings hard and issued calls of protest. Adahy then noticed that circling the group was a large tubular body that started to move around the group as if it were a wall to keep the meeting private. Then he noticed the great serpent's head, moving, hovering above the group. Tlanuwa watched. Its wings not quite resting, ready to attack. The serpent's head had two horns and its eyes glowed a soft yellow, coming around to face Adahy. Its body was adorned with spots of different colors one even rested on its head, not a spot though, a diamond shape, raised on Uktena's skin.

"Tlanuwa is always on guard," said a sweet female voice of Uktena. "What have had our battles and even though I lost in the end, they are still bitter."

"But wait, I have seen Uktena…"

"Yes Adahy death will come to your family. But that isn't important. What is most important is your survival. We know of what will come to the Cherokee people and we cannot stop it. The hardship of our people has been known to us, but we come to you, Adahy…Death. We know of your other duties and are proud that it has come to our people. But this must be passed on. If you do not go to the west ahead of the tribe, you will be lost. What you discovered after you came back from your last journey is a part of the future. It must be remembered so that it can never happen" said the invisible wind god, dancing around Adahy as it spoke.

"What does it mean?" Adahy questioned. "We do not know," Oonawieh Unggi whispered "but it is a clue that will keep our world safe for thousands of moons."

A child emerged from the group of spirit people but stayed close to the groups perimeter, "Adahy you must leave. We do not have all the answers. It is what we have heard from the others that has caused us to arrange this meeting with you. Remember what you saw, remember our words and remember that your duty is greater than that of all the tribes."

Adahy looked around the fire at the solemn faces each nodding, even Uktena overhead. "You have been gone too long already Adahy you must wake up…"

Adahy was back in the village, laying on his back with his knees over the log where he and Onacona had talked. It was night but that started to give way to the glow of orange on the horizon. The fire burned low as the disappearing stars twinkled in the last of the nights' light. Righting himself he sat back on the log as he stared into the flames and then looked up at the stars. A streak of light flew across the night sky. Adahy took this as a reminder to him of his dream journey. He had so many questions. He would meet with Dustu and talk about all that had happened. Between the cave and what he had just witnessed he knew that something greater was at stake here. He gave thanks there under the stars to each of the Cherokee gods who spoke with him, who guided him along a difficult path. Onacona was right about the raven. He thought about the call of the raven warning him of a journey and changes ahead. That these happenings were spiritual and mystic in nature meant they had to be taken to heart. Unsure of himself he went back to the woods to the spot where he would wait for the bracelet. Once he was there, the bracelet appeared. Adahy calmed his mind and prepared himself for the journeys ahead.

CHAPTER 22

Moving On

Adahy checked the gear again. He didn't have much but what he did have he took with him knowing that he would never return here again. He had never traveled too far from the tribe. His responsibility as Death took him to extraordinary places, faraway places. These places were on his mind as he made his preparations for the long journey, a journey without end, a journey taken on faith. His trips had always been short, a few days and back to the familiar settings of the tribe, but this jaunt would take him to an unknown place. With his bow, a few arrows and a day's worth of food Adahy looked over his horse. He would be able to hunt and forage for most of the journey. Onacona gave Adahy this horse. Adahy told Onacona of his vision and Onacona decided to help. The horse was not large, but it was young, still young enough to carry Adahy for many years. Word had spread throughout the tribe. There was a sadness but not about Adahy having to follow his own path but that he would be away from the tribe in the future. Some of the tribe came to wish him a safe journey, others waved and went about their business. Onacona had said his farewell with the horse. Adahy looked around the village as he had walked the horse out. He had been here for fourteen years, two thirds of his life. As he walked he saw places in the village that were significant to him while still not quite believing that he was leaving all he knew and loved. He had one stop to make outside the village before he started his journey, one he wasn't looking forward to. He put that out of his mind as he neared the edge of the woods that surrounded the village. He mounted his horse and started down the trail that would take him to town. He wasn't quite sure where he was going, but he knew he would be guided by Raven and the other spirits of the Cherokee.

As he rode, Adahy played over the conversation he had with Dustu. "If it were another member of the tribe my words would be different. But to you Adahy, who walks in two worlds, the Gods know. They knew you as Death, they spoke of a dark future if you stayed, then you must follow their words. I will not speak to anyone about what was said to you on that journey. I must speak with the White and Red government. Heyatahesdi *(be careful)* Adahy."

The ride took him the better part of a day. He passed through the town without incident and rode on towards lands that he knew, but hadn't been to in years. He had been on their land for a while now. Some of the landmarks were familiar to him even after all these years. He let out a sigh and nudged his horse on. There was the house. It was built up on a slight rise with its back facing a steep hill and thick forest. The front had been cleared for livestock, horse, cattle, sheep and goats, though many grazed not too far from the house. The chickens were kept closer to the house to prevent foxes and other animals from getting at them. The barn wasn't too far off from the house. That was George's favorite place. The name came to him like lightning, as he remembered playing in and around the barn. He saw himself as that child, George, running the fields and climbing into the hayloft of the barn. It was the name given to him by his mother and father. It had probably been since he left this place that he had even thought of that name. He had run away from this mother and father so many times that they both knew it wasn't going to stop, no matter what they did. As a child he would run into the woods and hope to spot his people and have them take him away. Sounds from the farm brought Adahy back to the present. The door closed and a woman was carrying a bucket and began tossing grain to the chickens. He put his heels in the side of his horse and started towards the house. Adahy was halfway to the house when the woman stopped and stretched her back as a call came from the house.

"I'll be out to help in a minute, just have to finish the last piece of pie. Can't have just one piece laying around" the man in the house finished. The woman looked across the field and saw Adahy riding slowly towards the house. She straightened and just stood there watching as Adahy closed the distance to the house.

"Did you hear me Marion," the man questioned stepping out on the porch. He too stopped in his tracks. Both of them were hypnotized by the rider they saw approaching their house. The horse and rider stopped just outside the fence. Adahy dismounted and tied his horse to the post. He touched the sign that was fixed to the post that made up one of many fences surrounding the house. "Willis" was scrawled into the wood. Black paint highlighted the engraved letters. He ran his fingers over the letters, that name too was much like George, a part of who he had been. He heard footsteps, he lifted his eyes to see his mother and father. They looked at each other for a while before Gerald spoke.

"It's good to see you, son," he said looking down to check his wife's expressions and then back to Adahy's face. Adahy's eyes fell on his father and then went to his mother. Awenasa or Marion, as she went by after she had met and married Gerald Willis. She breathed shallow breaths as water pooled and then streamed down her cheek. There were no sounds coming from Marion, just the silent tears

"Thank you Gerald," Adahy said looking back at his father, who flinched slightly. When Adahy went by his birth name he would use terms of affections for Gerald Willis, his father, but that was as much a part of the past as his birth name George. That didn't mean that it didn't hurt all parties involved, especially Gerald. Maybe it was Adahy's responsibilities as Death that kept him from feeling too much in this moment, or maybe it was that he truly didn't belong here. Marion and Gerald were both now wiping their eyes, Marion more so. "I have come to say my good byes. The government is most likely going to remove the Cherokee...."

"We are working to correct that," Gerald interrupted as if trying to reach his son, actually reaching his hand out to stop Adahy, to make amends for putting Adahy in this position. Adahy offered a nod and smirk.

"That is good, the Cherokee are going to need help. I am leaving, something else calls me to head west" Adahy said stepping forward offering his hand to Gerald. The man took his son's hand more in disbelief, as his mouth opened in an expression of shock, that then morphed into disappointment. By the look Gerald cast on his son, Adahy knew Gerald wanted more but that is all Adahy was willing to offer. Even as Gerald shook the hand Adahy felt a little pull after the third and fourth shake. He let go and turned to face his mother. Gerald went into the house. She spoke "Ayv asvnasdi uwedolisdi." "*I feel sad.*"

Adahy replied "Ayv asvnasdi utloyi." "*I feel the same.*"

They each said at the same time "Stiyu." "*Be strong.*" She reached around Adahy's neck and pulled his head down and she kissed his forehead. As he pulled away, Adahy took one last smell of his mother's hair. She dried her tears, looking sad but bittersweet, as she smiled at getting to see her son again. The door banged open as Gerald walked down the stairs toward the pair. Marion never took her eyes off of her son as Gerald said nothing and simply handed his son papers bound in string. Adahy smiled and nodded, putting the papers in his satchel. Adahy turned away from his parents and walked to his horse. He untied the horse, mounted and then put his heels to the side of the horse to begin his journey. He rode towards the setting sun, never looking back.

CHAPTER 23

Choice

Death continued to fall, as he had been falling for a while now, leaving behind the last place he had visited, nearly catching up with Marcus. In the blackness he saw nothing and felt only the cloth that surrounded his bony form whipping around his arms, legs and head. He wasn't sure how long he had been falling. Since there was nothing else to do, he tried to understand the events that he had been experiencing. His thoughts drifted back, to the impostors after Cerberus and after the building collapse. Before he could go too deep into these experiences, Death saw a white dot that he was falling towards, that dot cast a small amount of light to see with. He noted his position was like that of a sky diver, with his stomach facing the dot. As the dot grew in size, it was a perfect circle and he was heading right for it. Even if he wanted to try and evade the approaching circle he didn't have the energy to. He was tired. Tired of the uncertainty, tired of not knowing when he would see his family again. The portal as he could see it now was no longer white, but instead it was giving off a blue light. He passed right though the threshold and if he would have blinked or had eyelids for that matter he might have missed it. As soon as he passed the threshold he was no longer prone. His feet pulled him toward a brown spot surrounded by blue and he was picking up speed, being pulled down by his feet. Death looked around and saw ocean blue, and a single island fast approaching as he fell. He wasn't going to hit the island, he could make that out at least, as he fell faster and faster. He would come down just off the shore. He hit the water and was surrounded by a circular sheet of water from his splashdown.

The water settled and he rested atop the sea. Picking up each foot as water gently lapped over his feet he started to walk toward the island. He noticed a large house on the highest point of the island that reflected the light from all around. It was white, pure white. There wasn't a blemish on the houses exterior. Columns supported an overhang that shaded the front porch. There were large windows on the side of the house that he could see and smaller windows on the front of the house looking out on the front porch. Above the front porch was another area that appeared to have tables, chairs, umbrellas and probably a good view of the ocean.

Acting as a gateway to the house was an area that was decorated with two moderately sized man-made waterfalls. This area was slightly lower than the house. Around the waterfalls, were shade canopies. Four poles supported a white fabric that fluttered gently in the breeze while chairs and tables rested in and around these canopies where one could take rest from the sun. He looked over his shoulder and if Death wasn't mistaken, it looked like it could have been the sun in the sky providing light for this island. *Could I be back home? Wouldn't I have changed back to myself if that were the case?* He thought, for a minute, he could hear music and other sounds from around the waterfalls. He stopped for a moment to try and focus on the sweet notes of music that he thought he heard over the sounds of lapping water. *It feels like I haven't heard music in a lifetime. I wonder what's playing. That's odd. Besides the sound of the water and the music, there really aren't any other sounds.* The seemingly normal surroundings prompted a reluctant Death to investigate. It took him a couple of minutes to reach the shore as the surf gently caressed the sandy beach.

As his foot first hit the sand, he felt the granules under his feet, then the bone foot that brought him across the water gave way a fleshy foot, his foot. Without thinking, he brought his other foot to rest beside the first foot that was no longer bone and his other foot appeared, fleshy and whole, leaving his bony appearance behind. The guise of Death melted away. The form that was Death became grains of black sand and simply fell off Samuel. The black sand changed color and blended with the sand on the beach. Looking at his body, he saw his hands; fleshy aged hands. His arms and his upper body were covered by a light weight white linen shirt. His legs were covered in beige clam diggers that just covered his knees. He ran his hand over his head, feeling his hair, his nose, ears, eyes, and mouth. He stood there for a while. He must have finished with the trials to be standing here like this. Samuel let out a sigh and enjoyed the sun warming his skin. Samuel soaked in all the senses he could, feeling everything he had missed while wearing the guise of Death. It felt like forever since he had felt like this. He may have looked like himself in paper land, but he didn't feel whole in that foreign place, but he did now. He crouched and picked up wet sand, then let it run through his fingers accepting the cool mixture of water and sand in contrast with the warm air. Samuel knew he heard the music start again. It seemed to be coming from somewhere close to the waterfalls as far as Samuel could tell. It was island music of some kind; *fitting*. He walked along the beach toward the sound of the waterfalls, letting the music take him as he stepped in time and even hopped just a little letting the sweet notes fill his ears and his heart.

Life can chew you up and spit you out,

Man…I know what your talkin bout,

When you have the chance to celebrate,

Don't you dare hesitate,

The work is done, the labor through,

M.F. Thurston

Now party like you're always wanted to,
The clouds are gone, the sun is shining,
Release the troubles you've been confining,
So dance with your feet floating six inches high,
So dance, grab a partner, it's time to fly

    Samuel smiled. The song wasn't one he was familiar with yet he enjoyed the island style music. Samuel came upon a path paved with large gray stones that led up to the first tier. The warm stone steps took some of the sand off his feet with each foot fall as he ascended. There were a couple of tiers all leading up to the waterfalls and then the house. As he walked the path he heard a shaking and rattling just over the music ahead of him. He walked past the first couple of tiers, canopies and chairs. Now he clearly heard the water from the waterfalls as well as the music's clear sweet notes.

    In front of each of the waterfalls was a bar. Suddenly a man popped up from behind the bar on the right. The man was dressed in a white shirt with a black vest and bow tie. Samuel wasn't surprised by his appearance because, again it all made sense. This place, the house, the furnishings and now the bartender all fit. Well, it fit the strangeness of this journey and it fit the environment; an island getaway, beachy music and someone serving cold drinks, this all seemed to fit the end of the trials he anticipated.

    "Margarita sir?" the gentleman asked. Samuel looked around to see if there was someone else he was addressing, yet he stood alone, with a quizzical look in his face. "Me?" Samuel asked. The man simply chuckled and laid a glass on the bar. He poured a margarita on the rocks with no salt, and finished it with a lime on the side of the glass. Samuel tentatively walked the last ten, fifteen feet and looked at the drink.

"Help yourself sir," said the bartender with the music playing in the background. The bartender busied himself cleaning the items he used to make the drink. Samuel bent over and smelled the drink. He could smell lime and tequila. A drop of the drink was running down the side. While the bartender wasn't looking Samuel caught the drop on his finger and popped in his mouth. It was a margarita alright; *ohhhh that is tasty. How did he know how much I like my margaritas?* Samuel raised the glass looking at the bottom making sure there wasn't anything suspicious lurking at the bottom of the drink. The music played and Samuel took a sip. *Oh that's good, sooooo good.* It was the right mix, not too sweet, but there was something else besides the lime and tequila. That ingredient seemed to take some of the bite away from the mix, which didn't seem to leave that thick stickiness in his throat, as a normal margarita would. Samuel took an honest pull off the drink. The refreshing taste of lime and tequila, as well as the mystery ingredient, was all that he knew in that moment. The world could be burning down around him right know and he wouldn't know it. He set the drink down and then noticed a stool that hadn't been there before. Taking a seat, "Is it to your liking sir" the bartender asked.

"So good, thank you...." Samuel paused waiting for a name, but the bartender smirked and nodded just continuing the conversation. "It was my pleasure sir."

"This place is beautiful. Where are we?" Samuel continued to ask, but stopped once he saw the bartender simply smiling at him. "Right, no questions. Well, good to see that some things don't change," Samuel replied with a drop of sarcasm, a roll of his eyes and another sip of his drink. Samuel sat there enjoying his drink as well as the sights and sounds wanting to ask for the last ingredient of the magical margarita but he knew he wouldn't even get the answer from that trivial question. The music had changed to an instrumental piece with kettle drums and an easy beat. A breeze picked up just then. Samuel closed his eyes and enjoyed the breeze as it gently stirred the hairs on his arm. After a couple of minutes he opened his eyes and took in the view. Samuel raised his glass, toasted to the ocean, as he was close to finishing his drink while watching the water roll on by. He turned back around to address the bartender only to realize that he was alone again. Finishing the last of this drink, Samuel left the stool and glass and headed for the house. Looking back at the bar, he noticed that there was nothing there, just empty space. No tequila, no mixer and no glasses. *I may have imaged the bartender, but not the slight buzz I'm feeling.* The music volume was lower as Samuel approached the house and he could have sworn he heard the lyrics of Bobby McFerrin's Don't Worry, Be Happy.

Samuel paused when he was on the same level of the house and took a 365 degree look now that he was at the highest point of the island, besides the top of the house. The house was pristine even this close. The closer you got to something the less it appeared clean, but that wasn't the case here. It shown in the sun like a beacon of purity. The front porch was made of white marble that led up to a set of double doors with silver knobs. Samuel did his best to wipe the sand off his feet before he turned the knob and entered the house, but knew it was futile, as there was always sand inside at the beach. Inside the house, like the outside was white, pristine white, with no flaws. White marble squares made up the floor in the foyer straight ahead of Samuel. A large staircase that started on the right and followed the curve of the wall, ended on the left side of the house. To his left and right there were large open rooms. Each room had sand colored carpet, but no furnishings. He called out "hello" but no one responded. Samuel didn't even hear an echo as he considered how empty the house appeared. As he moved, the only sound was the slight whisper of his feet leaving the stone. As he looked back at the door, he was surprised to see that there wasn't any sand. To that, he lifted his foot and held his ankle to examine his foot. *Completely clean.* His feet seemed to have been manicured. There were no callouses, or dry skin and even his

Occupational Death

toenails were neatly trimmed which he neglected, more than his fingernails. Samuel went left first, walking into the room that was the entire length of the building. The large windows ran from the front all the way to the back of the house. Leaving that room and he headed back through the foyer past the stairs Samuel saw the other room was identical to the last with large windows all the way to the back of the house. From this view he could see that the back half of the island was not as expansive as the front. Samuel walked the interior of house to make sure that he covered all the first floor before moving to the second. The stairs didn't make a sound as he ascended. The only sound again was his slightly moist feet being pulled free from the wooden stairs. As he rounded the corner following the stairs, he saw a hallway that led to a door. Once at the top he could see that this hallway was decorated with doors and paintings. Framed paintings were hung between each of the doors. The first thing he noticed at the top of the stairs, ignoring the first door, was a painting of himself and Marcus. In the painting Samuel was reaching for Marcus. *This was the night that it all started.* The painting held Samuel's complete attention. His hand slowly moved to cover his open mouth. He wasn't sure what to make of the painting he was looking at, the shock of seeing the rendering was overwhelming. Swallowing hard and almost stumbling, Samuel went to the next painting, ignoring the doors. It was him, Death, battling the Minotaur's. The artist was different that much Samuel could tell. Samuel didn't know the first thing about art and not caring he ran to the next painting. In what he guessed were water colors he could see angel's wings talking to a black blot, which should have been him. *The garden. Am I the black shape?* He ran on not thinking, to the next and then the next, as each of the paintings showed him on his journey. The last depiction he came to was of himself sitting at the bar. This piece of art was a snapshot of Samuel as if someone was painting on a ten-foot ladder behind him as he looked out to the ocean. He could not see his face, just the view that he enjoyed as he was enjoying his drink. To the right of the painting was the last door. Samuel paced back and forth the entire length of the hall a couple times, his eyes going over each of the paintings again and again. He stopped. *Wait…the swamp…the pool of blackness…the egg…and the huge serpent…the light and the dark…why aren't they here.* Every other step of his journey was here except for the episode at the swamp. He walked the hall for a while looking at each painting to take in the breadth of what he had done. *Am I done? Have I succeeded? Do I want to go through that last door?* Samuel looked once more at each of the paintings, taking his time to look. He went back to the first door and tried it, turning the knob, it was locked. That is when he noticed that the paintings were animated slightly. In the first his hand was moving towards Marcus. The second, the Minotaur's swing, came slowly towards Death. Each painting showed a small animation part in its rendering. Then Samuel tried all the rest of the doors working his way to the last. Each door was locked and then he was standing at the last door and turned the knob, which wasn't locked, and then let go. After waiting a minute or two, he gathered his courage and then turned the knob. Samuel pushed the door and came into a room with a sweeping view of the water. A single large window took up the back wall of the room, the other walls were white and the carpeting was sand colored like the first floor. The rest of the room was occupied by a large desk, taking up most of the back wall of the room. Behind the desk was a chair and in that chair was a man who smiled with a joyful expression.

"SAMUEL," the man shouted. The man rounded the desk with a little too much animation and came and shook Samuel's hand; the handshake was firm. He looked at the man from head to foot. He dressed in a gray suit with a white shirt, black tie and what looked like white boat shoes. Samuel felt as if he should know the man, like he had met him once before or passed him on the street but he couldn't be sure. He just kept staring at the man as he went on talking. Awestruck, Samuel couldn't make out large chunks of the conversation. The host went on even though for Samuel it was as if the sound had been turned down on the moment. Samuel felt faint, his eye rolled ever so gently and another shake of his hand brought him back, slightly. The man was so exuberant with his gestures, with his speech, but still Samuel couldn't make out a word. Still holding his hand, the man led Samuel to a seat in front of the desk that he didn't think was there before. The man sat him down and let go of his hand. Samuel felt as if he were drunk or drugged, which confused him more. Just a minute ago in the hall he was frightened, surprised and concerned. Now he was just dazed. The man rounded the desk and took his seat, only then did the fog pass. The sound was turned up, Samuel felt normal.

"Whew. I can't believe you did it. You will have to forgive the hallway. Like I had said before this is kind of a special time. No one, I mean NO ONE, has ever done what you did my man. You came through like a champ. All that was thrown at you, you overcame. I wanted to make sure that this special time was documented. Again, please, forgive the hallway. I wanted to make sure this was recorded. Oh MAN...and please forgive how I appear. If you were to see the real me, well... that just wouldn't do," the man finished smoothing his tie and his hair. He then took a deep breath and just looked at Samuel with a wide smile. The man looked like he belonged on a game show or maybe selling insurance, but Samuel could have sworn that he knew the face, but just couldn't fit the pieces together.

"You've been watching me?" Samuel questioned.

"Guilty! I had to know that you were the real deal. After you took the watch from Marcus, to be quite honest I was really shaken. I never thought it would happen, because, quite frankly, it wasn't supposed to happen. I could tell that everything you went through was taking a rather heavy toll. I had my doubts. MAN! You did it." He finished looking like he was ready to jump out of his skin.

"Wait...you're Regus Argent?" Samuel asked. The man's

smile grew bigger as if it shouldn't but did and he simply nodded.

"I don't want to get into the details of how it happened I just want to celebrate with you that it has happened. You, Samuel, are a devoted father. There is nothing to question that now. If Maggie could see what you have done and what you had to go through, she'd be so proud of you. Look, I have some things that need to be attended to so, can you walk with me please?" the man asked, rounding the desk and patting Samuel on the back. *I have done it! Not only for the family but for me as well. Doing this I've proven I'm a good father.* Samuel got up and walked with the gameshow host. The conversation wasn't as before when they first shook hands. Samuel could hear every question from Regus but couldn't get a word in edgewise as he just went on and on. On about how Samuel had done this and done that. Stopping for a moment at each of the paintings as if to hit on the highlights and to congratulate him on each of the hurdles he had overcome. They made their way downstairs and the man continued to talk. Each time Samuel would start to ask something or say something Regus would cut in about something that Samuel had done on his way to this point or how proud his family would be of him. The man led him right down to the beach and right onto the water. The music was gone, the waterfalls too. Even all the furnishings that made this an island paradise had been removed. There wasn't even a house, just a path that they took towards the ocean.

There things changed drastically. With both feet on the water, Samuel was Death; black robes and boney features. He had stopped and looked down at himself. He shifted his hands to form blades as he had done before. When he looked up. The man was gone. In its place was a huge silver humanoid twice the size of Death. All conversation had stopped. The being strode towards a large square block in the middle of the water.

"Weren't you saying something?" Death asked. The silvery body continued to the walk. Death followed Regus' path and looking in the distance he could see two people chained, standing on the block. "Wait isn't that ..." his vision focused and there were Maggie and Marcus. Not fakes, not like the paper land or after defeating Cerberus, they were really there. This felt wrong. Regus was almost to the block. Death ran as fast as he could to try and get there first. Before he reached the block a blow hit him in the chest. As he flew back, his feet lifted just off of the water. His feet came down as he hydroplaned to a stop. Death finally stopped and was almost to the beach as the spray of water, pushed aside from his feet sliding on the water's surface, settled. Regus held a pose from the blow he had delivered Death, then with a glance over his shoulder he put his fist back at his side and then, in two short strides, was atop the block and turned to face Death. In the blink of an eye Death was in the water just a few feet from the block.

There was a kind of face on the reflective metal head. Red eyes were the first thing he saw on the silvery head atop the body. Then there was lavender that marked what would be the high points of its face; nose, cheek bones, forehead and chin. All of these features and the eyes were contrasted with an oval shaped black background. It really didn't have a nose or cheeks, just the colors to make Regus appear that it did. A mouth appeared as he spoke, "we are not quite done as I said before. I would apologize but it wouldn't be sincere." Death had heard that voice before, the voice that emanated from the painting of his family before he faced his first challenge. He just about fell over backwards when he was close enough to confirm that Marcus was on the left, chained to four cinder blocks with a gag in his mouth. On the right, Maggie was incarcerated in the same way. Death felt as if a stiff breeze could knock him over and buckle his legs not wanting to believe what he was seeing. He reached out his hand to steady himself on the stone block, and his gaze bore into Regus. It then shifted to Maggie, and he found some strength. Then he looked at Marcus, straightening himself and slowly he stood finding his legs again.

"Choice. That is the final test. Which will live and which will die? That is entirely up to you, Samuel," Regus finished. "You accepted this responsibility. You must see it through to the end."

"What is preventing me from tearing you apart?" Death growled as his hand changed into the blades that had defeated larger foes.

"I am. I would be foolish to allow power to go to anyone that would exceed my own. I could destroy you with a thought and then your precious wife and son, and then what would happen to Denise and Robert? I easily stopped you from reaching the block. That should be proof enough that I have power over you. Choose or watch them both die. You can save one Samuel and that should be a consolation to you. "

Both his son and his wife were in tears, they could hear everything. They were looking back and forth at each other and at Death. Their eyes were full of fear and confusion. Death couldn't accept this. He had to try and save them both. He ran with all he had to Maggie, he cut the chains and turned a sharp curve to free Marcus, only to be swatted like before. He sailed a shorter distance after this attack. Not stopping his legs as he flew back and ran with everything he had, his thoughts, his will, his love were all poured into the speed to take him back to his son. Regus picked Marcus up and gently set him in the water. The blocks took his son down under the small gentle waves as they enveloped the blocks, the chains and then the boy. Still he ran and stopped at the spot right by the block where his son disappeared. Death tried to reach his son but his hand stopped inches into the water. Blades tried to slice the barrier preventing him from saving his son. He thrashed, swinging with wild abandon whipping his blades in a frenzy desperate to reach his son. Death was on his hands and knees atop the water slicing and clawing with blade and hand. Everything he did and had done, amounted to nothing to save his son. He stopped to watch the fear in his son's eyes, after that moment the blackness of the deep water prevented him from seeing anymore of his son. Death stood and screamed falling back on the stone slab. He sat right back up and screamed again, going back to the spot where he lost his son. Death flew into another frenzy refusing to let his son go. After all he had done to save him, he failed. He sat back again screaming, weeping empty tears, his whole body shaking. He felt a hand on his shoulder. Ready to kill Regus he cocked his bladed hand prepared to rend Regus, but he stopped just short of his wife. Maggie's face was bright red with tears as well as snot that wet her face, and she almost looked nothing like the woman he loved. Death's hands reverted and he squeezed his wife. She squeezed back, screaming and crying, coughing, and pounding both the stone block and the bony frame of Death. This went on for what seemed like hours, although it could have been days with the depths of the sorrow and loss they felt. Regus had gone. Leaving only the two of them. Maggie had finally got some control of herself when she asked, "why didn't you save…"

CHAPTER 24

Home

"SAM!" Maggie called out, not a shout, but a startled outburst. Maggie was being squeezed by Samuel tighter than he had ever squeezed her. Once she got past that, she heard he was sobbing uncontrollably. She was trying to sit up, but her prone husband was preventing her from doing that. It seemed that Samuel would relax his grip for just a second only to move slightly and then reapply the same intense grip. Maggie found a position that was slightly less uncomfortable and embraced Samuel. "You have to talk to me honey. What's wrong? Did you have a nightmare? You have to talk to me," Maggie said trying to soothe her hysteric husband, kissing the top of his head. She kept one arm wrapped around him and the other went to the back of his head. The effect was almost instantaneous, his breathing slowed and deepened. His grip was still firm, not painful. He was still sobbing and that went on for a couple of hours; husband and wife holding each other. Maggie was doing everything she could to calm and reach her husband. Finally, the sobs stopped. Samuel picked his head up off of Maggie's shoulder. Her hair was soaked as was the pillow under her. With an arm still around Samuel, she reached for the lamp on her bedside table and with an audible "click", light poured on her and Samuel. Samuel's face was wet and red, as if it were almost ready to explode. His hair, wild from having his head buried on Maggie's shoulder sobbing for so long, went off in all directions.

"I'm so sorry," he stammered "I couldn't save him. I tried, I tried. I swear. I wanted to save Marcus. He was so cold about it." His voice, nothing but a whisper at the end of his statement, stopped and he started to cry again. Not stopping him or questioning him Maggie went back to rubbing the back of Samuel's head in efforts to get him back to another calm state so that she could make sense of this. Hoping that it would snap him out of his state Maggie said, "Marcus is fine. He's asleep. You would have seen him and the kids when we came home from dinner but we saw your note saying you needed to sleep. We knew we shouldn't wake you when you misspelled sleep. You must have been exhausted after your flight back from the convention to misspell sleep." Even if Marcus wasn't fine, Maggie had to maintain the calm in order to get to the bottom of what was upsetting Samuel. Maggie took a deep steadying breath mostly sure, but slightly worried, that something was in fact wrong with Marcus. That is what hysterics do, they could spread like a disease as easily as touching a germ ridden door knob. Samuel took a deep breath and steadied himself as his head came off of Maggie's shoulder again. "What? Are you sure?" Samuel questioned and leapt out from the bed and raced for the door. Maggie still not sure what was going on was right on his heels. Samuel was at Marcus' door and then through it, not even knocking. There was Marcus, still and quiet and for an instance Samuel thought the worst. He held his breath, wiping his tears, trying to still his heartbeat that was thumping in his throat. Then Marcus let out a little sigh and rolled over. Samuel fell, half on, half off of Marcus's bed. The tears started again as he reached out and touched Marcus' foot. Samuel felt the warmth, the life in his son. He shifted off the bed and kneeled on the floor and crawled close to Marcus' head and watched him sleep. Samuel was hypnotized by the rhythmic breathing of Marcus.

"Samuel, what is going on? You can see that Marcus is

fine" Maggie said in a normal voice knowing that nothing would wake Marcus up short of a hurricane. "Let's get you some water and we can talk about this. You scared me to death." With that she grabbed her husband's hand and after a couple of tugs she got him to his feet. He stood at the door of his son's room watching him sleep peacefully, the perfect picture of tranquility. Maggie came back with a glass of water, and Samuel held it as a wounded child would. He remained for another minute and then turned to follow his wife. Marcus could sleep through anything, but the twins were a different story. Samuel peeked in on the children wanting to make sure his family was whole and safe. Not wanting to risk waking them, Maggie grabbed hold of his hand and led Samuel downstairs to the kitchen. They both took a seat. The only light in the room was the light above the stove. They sat in the booth where the family shared its meals. As Samuel drank his water Maggie got up to get a glass herself. *What is going on? I know she is going to want me to explain all this. I could have sworn that Marcus drowned. I saw his face, not the face of someone else, drift to the depths of the ocean, it was so real. Not like when I was thin as paper chasing Marcus. I couldn't be sure if that was him. The same with Maggie on top of that structure. I thought I was freeing my wife, but it wasn't her. Is this real? Or is this another trick from Regus? Will he pull the rug out from under me again?* Maggie returned with a glass water, she kissed Samuel on the top of the head and took a seat across from him.

"I'm sorry that I frightened you. I don't quite know what is going on," Samuel said with a sniffle, taking another drink. He looked around the room, looking for anything that would tell him that this wasn't his house, hoping for evidence to disprove that he wasn't still participating in the trials. He looked at himself again, looked at his arms, stomach and chest and finally touched his face and neck wondering if this was real or some trick. Was he still trying to prove himself worthy to take over as Death? Was the paint going to peel and reveal yet another trial or monster to overcome?

"You've awakened from nightmares before Sam, but never like that. Screaming and grabbing me like that, it must have been one hell of a nightmare or maybe even a night terror," said Maggie looking over her husband. "Should we contact the doctor?"

"What was the first job I ever had?" Samuel asked suddenly.

Maggie looked at Samuel with a confused expression letting the question and why he would ask that sink in for two seconds before blurting out "Paperboy. Why would you ask me that? Samuel talk to me. What kind of dream would have you this wound up? You just about crushed me and I've never seen you cry like that, not even for your Mom or Dad," Maggie asked and started growing more concerned. *I have to tell her something, Maggie knows when even the smallest things are bothering me. If I don't tell her something she won't give up.* So Samuel told her about the last encounter that had him shaken so. Samuel did leave out Regus and his appearance as Death. Something told him that he couldn't, shouldn't tell her about anything more than the very end of the dream if it was a dream. That he had to choose between saving her or Marcus, that he had freed her but just couldn't get to Marcus in time. He started to cry again as he could see that last image of Marcus slipping into the deep, cold ocean.

"Hey Samuel Gerald Willis, look at me." He lifted his head and wiped his eyes after hearing his full name. "This is about what we were talking about with regards to Marcus withdrawing isn't it? You think that you won't be able to reach him, that he is slipping away. The fact that you freed me first is just a reflection that you want to free me of the burden of bread winner. Wow I actually sound like I know what I'm talking about, anyways. Honey, Marcus and you, all of us, will be fine. You just have to keep at it, being a father and husband, just like you should keep at the job searches. I know that something will come up, it has to. You just got back from the job expo and you'd texted that you had some promising leads." She got up and sat beside Samuel who was hanging his head low as he rubbed the back of his neck with both hands, elbows resting on the table. She put an arm around him and squeezed and gave him a gentle shake. She planted a kiss on the side of his head, then laid her head on his shoulder, rubbing his back with one hand; her other hand caressed his arm. "You're a great father and the only partner I would ever want. I have an idea. Why don't you have Marcus skip school today so that two of you can get back to a better place. I don't know, take him to lunch and then to the mall and just walk around and talk. None of his friends should be there so he won't be too embarrassed," Maggie finished with a smile and a wink. She looked at the clock on the coffee pot, "Coffee's about to start so no sense in going back to bed. Would you like some eggs honey?"

"Yes please," Samuel said with a weak smile. He started to let the realization in that he could be home. All seemed normal to him. The sounds of the kitchen were normal, the smell as the coffee started to brew, again normal. He put his head back and stared at the ceiling. The ceiling fan was spinning slowly, and Samuel noticed a crack in the dry wall that branched off where the ceiling fan was installed. *I said I was going to try and fix that crack in the dry wall a week ago.* The little imperfection in his house left Samuel comforted. He felt like this was where and how he should be. He got up and went to the powder room. He turned on the light, all was in its place. He ran cold water and splashed it over his face and head, then used the small hand-towel to dry his face and hair. *I know that Maggie really doesn't like it when I do this.* That too helped. Each minute, each experience no matter how small helped to bring him out of where he had been, and back to his life. Samuel was starting to remember what life was like before he removed the watch from his son's wrist. He took a good look at himself in the mirror. Staring at himself, he steadied himself; *everything is fine. You're home.* His eyes were red and slightly swollen. He smoothed his hair, replaced the towel and turned off the light. His eggs were waiting for him. The eggs were covered with a generous portion of salsa, just how Samuel liked them. *Maggie is so good to me.* These were his favorite with just a little cheese in the middle, covered in medium salsa. He started on his eggs and sipped his coffee. This was what it was to be normal. Maggie reappeared with her cup of coffee, and kissed Samuel slowly. She smiled, "you used the hand-towel didn't you? Well after last night I guess I'll let you slide just this once."

Samuel smiled. He felt better after eating. He cleaned up his plate and the pan that Maggie had used. He topped off his coffee and walked upstairs. Maggie greeted him "I'll take the twins this morning I don't have to be at the office until 10 for a meeting anyway." Samuel walked into Marcus' room. The craziness of what he had just gone through started here. Samuel looked around the room, it was just as he remembered yet it seemed like a lifetime ago. Samuel took a seat in Marcus' desk chair, facing his son watching him sleep. The sun was trying to find its way through the trees into Marcus' room. Samuel cracked the window and let a gentle breeze come into the room slightly pushing the curtains and pushing out the last of Samuel's apprehension. Samuel sat there and watched his son sleep, enjoying the peace, enjoying being home.

****

That afternoon Samuel went with Marcus to the mall and the afternoon was successful. They had enjoyed a good lunch, and walking around the mall was good for conversation. Marcus and Samuel were back to where they belonged, communicating as if nothing had even happened, not the watch, not the trials, and no longer any doubt. It carried into the weekend and even into the next week. Samuel had saved his son. It still hurt him, haunted him, that he didn't choose to save Marcus first. This was what Samuel needed to sort out, but could he really sort it out? He made his decision and he would have to live with that decision the rest of his life, even if it didn't yield dire consequences. *I was selfish, that's why I saved Maggie. I don't know that I could do this on my own, taking care of Marcus and the twins. Marcus had time with me and Maggie, how could I deprive the twins of their mother? How could I deprive Maggie of her first baby?* Every time Samuel went to that place he wasn't anywhere close to Maggie. She would pick up on the emotions of doubt, the regret that Samuel would be feeling about his choice and question him about it. He would explain that it was that dream, and he just hadn't quite gotten over it. He wasn't quite sure he would ever be able to get over what he had seen and done with his choice. Those questions he asked himself over and over again. *Why Maggie and not Marcus?* He would keep asking himself that probably until the day he died.

The next day Samuel received a call about the last interview he had been on before Marcus and the watch. The interview that led to the chaotic events in the garage was a bust. Recalling the events in the garage was like burping and having a little extra bile come up with the expelled gas. *I wonder if that poor man felt the burn of a belch, or more the burn of a fire being betrayed by his fellow man, mugged and tormented. I keep thinking about my problems with the garage, but that guy's month, year or maybe even his life could have been changed or ruined. I feel the same way when I think about Marcus.* His mind went over the events again. He felt guilty about not helping that man who was being mugged, which then rolled into guilt for not being able to help Marcus, leaving him to that fate even if it was a part of the trial or maybe even a dream. The guilt still smoldered in him, like some forgotten spark deep in the bowels of what used to be a raging fire. Samuel went back and forth between Marcus and the man in the garage. He remembered the drive and how he thought it impossible that he would make it home after being such a wreck. Walking that memory and seeing it happen did make him remember one thing he forgot to do, reach out to Mary Patricia. Samuel went to the phone to call Mary Patricia trying to put a positive spin on all the negativity in his thoughts. After the pleasantries and catching up Mary said she might have something for Samuel. "Do you have time in the next couple weeks to discuss it?" Mary asked on the phone. Samuel replied "sure I think Maggie is taking the kids to Funzone this Sunday so does that work for you? ... Good I'll see you around 11 on Sunday, bye." With the promise of something new, Samuel decided that they would have a cook out Saturday before he was going to meet with Mary Patricia since the warmer weather was on the wane. He wanted to banish the feeling of negativity and turn his thoughts around and felt that he and the family needed, wanted, to have some good food as well as some outdoor fun.

On that Saturday, footballs, Frisbees, bubbles, hula hoops and other lawn toys were brought out. The twins asked if they could have a couple of their friends over as well to play. The twins had hoped that Hope could come over, but she had an unexpected visit from her Grandmother. Samuel and Maggie always enjoyed having the neighborhood kids over. They had always agreed to let anyone, any number come over. They stocked all the good snacks to ensure that everyone wanted to stay at the Willis'. It was expensive and it was one more thing with less money coming in the house, but it afforded Samuel and Maggie a way to keep their eyes on the kids. Marcus was running with the little kids, being the tickle monster and helping them with their Frisbee throws when Samuel called to him.

"Marcus, why don't' you invite Thomas? It's been forever since we've seen him," Samuel said, as he put down the tub of ice filled with drinks. Marcus smiled. "You're right dad. It has been awhile since we saw or talked with Thomas," and went for his phone thinking he needed to finish that conversation with Thomas. Samuel went back and wheeled out the grill.

Thomas arrived at just the right time. There was food being pulled off the grill into the warming trays while Marcus was trying to get a Frisbee to one of the other kids. From out of nowhere, Thomas sprinted covering the distance easily just to intercept the throw. Thomas threw the Frisbee to Samuel who flipped the burger and ran a few strides to make the catch and then threw it to the next ready person. Thomas went up to Marcus and shook hands. They talked for about 30 minutes, catching up and mostly smiling though out the exchange. Samuel just smiled. It was the perfect day, family, friends and some good times. Marcus went after the kids as Thomas jogged over.

"Thank you for the invite Mr. Willis," Thomas extended his hand. "No problem Thomas you are always welcome. How are your folks? How are you holding up? I'm sorry I haven't reached out sooner," Samuel replied with a wink putting up his hand for a minute to flip a couple of burgers. "Or has Marcus reached out recently?" Thomas's older brother Isaac had died suddenly seven or eight months ago. Some questions were raised as to how and why. There was speculation that Isaac, being a young black man, had done something wrong. Samuel knew better. Isaac used to babysit Marcus when he was a child and there wasn't a more trustworthy or reliable young man than Isaac Jackson. That is how Marcus and Thomas became such good friends. Isaac would bring Thomas along when he sat for the Willis'. Samuel, finished with flipping the burgers, put his hand in Thomas' and gave him firm shake. "You need anything Thomas, don't hesitate to ask." Thomas held on longer than he should have. Samuel looked at their hands and then to Thomas. Thomas' eyes just looked deep into Samuels.

"Little help," someone cried. Thomas broke off and was able to make the catch on the run, behind his back no less. Samuel shook out the cobwebs and went back to the grill, enjoying the afternoon fun.

CHAPTER 25

Letters

"Honey how about this one?" Michael Lynx called to his wife. This had been the first yard sale this morning and Michael was already tired. Linda had been in search for the perfect piece to finish off one of the guest rooms. "I hope this is the one. This is getting tiresome" he said in a low voice which was followed by a sigh and a sip of his expensive coffee. It was all about the image for Michael and Linda. The right color to a room to elicit the proper response, the best window shades to ensure that the fabrics of the room wouldn't fade and the correct wood tones to match the rest of the furnishings. It had to be the right furnishing to accent the room and fill the guest's needs. Linda was looking for something to go at the foot of the bed in the last guest room. They had looked over quilt racks, foot lockers, wooden chests and even bedroom benches. She had seen a couple of foot lockers, very old that could fit her particular vision for this room, but the four previous yard sales this week and the eight last weekend along with a couple flea markets, drove Michael to the point of losing his drive and patience for the perfect piece, but not Linda. Once she had that itch there was no scratching it. It would be rubbed gently into submission because Linda was all about the control. Michael waved his wife over. The footlocker was old. He wasn't sure how old, but Linda might know.

The piece was unpainted, it was finished in a lacquer. It had clawed feet keeping it off the ground.

"What is it Michael?" Linda asked throwing her hand on her hip. She stopped and looked at the piece and stood straight. Her body and her eyes said wow, Michael could see that she wanted it. It would be the perfect piece. Then her body slouched, as if her body said "eh" it was an act, at least Michael thought so and to that effect he would be willing to lay a little money of the fact that she wanted the piece. Linda wanted the piece but acted like she didn't to try and drive down the price. This is how Linda worked the trades. She was as shrewd as an Iranian carpet salesman. She lifted the lid. It could use a good cleaning inside, but the outside was what was important. She walked around the footlocker, stalking it, like she was about to pounce on the furniture and claim her kill. She clicked her manicured nails together on the fifth lap around the footlocker when one of the organizers of this sale saw her waiting and started over. Michael knew as soon as the person was halfway to his wife she would walk away and Linda did just that, laying down the act so thick she could whittle down the cost the seller had in mind. After a lap with Michael in tow, she would return to the footlocker and get it for half the cost after pointing out mostly superficial flaws.

It was done, just as Michael had predicted, the only thing he hadn't predicted was how heavy it was. The foot locker was loaded in the back of their overpriced SUV. Unloaded and put in the garage for a cleaning of the interior and exterior, then it was put in the room. The footlocker was a perfect fit for the room. The wood tone matched seamlessly with the rest of the wood in the room, as if the footlocker was meant to be theirs. It sat for a few days and once it sat long enough Linda began to inspect the footlocker. There was a considerable amount of dust even with the first cleaning in the garage. After about thirty minutes of cleaning Linda was satisfied with the interior, again the exterior was the most important. Michael came in to check on his wife. He wasn't sure if she would keep the piece. She had a way of changing her mind and this wouldn't be the first time Michael would see that change of heart. He looked inside and saw something curious. He took a couple steps back and let out a "humph".

"What is it Michael? Don't you have anything better to do than watch me clean this? If that is the case, I'll turn it over to you" she finished with a certain amount of sass flipping the rag over in her hand offering it to Michael. "I'm not certain, but I think this footlocker has an extra space on the bottom of it." Michael bent over to inspect the footlocker. With most of the dust was gone, Michael started to probe the bottom. He ran his finger along the border pressing down knowing that something was just out of place about this footlocker. "Nothing," he continued by lifting it up and confirmed that there was something he was missing. He set the footlocker back down and pressed right in the center. The left side panel covering the bottom popped up ever so slightly. A seam appeared after the panel came to rest. Michael went to his office in the next room and plucked the letter opener from his desk, pushed the spot again and slid the letter opener down along the left wall. He found purchase with the tool, twisted it ever so slightly to make sure the panel wouldn't fall back. The panel came up and he was able to get a fingernail in place of the letter opener. The panel came free with a little effort. In the bottom were old, quite old pieces of parchment. Linda reached in to grab them, "STOP!" Michael shouted. "These letters might be valuable and if you touch them the oils from your hand might degrade their value." "Well you don't have to shout Michael," Linda finished with a sigh. There was writing on one of the letters, it was hard to make out. Michael got closer to get a better look. He read the name Willis, the rest he couldn't make out.

Now Michael, being a salesman was really good with names. He could meet someone on a sales call and three years later he would remember them. It was the hidden talent he had as a salesman, which made him one of his company's best. "Willis, I know that name. Willis, Willis...wait." Michael had heard the name Willis from a lady he had sold software support to. Her name was...he could see her face. She had the cute librarian look down pat. "Mary Patricia, she and Sam...no...no that's not right. Samuel! That's it, they bought support for several servers last year. Yea. I wonder if Samuel is related to the person who wrote these letters."

They read one of the letters which Michael held with a handkerchief. It revealed that someone named Felicia Willis whose favorite Uncle who helped raise her and treated her like daughter was the one that died and she received Death from him, not from Peter. "How do you receive Death?" they asked in unison.

CHAPTER 26

Sorted Emotions

A scream caught in Samuel's throat hurt, as he was jarred awake. He could feel the air rush from his lungs up to his throat, but it stopped, and he couldn't breathe. He stumbled out of bed almost knocking the lamp off of his bedside table. He stumbled into the bathroom and turned the light on, Death stared back.

Samuel woke up. Then took a deep breath in and let it out. Maggie was sleeping undisturbed next to him. He rubbed his face and looked at the alarm clock. The ruby colored numbers, 3:45, rested on the face of the clock. The house was quiet so Samuel stopped his breathing just for a minute to make sure that was entirely true. He knew the house was quiet when he could hear the grandfather clock in the dining room below ticking away. It had been a week since he had returned from a world that was more fantastic, more strange and interesting than Samuel had ever known. Nightmares haunted him. The worst was Marcus slipping under the water. Samuel could still see his son's nose as tiny bubbles of air rested on the cusp of his nostrils as he drifted silently to the deep. His hair waved slowly, deliberately, as he thrashed and tried to free himself. These were the images that Samuel saw when he closed his eyes. He heard the question Maggie had asked, or started to ask before he woke up escaping the last nightmare. "Why didn't you save…" Samuel ran from that answer just like all other confrontations in his life. He knew the reason he went for Maggie first. He just didn't want to admit it. If he did, then all that he had done to save Marcus might come crashing down. His weakness, fear, influenced his decision, just like in the garage. He was tired of feeling that way, uncertain, frightened and unable to act. His feelings since returning from the start of his journey were that of a nerve exposed and plucked like a guitar string ready to snap. As these thoughts raced through his head, he knew there would be no more sleep tonight.

    Samuel had gone to bed a little early and that coupled with the dreams that kept haunting him made him come to a realization; *I'm not getting back to sleep, am I?* He could survive on 6 hours or so. What he couldn't survive on was the constant worry of his inability. A job, saving his son, or the act of helping a fellow human being out of a bad situation seemed evasive and elusive. He got up swinging his legs over the edge of the bed. Maggie rolled over and smacked her lips. The house was chilled, he preferred it that way. He could sleep in 65 degrees and not bat an eyelash. The rest of the family, not so much. The thermostat was set at a compromised 69 degrees that was displayed on the thermostat in the hall outside his and Maggie's room. He grabbed his house pants and his tee shirt, he dressed and headed for the kitchen. When he reached the kitchen Samuel grabbed a glass of water and sat at the table where the family took most their meals.

    He let his mind drift back to the beginning of his journey in Grayland. He thought he would have been so afraid, but he was acting on instinct. There was little to no fear, no worry, that he acted appropriately and it worked out that his actions were faithful and correct. That feeling stuck with Samuel for a few minutes as he sipped his water. He was in control of his emotions at that point on his journey, he had tools to cope with the difficulties, and the emotions weren't so overpowering as to let fear take him over and stifle his actions. He sat forward, thinking of the journey from Grayland to the garden. How the garden threw him into a spin of desperation and hopelessness, then spun him back to joy and elation. The journey was confusing and difficult, not only because he sampled all the new sights and experiences, but the feelings that would manifest at different places in the journey. When the feelings weren't thrown in his face he had a purpose to get back to his family, but the feelings didn't control him, they guided him, or was it his choice? Choice to confront Marcus, choice to just keep moving towards a goal, and choice just not making it about the family, but about his mental well-being, his thoughts of self. The boatman tried to instill him with a fear of knowledge. It was a form of control, but was that Regus' control being asserted or the tasks at hand leaning, influencing, his choices? How much did Regus dictate what happened during the trial? All, Samuel expected. He made the choice to confront Marcus so the other circumstances he had to accept. Either way he was able to put that doubt aside and move on to Cerberus.

Then he stopped and thought of the swamp and the walking corpse that helped him. He felt there, not the over powering, merry-go-round of feelings like the garden, it was him, it was how Samuel would express his emotion's on any normal day. He felt the pain of being freed from the forgetting fog, the disappointment of self when he almost failed himself, his son and family. He felt self-doubt and wonderment when witnessing the phenomenon and scope of the blackness on the rusty colored shore and what it birthed. He shook his head and smiled when he thought of the little bit of joy he felt with the chorus line of Deaths. *I have to admit that was funny. That was something I would do with the kids, like skipping through the parking lot or splashing in mud puddles.* The awe he felt witnessing the light and the dark. He wasn't sure why he was to witness that grand event, but there had to be some purpose. When he saw the events at the end of the swamp he felt small, like he could be swallowed up by the universe at any minute and he didn't want to feel those emotions anymore. He wanted to do what he needed to do without all the doubt that feelings brought.

He took himself back to Paperland. He just wanted to get to his son, to see him safe. He didn't feel the emotion of need; it was a call to action that he had to fulfill, an energy born from within, simply put, love. Samuel was sure it was love as much as he was uncertain of his son's fate in Paperland but after the battle with Cerberus and the fake Maggie, he had suspected another counterfeit family member. He was upset sure, but was it because he didn't reach Marcus or was it that he was led astray again, duped into feeling something for someone that wasn't one of the family? He failed that person but did he really fail the family or himself? But Samuel hadn't failed, because it wasn't Marcus it was someone else and with that thought he allowed himself to relax just a bit. His focus was on saving his family, he couldn't save everyone, just like he probably couldn't have saved the man in the garage. When he wasn't overwhelmed with fear or uncertainty, he could act and own those actions. Had his emotions been his downfall all these years? Before Regus put him through the last of his trials he was human and felt all the things he would if he were on a normal beach somewhere bright and sunny. He felt slightly relaxed when he finished the margarita. He felt empty watching Marcus drift below the water out of reach. Samuel could feel the tears start in his stomach, then they creeped up his body to the back of his throat, then he swallowed, trying to put the emotions back in their place.

Then he took a couple of swallows of water and thought about the journey beginning to end. He was shocked at the scope of all he had done as Death. Samuel was beginning to see that emotions weren't the best thing for him or were they? That is what he needed to know. The tears that had just tried to run to the surface wouldn't have helped him here and now. He needed to check out of his own mind in order to do what needed to be done, not to feel his way through, but see a course and put his conviction in the path and Death was that path. He would take the steps necessary to quiet the feelings of doubt and fear that would be better than feeling regret for not helping that man in the garage and the regret of not getting to Marcus in time. Staying the course and not letting his emotions overtake him would have helped Samuel not to feel the fear that nearly caused him to fail his family in the swamp and it would snuff out the feelings that betrayed him on the final steps of the trial for Regus. *Or was the entire journey for me? Growth for me? Am I really trying to save myself so I can save everyone else? At first I was cast into the mix to save Marcus. Could I have saved both Maggie and Marcus at the trials end? As Death could I have saved the man in the garage? As Death with no feelings, it is most assuredly possible, as Samuel Willis, feeling gets in the way. I wasn't able to save them both because I was feeling too much. I was irrational and let that fear drive me. Regus said I had to choose, but it wasn't about his choice, it was about my choice of letting emotions rule my outcome, I won't let that happen again. I will take the steps when I am performing my duties as Death not to feel, not to let any feelings get in the way. I am unsure if I have that option or decision, so I am making that choice now. I felt several emotions as Death and maybe that is a good thing and maybe that was my inoculation from emotions. Could that one glimpse show me the folly of feeling as it leads to indecision? Could that indecision mean the end of me? Can Death die, can I die as Death? If I die will Marcus have to assume the responsibility once more? I can't let that happen. I can't let these hesitant feelings rule me. I must control them.*

    Samuel sat straight. He looked forward, finished his glass of water and deposited the glass in the sink. He went to Marcus' room and looked in on his son. Marcus didn't move except for the rhythmic movements of his chest rising and falling. He went to the twin's room. The nightlight provided more illumination than the streetlight that shone in Marcus' windows. Toys were scattered in the room and two beds without frames rested on the ground. Maggie and Samuel didn't want the kids to fall far if they happened to roll out of bed. The twins were fast asleep, each of them still clinging to their blankets. Then Samuel went back to his room, used the bathroom and looked at himself in the dark mirror. The traces and reflections of light from outside his bedroom windows, the street lights, through the mirror cast a dim light on Samuel. He couldn't afford to feel when he was Death, maybe even in life. He would have to consider that as time went on. Samuel laid in bed after disrobing. He pulled the covers over the left half of his body and settled in. He wasn't sure why but the dreams had faded and he felt that sleep might come to him again tonight. His confidence was swelling, he was feeling less and less anxiety when it came to his responsibilities as Death, maybe even in life and he liked it.

CHAPTER 27

Then There Were Four

    Several days had passed since the cookout. Samuel kept going back to his handshake with Thomas. These thoughts rolled around in his mind as he woke. It was Sunday, Maggie lay beside him her breathing steady and deep, she was still asleep. *That handshake was something else. When Thomas looked at me I thought lasers were going to come right out of his eyes and burn through my head. Then it was gone as soon as he went for the Frisbee.* Samuel swung his legs over the edge of the bed and shrugged it off, or tried to, starting his Sunday routine. He dressed in his house pants and tee-shirt heading for the kitchen. The coffee was already brewing as Samuel got the oven heated and ready for the cinnamon rolls. *Cinnamon rolls! Yum! Just hate opening these containers.* Samuel had trouble pulling apart some of the cinnamon rolls which was a somewhat regular Sunday affair. The generics seemed to cook and taste better, so why spend extra for a name brand. With everything laid out, Samuel just waited for the oven. He started toward the front of the house remembering the Sunday paper should be waiting for him. He stepped out into the cool morning, there was dew on the grass that shined like glass beads. He bent down to get the paper. When he came up one of the neighbors was jogging in front of the house. He waved and then took a moment to be in the moment of the morning in with a deep breath of cool crisp air. It would be a beautiful day. He would meet with Mary Patricia and he felt confident that things would work out, that Mary Patricia could help him as she had in the past. Then the kids would come back from shopping and their trip to Funzone with Maggie and the family could enjoy the backyard for a while, with either Frisbee or some light chores until it was time to fire up the grill for some Sunday steaks. *That could just be my perfect Sunday. The cherry on top would be if I came out at the end of the day with a job.*

Samuel remembered the task he had started and headed back to the kitchen tossing the paper on the table. The oven was ready, so he popped the rolls in and Samuel slowly, deliberately got a cup of coffee enjoying the peace for a moment. After a couple sips Samuel heard the tell-tale thumps of little feet heading to his and Maggie's room. Then more laughter erupted from the top of the stairs as little feet started flying down the steps. Samuel walked to the bottom of the stairs. The twins, much to his surprise, jumped from five steps up with blankets trailing behind like capes in the wind. Samuel caught them both and embraced them. Samuel's strength and balance were tested as the kids flailed in his arms as he made his way to the kitchen. Samuel took a step away from the kitchen counter to prevent the coffee from being knocked over as Maggie came around the corner laying kisses all around.

"Thank you for making cinnamon rolls" Maggie said rubbing Samuels back and heading for the coffee. Cheers erupted from the kids as they heard the magic words. The kids just about leapt down from Samuel's arms and made for the booth. Samuel didn't use a timer when cooking the rolls, his nose was better than any timer, not with everything but with the rolls it was. Samuel paused sniffing the air. "Close," he said to the kids with a wink. Samuel paused, there was an uncomfortable sensation in the room. As he thought about his ideal day he remembered, Maggie always had just a hint of jealousy with regards to

Mary Patricia. It was completely harmless between Mary and Samuel. Mary was a few years younger than Samuel. They had worked together but they were only friends. No one could replace Maggie. She was the only woman for Samuel. He looked at her, she was sipping her coffee looking at him over the top of her cup and then she looked away. Samuel chuckled to himself. He walked over and planted a long slow kiss on his wife. She seemed to relax just a little. She put her coffee down, wrapped her arms around Samuel's neck and moved to kiss him. He put his hands on her hips and moved to kiss her. Maggie opened her eyes just before their lips touched, Samuel had stuck out his tongue to intercept her lips with a playful lick that he hadn't done in a year or two. She pulled back with a smile wiped her lips and stuck her tongue out at Samuel. "I love you," Samuel said pulling Maggie back and planting a quick kiss on her lips. Samuel pulled away "the rolls are ready." He grabbed the oven mitt and pulled the rolls out. Then got juice for Denise and milk for Robert.

"I'm going to take the kids shopping with me round 10:30 and then on to Funzone" she mouthed the last word not wanting to send the kids into hysterics before reaching the destination of inflatable slides, obstacle courses and video games. If the kids were alerted too early it would be non-stop questions 'when can we go? Is it time yet?'. Maggie continued "I have a grocery list on the fridge, just add anything that you might need since you will be busy getting that great new position," Maggie raised her eyebrows on "busy" and sat with the family to enjoy breakfast. The family joked and got their fill of the cinnamon rolls. Each of the kids had three, they would have had four if Samuel and Maggie let them. Maggie was satisfied with one as was Samuel. The next batch would mostly go to Marcus who could eat five in a sitting, with Samuel helping to finish them off. Looking at the clock and hearing the toilet flush in the kid's bathroom he started the second round of breakfast. Maggie, Denise and Robert went upstairs to watch a little TV and then would get dressed for the day, TV was the kids' Sunday morning treat, an hour or two of television. The breakfast would differ but not the routine. Marcus appeared zombie like, and sat at the booth with his old man. He slouched down to a semi reclined position so that his head could rest on the back of the booth. Samuel kissed Marcus on the side of the head. Marcus' eyes went wide, fixed on a point on the ceiling as he opened his mouth wide. He rolled his head to the side looking at Samuel with that frozen face. Marcus made a quick motion like he was sick and then smiled at Samuel. Who then got up and laid out the second batch of rolls and a tall glass of milk for Marcus. Samuel who should have stopped at two, had a third. He accepted that he was thirty, forty pounds' overweight and just enjoyed the food and the time with his son.

The hour of Mary Patricia's visit was fast approaching. The chaos of trying to get the kids out the door to Funzone and shopping was in full swing. Now that the kids were aware of their destination the volume rose only slightly less than the energy to get out the door. Hugs and kisses were exchanged all around in the kitchen as Samuel, dressed and ready for the day, looked through the paper and Marcus, still in his house clothes, was cleaning up from breakfast. Finished in the kitchen, Marcus left to start his laundry. The doorbell rang. Samuel looked at the stove and saw it was quarter past 11. Laying down the paper he went to the front of the house and as he expected it was Mary Patricia. He looked at her and smiled. "Good morning Samuel." Mary always spoke with little slang or contractions. "I have a friend maybe two stopping by as well. They wanted to have a talk about other positions they might have at their companies," she replied as Samuel stepped aside and let her in. She stepped in and Samuel motioned to the formal dining room. She was dressed in business professional attire, skirt, jacket top and a modest shirt under the jacket. Mary Patricia was always well put together and well dressed, Samuel couldn't recall seeing her otherwise. "Wow, really? Three chances are better than one.

Coffee? No that's right you like tea. Can I put some water on for you?" he asked heading for the kitchen.

"Thank you," she replied taking a seat. After starting the kettle, he returned to her in the dining room. Mary had produced a large brown accordion envelope. "What is that for?" Samuel asked. "Documents about the company as well as business models." They continued with more small talk, mostly about Samuel's family. Samuel asked if Mary Patricia's grandmother's condition had changed at all. Samuel had remembered that she had been in a coma for about five years now. Mary took a sip of her tea, "sadly no. She is breathing on her own with the feeding tube still in place."

"I'm sorry," Samuel replied. That kind of killed the mood and lucky for Samuel the doorbell rang.

"Those should be my friends," Mary said setting down her tea and straightening herself. Samuel walked to the door. He was completely surprised when he opened it to find Thomas Jackson and Hope Osborne.

"Hey guys. Marcus is upstairs Thomas, and Hope I'm sorry but the twins have gone to run errands with their mom," Samuel said with a chuckle looking in at Mary Patricia and then back to the kids. Thomas walked in as Samuel stepped back and revealed the stairs. Thomas, in a plain white t-shirt, jeans and sneakers, walked past Samuel and then turned towards the dining room where he sat at the table with Mary Patricia. Samuel followed his path confused and started to shut the door forgetting that Mary said she had two friends.

"May I come in Mr. Willis," piped Hope Osborne as she rocked from heels to toes and back again. Samuel wasn't sure what was going on so he just kept looking around like someone was playing a joke on him. She was dressed in shorts and a sky-blue hoodie. Her blonde hair was braided and came over her shoulder. Samuel stepped back from the door, not quite sure what to do. She stepped in and smiled and headed for the table.

Samuel stood there for a several seconds looking at the trio sitting at his dining room table with the door open as well as his mouth. He closed his mouth, looked outside and then closed the door. Still quite confused Samuel took a seat at the table.

"Sorry for the slight deception Samuel. There is a job of sorts, but it is not what you are thinking of. I even hear that you have already interviewed for the position. I was unsure, but Thomas was certain the time he came over for the cookout. He told us about it and we knew that things had changed," Mary Patricia said setting her empty tea cup down, she then shifted her sitting position. She then rested her hand on the stack of papers she produced earlier. "This is related to what we are talking about now, although I will ask you not to interrupt until I have finished explaining everything. Agreed?" Samuel chuckled and nodded not sure where she was going with this.

"Grace Williams sent me these documents 14 days ago at the behest of her husband, Richard."

"How..." Samuel's face transformed, it was light and jovial, after he spoke it was serious with wide eyes and a straight mouth.

"Samuel you agreed, so please let me finish. Richard was Death, as was Marcus, as you are now. We know that the responsibilities are passed down through the generations. Richard's research has confirmed the positions are passed down along the bloodlines. Hope's grandmother and Thomas's brother have corroborated what Richard is saying in his research. Some of the information regarding the Horsemen has been passed down by word of mouth, but a lot has been forgotten. The Willis line is an interesting one. Richard's research goes back to a half Native American, half white ancestor of yours named Adahy. From there Death split from the Willis line. You can look at the documents afterwards if you like. The Death bloodline has been riding the Williams side for a few generations, just a ball park

Occupational Death

estimate. Maggie's maiden name is Williams correct?" She went on not waiting for a response, for Samuel's expression hadn't changed it was still wide eyed with a non-existent expression on his mouth, as Mary's speech became more animated. Samuel went back to the other night, to his thoughts. He couldn't, he wouldn't show or let the emotion ready to run to the surface rule him. "Here is the interesting part, you and Maggie, are 4th or 5th I cannot remember which, cousins. The bloodline went to the Williams and now has come back to the Willis line. Now there has to be some precedence, some divine …power or hand at work here to bring this legacy back to your name and bloodline." Mary Patricia finished, showing uncharacteristic energy and bliss.

Samuel looked around the table. Thomas shrugged "I know, dizzying isn't it." Hope just yawned while tracing lines in the table where she used her breath to fog up the surface. Mary Patricia sat back, looking physically exhausted from the explanation as she smoothed her clothing. Samuel hadn't moved, he was still digesting the information that Mary Patricia had just vomited at him. *Horsemen, Death? Divine…just keep calm you can do this.*

"You can't be serious. This all has to be some joke right? How could you all possibly know all this? I know that you are a catholic Mary, but divine?"

Thomas spoke up "Samuel, sorry Mr. Willis, this is going to take some getting used to, but my brother told me all about his adventures, well that's what he called them. All the things he and the other horsemen had done. It's awesome. Right Hope?"

"Yea, sure," Hope replied rather bored of it all. "My grandma had told me it went from her husband, my grandpap, to my dad and then to me. No big deal really. Just things need doing elsewhere and we take care of it." Samuel sat back from the table. *This has to be a dream, I'm going to wake up, I'll still be*

Death but Mary, Thomas and Hope will have nothing else to do with it, yea, I'm convinced. With that Samuel just smiled and nodded sure about the situation, sure about nothing else really, but sure that this wasn't happening right now. As if on cue they all shifted in their seats. Samuel realized that they were all sitting in the same way. All were leaning forward, with their elbows on the table, one hand cupped inside the other. *They all look like they are expecting something.* Samuel was still sitting back was trying to take in all that he had heard, certain that all he had been told was made up. He reached to get his coffee, but stopped before his hand got to the mug. There on his wrist was a watch; Samuel didn't wear a watch. He looked at the time and then his eyes drifted up to look at his guests. Everyone else was wearing a watch as well. Mary Patricia a lady's gold watch. Thomas' watch appeared to be some kind of sports watch. Hope's was pink and had rainbows and unicorns on it, Samuel really couldn't make out the details with the shock of all he had heard and now seen. "What's going on?" Samuel asked. "Mary I know that you don't wear a watch. I don't wear a watch." He looked at the clock across the way and noticed that his watch was about five minutes, now four, fast.

"I don't wear a watch either Mr. Willis. Hope do you wear a watch?" Thomas shrugged at Hope and then he went back to looking at Samuel, as he shook his head in disbelief.

"I don't", Hope replied. Samuel tried to remove the watch. "That won't help Mr. Willis. It will go away in time." Samuel let go of the band and sat looking at all seated at the table one at a time. He looked at the watch and notice that it actually wasn't moving. He looked at the grandfather clock and there was about one-minute time difference between the watch that had appeared on his wrist and the clock in the room. Samuel didn't know whether he should just sit there or get up and flee, either way he was shaking, like he was filled with pent up energy.

"Dad? Are you talking to someone?" Marcus called

from the top of the stairs. Mary, Thomas and Hope all looked at their wrists and then presented their watches so that Samuel could see that the times of all four watches where the same. Samuel gasped. Marcus' foot falls started down the stairs. "Dad?" Marcus called looking into an empty dining room.

EPILOGUE

The vast jungle was alive. Trees moved slowly inching across the ground, crawling for a better spot of light or a better place next to the brook that trickled by lazy and clean. The trees were huge, their trunks several meters around at the base. Insects hummed and went about the work of the day, hunting and collecting food or mating to continue what had begun on Ephesus for as long as time was measured on this planet. Three moons and two stars circled the planet dancing in concert with the rest of the universe. With the two stars there was very little time on the planet where the light wasn't shining bright. This allowed the trees and insects to go about their business without worry, that the stars would continue to shine their life giving rays to the planet's inhabitants. Even when the suns would rest below the horizon, the moons allowed the trees or insect's cycles to continue with its less than brilliant light. This was the concert here on Ephesus and it took place every day, it was the way of life. The flow, the rhythm of life was conducted by all of the species of the planet doing their part, living, breathing, and working.

The Knoevors were a part of this planets concert. The Knoevors did not know how they came into being but they were a part of this concert just as the much as the trees and insects. They were made from the branches of the Mother tree, lovingly grown and encouraged to take the shape of cats. The

Mother tree plucked them from their boughs high atop her crown, breathed life into them and they went about skittish of the lightless areas, seeking the perpetual light. They kept to the areas where the trees and the insects were thin just as they were made to do, they left the deep dark hidden parts of the forest closest to the Mother tree alone. The Mother tree was the oldest and largest of the forests her trunk was as thick as hundreds of normal trees. She was the first on Ephesus. The Knoevors stayed away from the shaded forests out of a deep seated respect, as they were partners with all the rest of the living things on Ephesus, they knew enough not to intrude or change to the base levels of life on this world. The trees where here before the Knoevors made the transition from four to two legs, so they and the trees came to an understanding, whispering to each other as Mother tree expected they would. This was done so that a balance was kept and it was kept years before the Knoevors really understood themselves and their place on Ephesus.

The Knoevors were a race of bipedal cats who had been the keepers of lore for this vibrant and wild planet. Knoevors had come a long way from their ancestors, who walked on all four legs and hunted to survive. The first to take these steps on two legs was Adonna. She took the first steps towards a new future while her fellow cats followed her out of the dirt and muck to be in a better place and have a better understanding. Her first steps were recorded in mud to remember that it wasn't always this way, they had grown in awareness and purpose. From then on the Knoevors used clay and sticks to write out their history. These clay tablets where used to build the only structure on the planet, the Temple of Keeping. Even Adonna's first steps, recorded in clay, were hung in the Temple of Keeping as a reminder of where they had come from. The Knoevors sought the wisdom of the Mother tree speaking to the smaller trees that surrounded their temple close to the river. There was no need for shelter as the weather was always pleasant and the inhabitants were bathed in the light of two stars circling the planet

Occupational Death

contributing to the perpetual cycles of this planet, cycles that just were, that just worked as all did their parts. The water from the planet came from below the surface, bubbling up and anything not used was returned to the planet. They took rest in the Temple of Keeping, the dwelling built only of the clay tablets that the Knoevors recorded their history on. They were allowed to use the trees that had passed on to support their primitive clay metropolis. Trees passed on, the Knoevors did not. They were the same number of Knoevors as long as was recorded. The Knoevors used to fight for areas of better shade or sweeter water, but when the fight would end, even the most severely wounded Knoevors would rise, lick their wounds, and live as if it had never happened. They learned after this that they had no need to eat. The water kept them from thirst and the trees, while living close to them, but not too close, being in their proximity, fed the Knoevors in a perfect symbiosis. This was the balance and peace of this world.

What the Knoevors would never know or never understand is why the Temple of Keeping came crashing down on a day just like all the rest. It stood simple and straight as it had for all the time that time was recorded. It took an event across the universe, on a small blue world called Earth, a world they would never know or understand. It took a man, not that they would even understand what a man was, what a man looked like or even what they thought. That man Samuel Gerard Willis, did something that no one had ever done, he removed the summoning watch and that caused the Temple of Keeping to fall.

After that the Knoevors talked and inquired about the happenings of Ephesus, particularly why the temple had fallen, with the trees who had been on this world longer that they could remember. The trees were the world before the Knoevors came to being, came to knowing. These queries and conversations were left unanswered. The Knoevors were frightened. Adonna, the first who walked on two instead of four legs tried to quiet the fears of her people. They could rebuild the Temple of

Keeping, she told them, they could start to write a new history and try to piece the old back together again and preserve something of what was. So time past, the trees remained quiet. They no longer moved or spoke to the Knoevors, in fact more trees than usual were passing on. Dead trees were everywhere. This added to the worry among the Knoevors. The fear consumed them, they fell into disorder no matter how much Adonna tried to keep the peace. As the Knoevors were in a time of confusion and were frightened, a fight broke out involving many of the Knoevors. When the dust cleared, when the fight was settled, one Knoevor laid on the ground unmoving. Adonna went to the body that was still. She tried to rouse the seemingly peaceful body, she felt that its frame was empty and limp. She put her head to the body of the fallen Knoevor and heard no heart, no breath. Adonna wept, she had never cried before she was shocked at the tears in her eyes and even more shocked at the strong wind and rain that fell from the sky that day.

    This was about the time when Samuel, Mary Patricia, Thomas and Hope were first summoned to perform their duties as the Horsemen of the Apocalypse. The ground started to shake and heave. In the distant forest, in a place the Knoevors had never been, the Mother tree fell over. All the leaves in the magnificent crown were gone as were the branches that bore the Knoevors. Its trunk was half of what it used to be. As Mother tree fell, the world the Knoevors lived and survived on for countless years, hundreds of years, tore itself apart. They all perished and the last large remnants of the planet drifted into the cold dark of space.

First, thank you for taking the time to read my book. You have journeyed this far with me, would you be willing to go a little further? I have shared my words with you now I ask if you could share yours with me. Please write a review. Good, bad, or indifferent I would like to know your thoughts.

Sincerly,

M.F. Thurston

ELLIOTT
5902 HARFORD AVE
GWYNN OAK   MD
21207- 5023

Made in the USA
Middletown, DE
05 February 2019